Like my life, this book isn't perfect…

I'd like to thank my husband Tim for **ALWAYS** supporting my dreams & loving me

My sons, Gerald & Knicolus for loving me & letting me love them back

Special thanks to all the wonderful people who read my first book, *"The Plan"* and still encouraged me to write another!

Denise, Esther, Stephanie, Rene', Yvette, staff at Fenwick Landing, Heather, Karen, Lynn, Tammy, Pickles, Sandra, Cindy, Tina, Ce Ce, Audrey, June, Penny, Nita, Hadley, Beverly, & Drs. E/I/S.

I can't name you all but please know I appreciated your feedback.

Special thanks to Ret. Sgt M. Creager for your help with the law enforcement jargon and policies.

Special shout out to my purple sista…Wendy! Girl I'll need some Sulfur 8 after this☺

Ruth H. thank you for allowing me to take your name with me on this twisted journey!

#8 you will always get the credit for pushing me over the edge

For those who do the daunting work of child protective services...

What you do matters...

The way you say my name for the first time...matters

The way my parents or guardians feel about you & the things they say (when they think I'm not listening)...matters

The way you look around my home...matters

The way you show me you are here for me, may make me scared but ...it matters

The way you come down to the waiting area and walk me down the long hallway...matters

The way you look at me or don't look at me...matters

The way you allow me to be quiet/cry/look mad/ask questions...matters

The way you treat the person, who you say hurt me but they've always said they love me...matters

The way you promise to "do something" so this won't happen again...EVER? Really?...matters

The way you say taking me away to live with strangers is better for me...matters

The way I see the "stuff" done to me by that person...over & over again when you're not there...matters

The way my fear/self-loathing/sadness/body image/unable to trust...matters

But there is one more thing, that one day, will matter to me...

The way my adult life might turn out...because today I matter to you...

Thank you by deed and/or word, for showing victims that their becoming a SURVIVOR...matters...I wish you were there for me...Toki Smith

2

Organized and ready…

Well here it goes I've got my lunch box, IPod and my diary. Just another day in my life, ok, not exactly a "regular" day but actually "the" day in my life. This is the day when I make all my dreams come true. This day, October 17th, changes my entire life. This is gonna be one of those domino type days, where one action will affect everything else. I'm gonna be a little full of myself and say this is the day that will be on the lips of people for a long time!

So look, I'm Penny Darling or as my birth certificate says, Penelopie Florence Darling. I'm 32 years old, single and I love to cook.

People love to be around me. I've got this weird ability to make immediate friends and I can somehow sense when people are in need. I also have one of those internal "bull-shit" meters which more times than not I ignore and then I get hurt. Yes I do get hurt and it's not pretty when that happens because it usually presents itself as anger. When I'm angry my head starts to hurt and then whatever I feel is what I say!

Now let me tell you more about this wonderful day I'm going to have. I've been planning this particular event for about three months but it seems my whole life has led to this day. For a long time I've wanted to take control of my destiny so I don't get old and boring.

I still listen to Luther Prince and dance around my bedroom. Not taking notice to the medium amount of belly fat I've acquired since I stopped running track in high school. But still I'm 5'7" and I weigh 160lbs so I'm not a slob or anything. I mean I really look good in my size 7/8 jeans.

Guys do watch when I walk by! At least I think they do. It's not like I turn around to see if they're checking me out, but I'm sure they are. Ok, I think they are…aren't they?

Is it ok to want a little attention for the way I look? Or am I just asking for trouble by wanting to be noticed for my physical appearance?

Why do we stop doing the things that bring us joy and then sit around complaining about being unhappy? I used to like to run and exercise. What happened to me? Now I watch TV and read. I don't sing as much either. I used to sing and dance when I cleaned the house as a kid. I miss those carefree days.

Anyway that changes today!

Now back to my day. It's a Sunday and I went to church like a good girl. Sat in the middle so I wouldn't draw unwanted attention to myself because everyone knows if you sit in the front you're trying to suck up to the preacher and if you sit in the back you really don't want to be there. You pay more attention to the exit sign than to the "word."

Today I sat in the middle…just listening, singing and clapping along. I love gospel music but I get embarrassed when they get "happy" and start shouting and the song goes on for so long you forget what they were singing.

Now after church, I come back home to my house in Morganville West Virginia. I moved here after four years in the Navy.

The Navy was good for me, just not always good to me. I mean there is a difference so we need to put that out there.

I learned a lot of great life lessons and employable skills. It's just that some of those life lessons were painful and grossly unfair. But all-in-all I got more good from the experience than bad.

Once I ended my enlistment I moved to Morganville and took a job with the Veterans Affairs Community Based Out-Patient Clinic as a security guard.

I used my GI Bill Educational Benefit to pay for college and then I joined the Morganville Police department. I'm one of four detectives in the 15 police officer force. We serve the 11 miles associated with the West Virginia Science and Agriculture University (WVSAU).

After changing my clothes I got in my car and I drove down to visit my grandparents. See I want them to share in my day's accomplishment.

They live in Harmony Grove, WV which is 15 miles from my house. I try to get home often but sometimes I don't visit them for long periods of time. Lately, they always seem to be at church and my work hours vary.

Today I found them at Mulberry Baptist Church, their "home church". I sat with them outside and told them of my plans and how happy I'll be when I'm done so we can spend more time together.

After I leave my grandparents at the church I drive back to their house. It's not really a house, more a double wide trailer.

It's kind of big, four bedrooms and two bathrooms and it's where I grew up.

You didn't think I came to live in Morganville "just cause I couldn't wait to work in West Virginia" did you!! No offense, but I've traveled as a sailor and if not for this being home, I'd be somewhere else.

Home is safe, familiar, and my only real family is here, my grandparents. I had to come back.

I love coming home to the smell of good cooking and the warmth of the memories left behind. But today it's cold and I am alone. So I'm sitting on the floor, of my grandparent's home, with my lunch box, IPod and diary, just waiting for 6 pm. That's when my old life ends and my new adventure begins.

That's when I'm going to kill myself and join my grandparents at the church, where we'll be together again. Forever…

Of course you want to know why…

Well first off I'm not crazy…I'm not even depressed today. Actually I'm very happy that I'm taking charge of my situation and I'm planning to move forward. Look, don't judge me since you've never walked in my shoes.

Here's my story and I hope that when someone finds my body they can have a little sympathy for the life I led.

I've really tried my hardest to stay alive but sometimes it's just not in the cards for someone like me to recover and be able to live a normal life.

Do you understand? Can you imagine what it would be like for you to have been me?

I grew up ok for the most part. We lived in a quite suburb of Philadelphia, Pennsylvania.

I had both my parents and they were healthy so no undue burdens in that regard. Both my parents worked and helped out in their community.

Now my daddy…well I thought he was a giant. He invoked respect and love from me. He taught me how to do everything! He was so patient and always encouraged me to "do the right thing little girl."

I learned to write my name in cursive by the time I was four years old. He also let me help out in the kitchen. Well help out is an exaggeration, I mean I got to hand him the vegetables and cutlery. But I wore my apron like a proud souse chef!

My father wasn't a tall man but I thought he was the strongest, best daddy ever. My mom used to say he had a "napoleon complex" and that's why he wanted to be the best at everything.

He was always well dressed, even his construction work clothes were always clean and pressed. He kept his nails trimmed and cleaned cause he said, "I can't cook with nasty nails, might get my girls sick." He would smile and kiss my forehead then start making some kind of amazing meal. My favorite was his spaghetti with marinara and crab sauce.

Even though my mom was from the country she couldn't boil an egg. So my dad did all the cooking. He really enjoyed it and mommy and I enjoyed eating it so it was a win-win for all of us.

I miss those days. When I was 15 years old, my father died while vacationing with my mother. They were visiting a resort in Massanutten Mountain, Virginia for an extended weekend. My dad went for a walk one morning and never came back. My mom just seemed to stop living after that.

She sent me to live with my grandparents in Harmony Grove, West Virginia and she continued to live in the townhouse in Philadelphia. Later she moved to Ohio so she could visit my grandparents more often. I haven't spoken with my mother since shortly after my grandparent's funeral.

After my dad died my mom was distant and shut down, but we still spoke on the phone and she used to come to visit her parents. Once they died, she became so negative toward me that I had to let her go.

The last time we spoke she said, "It's your fault your daddy never came back! We went to the mountains to spend some alone time together. I thought I'd finally have your dad to myself and all he talked about was you. He probably had a heart attack or something from worrying about why you were acting strange before we left home."

I was and still am shocked that a mother could feel that way toward her only child. Looking back, I realize she never tried to comfort me when my daddy disappeared.

She would turn away and cry whenever I tried to talk to her about if daddy was dead. She then she would buy me something and tell me to forget about bad things and focus on the pretty new whatever she bought for me.

I never got the chance to tell my parents I was raped by…shit, my phone is ringing…"Hello, this is Penny."

"Penny, its Ruth, look we caught a case. Where are you?"

"Ummm…I'm at my grandparent's house."

"What are you doing down there Penny? Are you trying to kill your crazy ass again?"

"Whatever, what's the address Ruth?"

"I mean it Penny if you're having a mental health crisis moment, I'll call someone to come down there, get you, and take you to the hospital."

"Oh seriously Ruth, just shut up! Now give me the address PLEASE!"

Backing out of the driveway Penny says out loud, sorry grandma and granny, I have to leave for work but I'll be back soon.

Penny hits the siren and lights as she leaves Penny Darling's world behind and steps into the world of Detective Penelopie Darling.

On the scene…

The storage room had, what looks like, a gray concrete floor that was now covered in Raymond Jones' blood. There are boxes of liquor, peanuts and alcohol mixers stacked at least three feet high along the walls.

Raymond Jones, the bar's owner, was laying on his back, pants and underwear pulled down to his thighs. His hands bound behind his back with what looked like a zip tie. His legs were bound the same way at the ankles. He's approximately six feet tall, skinny and skin the color of parchment paper; kind of yellow, not brown or white…old yellow and dry looking.

At one time he looked like he had a head full of white hair but now his hair was red from all the blood that pooled on to the floor under his head.

His eyes were slightly open and his mouth duct taped shut. His genital area was exposed, but no genitals were there, just a lot of blood and indiscernible flesh. It was a disgusting mess to look at.

I drew my focus back to what was being said, "Hey you ladies want to see him from behind?" asked the medical examiner technician.

"No the ladies don't want to see him from behind," snapped Ruth. "The *detectives* want you to roll him over if there is some pertinent evidence you want us to see."

She gave him the "I'll smack the shit outta you if you continue to patronize us" look.

He obviously got high marks in the "read my face" class because all he did was nod and turn good ole Mr. Jones over.

I really wished he hadn't.

We saw what looked like the base of a finger sticking out of his very bloody anus.

9

"As you can see the middle finger area on his right hand is bloody so I'm thinking this was that finger and this much blood suggests to me the victim was still alive during the mutilation and amputation. I'm sure the medical examiner, Dr. Ellis, will contact you with the final conclusions. Will that be all...*detectives*?"

He says "detectives" like it's now a nasty taste in his mouth.

I glare into his smug disrespectful face and say, "Yes, thank you "fuck face," that's it for now."

I looked at Ruth and said, "I know you were thinking the same thing."

"What? No, I was thinking this is just the beginning of something big. My liver is quivering and that's never a good sign."

I look up at Ruth from Mr. Jones' body, "OMG you have all kinds of education and awards, yet you are tossing all your detective skills out the window for your LIVER!"

Looking up to the ceiling I ask, "Lawd what did I do to deserve this shit?"

Here it comes…

Dr. Wayne Ellis, Morganville Medical Examiner states, "According to the preliminary autopsy report, Raymond Jones, 73 year old black male was hit on the back of the head with enough force to knock him down which allowed the assailant to subdue him with plastic zip handcuffs also known as zip ties. No other obvious trauma to his head or torso so I'm concluding he wasn't beaten.

His stomach contents were consistent to the time of death which I believe was within six hours of his body being found. I do believe he was killed by someone who was shorter than he was hence the angle of the blow to his head."

Ruth says, "So the perp got Mr. Jones in the storage area, probably after the bar closed, knocked him over the head with something, bound his wrists and ankles.

Then pulled down his pants and underwear, cut his junk off, then cut off his middle finger and stuffed the finger in his ass? Is that how it happened?"

"Yes, but I can't really be sure if his genitals were cut off before or after his finger. His penis and testicles were cut off and removed from the area."

"You mean they weren't found at the scene?" says our Lieutenant who must have come in while we were reviewing various autopsy photos.

"Hey Lt. we didn't hear you come in," I say reaching for his hand. He looks at me and around the room without taking my hand.

Lt. Brogan hated anything to do with "nasty medical shit" as he once said to me. He will come to the crime scene but keep his distance. Once the medical professionals arrive and start messing with the body, Lt. Brogan is outta there.

Lt. Brogan is a 22 year police veteran with five of those years as the chief of the Morganville Homicide department. He answers directly to the Chief of Police, Chief Ritchie; who in turn answers to the mayor.

Lt. Brogan is a good enough cop and a very understanding boss. I mean he hasn't fired me yet!

But to look at him you'd think he was a cartoon character come to life. All his body fat has landed on his torso while every other part of him is skin and bones.

The man has skinny arms and legs plus absolutely no ass to speak of! His pants are so baggy that when he farts his pants balloon out!

When he lets one loose in the bullpen someone will yell out *helium balloon*! Of course that's when he's out of ear shot!

We are loyal to him and he is to us…we really like and admire him as a person not just as our leader.

"No Lt. Brogan, our guys combed the entire area and they didn't find anything" said Ruth.

"Ok, so what kind of sick fucker does something like this?" He says looking at anything beside the photos.

Dr. Ellis shakes his head and says, "I don't know, that's what the police are supposed to find out."

Lt. Brogan shakes his skinny finger at Ruth and me saying, "I want you two to get back to the office and check the National Information Crime Center for any other victims with the same M.O.

You know I'm going to have the mayor breathing down my neck as soon as the media gets whiff of this. I'd like to have something for the brass before the shit storm hits.

You need any more resources just call…ok? I'm counting on you two to shut this down immediately!"

Lt. Brogan is just three years shy of collecting his pension. He's not going to be happy if this leaves a skid mark across his otherwise stellar career. He doesn't like murders that aren't of the garden variety type. His famous line is, "If the victim ain't shot or stabbed send the file to the FBI, cause I ain't got the stomach for that kinky shit!"

Looking a little green, he turns and walks out just as silently as he came in. Lt. Brogan would've made an excellent criminal…you wouldn't hear him coming.

Ruth and I drove over to the medical examiner's office in her car so she has to take me back to the bar so I can retrieve my car.

"Look Penny I know this is bad timing but I've spoken to Lt. Brogan and he agrees it's time."

"Time?"

"Girl, don't play dumb with me! It's time for an intervention to this suicide game you keep playing."

"I don't…"

"Nope we're not going to pretend you don't know and I pretend I must have been mistaken. This time it's like this, per the department shrink, are you going to attend a weekly support group for victims of sexual assault?

Give me your answer right now. But make no mistake girl if you don't say yes, I'll formally report you to the Chief. I mean it Penny, you are about to blow and I don't want your brains on my hands.

You're a great cop and an amazing friend. I love you dearly but you are crazy as hell right now and have been for too long. You've got to find a way to deal with your past."

Penny looks into Ruth's amazingly dark brown eyes and sees nothing but love and pain. How could I have caused this?

Ruth continues, "You've never wanted to use me as your therapist, even though you know I have a degree in counseling, and I can respect that. But you did share enough for me to deduce that you're still affected by the assault.

Penny, your self esteem is low enough that at least three times a year you make elaborate plans to kill yourself.

Internal dialogue…

Penny…How does she know how many times a year I plan my escape? I thought I was being stealthy! Oh! I get it, that's why I haven't been successful! Ruth finds a way to screw-up my plans every time! Oh she's a sneaky one…

Ruth says, "Honey, it's time to deal with the aftermath of the rape."

Parking at the curb of the bar, "Ok, we're here…what's your decision?"

A week later…the group…

"Cindy can you please give me a copy of the next women's support group roster please? I'm going to facilitate this one myself since all the other therapists are full right now and can't take on another group," said Denise Wallace, Licensed Clinical Social Worker and Acting CEO of the Morganville Rape Crisis Center.

Denise is a black woman, 5'7" with absolutely no body fat on her 120 pound fit frame. She favors leggings and tunics with flat shoes. She's always accessorized with chunky jewelry and bangles. Today her hair is in a ponytail, but usually she wears it down in a bob style when she's working with clients. Her makeup is always at a minimum, eye liner, mascara and lip gloss.

Cindy gives Denise a copy of the support group roster and returns back to her desk.

Denise doesn't know the participants, so she will have to rely on a summary of their stories to give her some information about their trauma.

The group will meet for eight weeks in the conference room of the women's health clinic. This location was picked after discussions about having it at the rape crisis center. The feedback was women didn't want to run the risk of being seen coming in the center by their family, friends or coworkers.

Seems that even in 2016 there is still a stigma attached to sexual abuse and no matter how many initiatives are written and vigils are held, victims were still too afraid and/or ashamed to be the face of this awful epidemic.

Even sexual assault survivors are not as vocal as other survivors, like cancer or even domestic violence.

Domestic violence used to be one of those things no one talked about, like abortions but now they are so common place it's not even anything to discuss, especially since celebrities have made it a badge of honor to wear for the media.

No, sexual assaults and the after effects are not just swept under the rug,the events are vacuumed up like they never occurred; except by a few victims' advocates, psychotherapists, police departments and if the victims are lucky, some family and friends.

Unfortunately, most victims don't acknowledge the abuse or understand the after effects of it, which is why these ladies have been referred to this group.

Most have not fully made a link between the trauma and the effect it has had on their lives. Others know their anger and inability to have positive relationships are directly correlated to their sexual assault, but they have been unable to break their negative and hurtful behaviors.

I hope through this group they will find a safe place to move toward more healing.

Each lady was asked to write one or two statements about how they feel about their trauma.

Denise looks at the list and reads:

Penny Darling: 32yo African American; raped by a cousin; local police detective; single.

Penny Darling writes: *"Oh, no, there is so much more to my story than a few sentences. See I have feelings of being lost and empty. I feel dirty and marked for life. I feel like there is an invisible sign on my back and forehead that only men can see. When will I get a break?*

Dawn Walsh: 56yo African American; raped in college; high school principal; married.

Dawn writes: *"I am successful and 98% healed and I don't understand why my therapist wants me to come to the group. How do I feel about my event? Well I don't feel anything so I think the next 2% will be easy."*

Holly Chism: 26yo Caucasian; raped while a college intern by a janitor; court house clerk; single.

Holly writes: *"I'm so tired of looking over my shoulder at my past. I feel like I'll never be a normal person. I'm so scared all the time."* She scratched her next few words out.

Dani Bauer: 27yo Caucasian; engaged, raped by ex-husband three years ago; fitness trainer.

Dani writes: *"My fiancé is so good to me. He buys me anything and says he just wants me to feel whole and well. I love him and I feel safe with him. He's nothing like my first husband and I feel so blessed to say that."*

Cheryl Randall: 45yo African American; raped by husband's brother the night before her wedding 10 years ago; probation officer.

Cheryl writes: *"Where am I about that shit now? Well my brother-in-law was a fucking crack head and his ass died 3 days after my wedding. I didn't say anything cause what was the fucking point. Shit I wasn't gonna let that asshole ruin my marriage. I've known my husband since 8th grade and I'm gonna continue to be with him no matter what. This shit ain't gonna get me!"*

Ayda Espina: 58yo Mexican American; raped by her girl-scout leader 43 years ago; professor; single.

Ayda writes: *"It's a sin against God what happened to me. I've prayed for God and the Holy Mother to forgive me. I strive to live a holy life. I try to tell myself I'm a special person picked to carry this cross for some divine reason. How can I feel special and be marked at the same time? God puts his saints through things to test their faith so they say. My faith has been tested through and through, yet I'm still suffering. "*

Lynn Febus: 60yo Caucasian; raped during third month as a foster care worker 25 years ago; self employed tax preparer; married.

Lynn writes: *"I'm so tired of being a victim. I want to move on but I just can't. I wanted to help people but I couldn't do it the way I wanted. Where am I now? I'm embarrassed this still affects me."*

Karen Philpot: 22yo Biracial (African American/Caucasian); sexually assaulted by another Navy sailor 3 weeks ago; continues to serve; dating.

Karen writes: *"I'm still scared and confused. I've been reading all the flyers about reporting this type of thing but the female shipmates tell me not to believe it. It will be harder for me if I report it. So I want to come to the outside to deal with this. Should I even tell the guy I'm dating? Oh, right, where am I now? I haven't had sex with my friend since the assault. Maybe I'm gay now. I don't know but I want to find out.*

Yvette Dyson: 41yo African American; molested by her great uncle when she was 7yo; a registered nurse at a local hospital; married.

Yvette writes: *"I am at the point where I'm finding peace in my life. I want to make sure that if anything else is left, I am able to deal with it. My husband is available but I need to do this myself."*

Imani McCollin: 22yo African American; molested by her father when she was 4yo; graduate student @ WVSAU.

Imani writes: *"I feel like a fraud going to school and acting like everything is ok with me. I don't fit in with anyone because I'm so different and broken."*

Denise places the forms in a folder and puts them in the top drawer of her desk. She glances up at the clock…time to get ready for the ladies.

Just as Denise finishes setting up the chairs in a circle, the first person walks in. She's hesitant and looks around like she'll bolt out the door in a second.

"Hello, welcome! I'm Denise the facilitator for this group. Glad you've decided to attend."

"Ummm," biting her cuticle, Holly Chism fervently looks around. "I'm not sure I'm in the right place." She says while backing toward the open door.

"My name is Holly Chism and I was looking for the ummm…"

"Well are you here for the support group?" asks Denise.

"Ummm…yeah I guess so" stammers Holly. "I'm a little nervous."

Denise says, "Well that's to be expected. Everyone else who arrives will be nervous too. Why don't you sign in, your first name only, grab a snack, water whatever you'd like then take a seat?"

Denise smiles and walks toward the windows where she draws the blinds shut. She then goes over to the wall switch and dims the lights midway. Lastly, she walks over to the CD player, selects a CD and soon light classical music is playing.

Holly says, "I'm sorry, I got here so early! I can leave and come back if you want me to." She slowly starts backing toward the exit again.

Denise says, "Absolutely not." She continues in a gentle tone and a welcoming smile, "I'm just running behind and that's not your fault. Please don't worry and PLEASE don't leave!"

Holly murmurs, looking at the floor, "Ok, then if you're sure."

Holly signed in as she was told, got a bottle of water and sat down. Once seated she worried that she was too close to the refreshments and would be distracted by the smell of cookies. She stood and

19

moved to the opposite side of the circle. She sat for a few minutes and then began to worry that her back was to the door so she stood and moved again.

Once seated in between the door and a window she took several deep breaths and tried to calm her anxiety. But she continued to worry if coming here was the right thing to do and was she sitting in the right chair. What if something bad happened, would she be able to get herself out?

Holly looks down at her shoes and wonders why she wore them. There is a spot where they are worn down a little and she's sure everyone will see that she tried to cover it with black marker! But she didn't have time to go home from work before coming here. At work her feet are under a desk all day so no one pays attention to her feet. No one pays any attention to her really.

Denise goes into a closet and returns with some easel type paper, the kind that looks like a big post-it and has sticky stuff on the back. She hangs three sheets on the wall. In a box nearby, Holly sees various colored markers. Holly begins to sweat and thinks, I hope we don't have to stand up and write stuff. Lord, people staring at me! Why did I wear these pants? I bet everyone will see the cellulite on my thighs!" She feels sweat pooling under her arm pits.

Holly begins to fidget and thinks; maybe I'm too close to the wall where Denise has placed the paper. If I sit here, then everyone will always be looking at me when they look at her writing. So Holly gets up and moves three more times before settling on a final seat in the circle.

Denise sees all this but doesn't say anything. Observations are a big part of being a clinician. Another part of group therapy is to trust the process, so for now, Denise thinks, I will trust the process and pray it helps Holly.

Next walks in Cheryl Randall, she strides over to the sign-in table, signs her first name, gets a cup of coffee, loads it with sugar, puts two cookies on a napkin and grabs a bottle of water. She takes the seat closest to her which is opposite to Holly and immediately pulls out her cell phone and begins texting. Cheryl is dressed in sweat pants, sneakers and a decorative scarf around her braided hair.

While Cheryl was getting her coffee sugared, Dawn Walsh and Ayda Espina come in. They are politely chatting and after signing in, they both take their bottled water and sit next to each other.

Both say hello to Holly and Cheryl. Ayda and Dawn continue chatting quietly.

Holly thinks, see no one likes you already.

Next come in Lynn Febus, Yvette Dyson and Imani McCollin. While Yvette and Imani are signing in, Lynn asks if they want anything from the snack area. Both decline but Lynn stresses they should have something since they will miss dinner and events like this can be stressful she adds.

Yvette and Imani both ask for a couple of cookies and each take a bottle of water. They thank Lynn for looking out for them. Lynn smiles with satisfaction.

Lynn asks Imani if she'd like to sit next to her and she agrees. "I'm glad I came in with you Lynn, if not I wouldn't know who to sit by." Imani smiles gratefully.

Yvette thinks that chick Lynn ain't gonna mother me to damn death. I'm glad there are some other seats still available away from that one!

Yvette sits down and nods to the other ladies.

Penny is the next to arrive, but before going in she stands just outside the door to the meeting room. Am I really going to do this and if I get better, then what? She starts unconsciously picking her cuticles. I'm a detective, I should be doing better. What if these women see me outside of here? What will they think of me?

21

They'll lose respect for me as a policewoman…shit! I hate Ruth for making me do this!

She begins to pull at the skin above her cuticles with her teeth. A long strip of skin comes off and immediately her finger starts to bleed. Penny sucks on it a few seconds then using her other hand she pulls out one of the four band aids she has left in her pants pocket. Every morning she packs 10 band aids just in case she's faced with a stressful event. Just thinking of this meeting, she used six throughout the day.

Looking at her bleeding finger she is momentarily mesmerized by the perfectly shaped circle of blood. She sucks at it again then quickly places the band aid over it. Then she shoves the band aid wrapper back into her pocket.

Ok, well…it's either this or I lose my job…she walks through the door.

Once in, Penny heads directly for the first empty seat she sees. She sits down and crosses her leg. She's promised herself she will not bite her nails or cuticles in public so she sits on her hands.

Lynn leans toward Penny, who is sitting opposite her in the circle. She clears her throat and says, "Excuse me ummm Miss, did you sign-in?"

Penny, looking perplexed, shakes her head no.

"We all have to sign-in, with our first name only, then get a goody and beverage; but that's only if you want, I mean the goody and beverage. I can make sure your seat is saved if you want."

Penny says, "Thank you I didn't realize about the sign-in and for sure I'd love some sweets! Thanks again." Penny quickly heads to the table, signs in and gets five cookies and a cup of coffee with creamer and no sugar.

Karen Philpot arrives two minutes before group is about to start. She looks straight ahead, marches over to the sign-in table. She makes a cup of coffee, keeping her gaze on her cup. She hesitates before signing her name and contemplates using an alias but remembers she's already given them her real name on the initial paperwork. She signs "Karen" and takes the first open seat she sees.

Soon as Karen sits down, Dani Baurer rushes in and stands in the middle of the circle. "Sorry I'm almost late ya'll. My exercise class ran a little long. Is this the rape victim support group?"

Holly can't believe she is asking that out loud! I would rather die than admit I was here for a rape support group. I mean I know I am but saying it out loud is a bit too much! See this was a terrible idea thinks Holly. She closes her eyes and tries to steady her nerves but it's not working!

Cheryl looks up and says, "We aren't doing anything yet, we haven't started."

Lynn speaks up, "Ummm you should probably go sign-in, get a goody and a beverage then take a seat. It's almost 6pm."

"Ok, thanks," says Dani sounding like an over sugared cheerleader. She rushes over to the table scribbles her name, grabs two bottles of water and sits down in between Dawn and Penny.

At exactly 6pm, Denise joins the group and takes the remaining seat.

"My name is Denise and I will be the clinical facilitator during our eight week group meeting.

She has been observing the group settle in and has developed some first impressions of them.

The "I'm a bundle of nerves" twosome: Holly and Penny.

The "I don't appear to give a shit" group: Cheryl, Yvette, and Karen.

The "I'm going to get on everyone's nerves" group: Lynn, and Dani.

Not sure where little Miss Ayda fits yet...

Denise is interested to see if she was accurate.

She clears her throat, smiles and says, "Welcome ladies I am looking forward to our journey together. Please note that I am not the "leader" of the group but the clinical facilitator. My role is to help you stay on topic, watch the time, and provide clinical interventions if needed.

As we grow as a group you will see what I mean. My role will diminish as your cohesiveness increases. Of course this depends largely on your openness to discuss your stories."

"Now," slapping her hands together and smiling broadly she says, "First things first! Let's relax a little by doing a calming exercise.

Then we'll go around the circle and introduce ourselves, remember first names only.

Then we will start off our group by identifying a foundation of ground rules that will help to keep us safe and balanced.

Once we've finished relaxing, introductions and developing ground rules, we can begin discussing why we are all here tonight.

Internal dialogues...

Holly...No I'm not ready to discuss anything with these people. They will think I'm stupid.

Ayda...I pray I will have the strength to do this! Lord please guide my steps tonight.

Cheryl...Fuck it, let's get this party started! I don't want to do no stupid relaxation shit!

Dani...I wonder if I can get some of these ladies to sign up for my exercise classes at the gym. This might be a great opportunity for my business!

Now everyone place your hands flat on your thighs, palms down. Take a deep breath in, hold it...now let it out. Again breathe in, hold it...now let it out.

Ok, while breathing normally, let's do some shoulder shrugs. Hands stay palms down on your thighs while you pull your shoulders up toward your ears. Hold it...release; ok, let's do those 2 more times."

Internal dialogues...

Yvette...Really this is embarrassing!

Lynn...I have to remember how to do this...it feels amazing.

Imani...this is weird and I don't feel any different.

Holly...I don't think I did it right cause I don't feel relaxed!

After the last shoulder shrug Denise exclaims, "Great job! So you've just done two great relaxation techniques and you can do them any time prior to, during or after a stressful event."

Looking around and still smiling she says, "So let's get to know each other by starting on my right, remember, first names only."

One by one each lady says her name.

Once back at Denise she says, "Again, welcome ladies and it's truly my honor to be here and support you toward your goals. Now let's work on those foundational ground rules I mentioned earlier." She stands and walks toward the paper on the wall and grabs a marker.

She writes, "house-rules" underlines it and then turns to the group.

"Please raise your hand, say your name again then make your suggestion or comment."

First hand goes up is Cheryl's, "My name is Cheryl and I'd like to suggest we start and end on time."

Denise writes "start at 6pm and end at 8pm"

"Is that the start time and end time everyone agreed to during their interview session?"

All heads nod affirmative.

Denise says, "Thanks Cheryl, anyone else with a suggestion that would benefit the group?"

Lynn says, "I'm Lynn and I'd like it if we don't make judgments about each other."

Denise, "So are you saying let's make "I statements" versus "you statements?"

Lynn, "Yes exactly, "I feel…I think…I heard…etc."

Denise writes this on the easel paper.

Denise asks, "Anyone else?"

Holly asks, "Can we sit in different seats each time? Oh, sorry my name is ummm Holly."

Denise writes, "First come first seated." Does that work for you all?"

Again everyone nods in agreement.

Denise asks, "What about profanity?"

The group starts mumbling out answers…

Denise says, "Ok, I'll reword it…if someone uses profanity…"

Dawn says, "I'm Dawn and I think as long as they are cussing "about" something or someone outside the group and not "at" someone in the group, I think it should be allowed. I know I'm known to drop a few choice descriptive words now and then!" She looks around the group smiling.

Ayda says, "It's against my religion to use profanity, but I'm not here to judge others. Oh, and my name is Ayda."

Others nod their heads as a way to show understanding to what Ayda has said.

Denise writes on the paper, keep profanity within the context of our discussion and be respectful of others.

Karen raises her hand and asks, "Hey I'm Karen, what if I need to miss a group cause of my job? I'm on active duty and sometimes things come up."

Denise nods and says, "Thanks Karen that's a really important question. Due to the nature of our group and the limited time we have together, if a member of our group misses two meetings they will be discharged from our group. This is for continuity and a feeling of safety for all members. When we share and elicit feedback from each other, it's important that everyone show respect for each other. Anymore than two missed sessions will make it difficult for that person to catch up and it's not fair that the members have to re-cap sensitive information. Anyone have any questions or comments about this?"

No one responds so Denise adds it to the list.

"Well anything else you would like me to add to our list of norms?"

Lynn raises her hand and asks, "What about food? Some of the ladies probably come here straight from work and it is during the dinner hour. Can we bring food to the meetings?"

Internal dialogue…

Yvette…Really grandma shut the fuck up! We will never get to shit if she keeps running her mouth about feeding people!

Imani…She sounds like my mom, always worrying if somebody ate or not.

Denise says, "Good points Lynn and it's a yes/no answer. Research shows groups need focus with limited distractions; hunger is certainly a distraction; however, so is someone chowing down on a slice of pizza or crunching a salad. Our center will provide water, coffee and cookies. No other food will be allowed during our meetings.

Anyone have questions or comments?

Lynn raises her hand again, "I'm sorry but if they get here early can they eat before the group starts? I just worry a lot about the ladies that are working or caring for their kids. I'm retired so I have time to eat before coming here. I'm just trying to be helpful."

Internal dialogue…

Yvette…See that's what I'm talking about! Shut up so we can move on PLEASE!

Cheryl…Really?

Dawn…She's deflecting so she won't have to discuss why she's here. My therapist says it's one of the ways a person denies a traumatic event.

Imani leans over to Lynn and whispers, "Thank you for being so kind."

Cheryl and Yvette make eye contact and smirk at each other.

Denise smiles and says, "Sure Lynn that's a wonderful idea. Whatever happens before group is fine. The room will be open 30 minutes before each group so if you want to come in and eat prior to the meeting please feel free to do so."

She smiles and looks around the group for any body language feedback but finds none.

Well let's see if this next item shakes them up a little.

"Now the last thing to discuss, confidentiality and what it means to the success of our group."

Penny raises her hand, "I think we shouldn't discuss what we say or hear outside the group."

Dawn, "Is there anything wrong with sharing our group experiences with our spouses if we don't use names?"

Cheryl, "I don't see why we need to discuss this. There ain't no way to monitor what people are going to say when none of us are around."

Dawn, "Yeah that's what I'm saying."

Ayda raises her hand, "I believe that if we say we will keep each other's confidences then we should."

Others just look around the group or at their laps.

Internal dialogue…

Yvette…I bet these heifers can't keep water so that's why I ain't telling them anything I wouldn't want to tell everybody.

Dawn…I tell my husband everything! No one should expect you don't tell your spouse everything that goes on during your day.

Karen…I'm gonna tell my shipmates everything anyway so piss on their little rules.

Lynn...I don't think we should say anything to anyone. I'm not going to talk about what I hear in here to anyone.

Holly...I want to get some more cookies but I'm too scared to move.

Denise thinks, wow this is usually the topic that creates the most discussion during the first meeting. What's going on with them? Maybe they don't know that they are entitled to respect and privacy.

She writes on the easel paper, if stories are shared, we will only share with people we trust and no identifying names or descriptions will be given.

She turns and looks at the group, "Can everyone agree to this?"

They all nod their heads.

Denise places the marker in the box and takes her seat.

"Ok, who wants to begin telling us about why you are here and what goal you would like to achieve by being here."

Penny thinks, I'm here to keep my job long enough until I can successfully kill myself! I bet she wouldn't expect me to reveal that truth!

Penny raises her hand, "My name is Penny and I'm here because my job made me come. " Laughing and looking around she says, "Ok, that's one part of my reason for being here. I'm also here because I'm still feeling broken by the family member who assaulted me. My goal is not to feel this way anymore." Penny looks down at her hands and starts to pick at a hang nail.

The room is silent until Cheryl says, "Ok, so my husband's crack head older brother raped me 10 years ago, the night before my fucking wedding. I mean the night before my wedding! Can you believe that shit? Well the mutha fucker is dead now and I'm not

30

sure if I should've told my husband when it happened or ever tell him.

My goal is to make a decision about what to do and stick with it. All this back and forth I go through each day is stressing me out and pissing me off. It's starting to affect my work. I'm a probation officer and I find myself not having much patience with the cons assigned to me."

Dawn says, "Penny and Cheryl thanks for breaking the ice. Cheryl, I'm married and I work full time too. I've been in therapy for the last 20 years."

Dawn is a short plump African American woman. Her hair is cut short in a natural curly style. Her hair is died a deep red color and she has over exaggerated eyebrows. She's wearing jeans and a tie-died sweat shirt. On her feet she has spike heeled red boots which look dangerous to walk in. Dawn is barely 4"11' so she wears spike heels to elongate her frame; which is what she read in one of those high-end magazines.

But Dawn isn't tall and thin like the models in the magazines so she looks like a cue ball on spikes. To top it off, she sounds like she's been sucking on helium! Her voice has always been high pitched and whiny, even to her own ears but she has made peace with it. Her therapist told her to own herself and she has…98 percent worth!

Here I am 56 years old and I'm still dealing with a rape that occurred while I was in college. I've become very comfortable exploring my feelings. I also welcome the perspectives of others, so I guess that's why I'm here. I want to hear from you all and maybe, just maybe, I can get that little something I've been missing that will help me move to the next level of good mental health.

"Hey Penny", Dawn shouts, "My job didn't make me come," she says smiling at Penny, but my therapist strongly encouraged me to attend. Not sure but I think she's tired of me and wanted a break! At least that's what my husband says!"

31

Yvette…if I was your therapist I'd be tired of you too…I'm already tired of your whiny voice.

Imani speaks next, "Hi I'm Imani and I'm a grad student at the University. I just turned 22. Imani's dark ebony skin looks like silk more than skin. She is beautiful and exotic looking with the long flowing summer dress she's wearing topped off with a denim jacket. Her make-up is perfectly applied and she smells like fresh coconut.

"I'm here cause of what my dad did to me when I was four years old. My parents took me to counseling and they even went to a therapist too. Our family stayed together and my dad never touched me again.

My parents are really supportive and very good to me but I guess that's why I'm here. My life feels like a really good lie. My goal is to truly *believe* that my life is good." Imani holds her head down and cries into a tissue.

Internal dialogue…

Penny…of course your life is good you have parents that love you. I would kill for that!

Dani…I wonder if her parents would like to come to the gym too. It could be a good bonding experience for them.

"Imani, says Ayda, "I praise your efforts to continue school despite the issues you are dealing with. I am a professor at WVSAU and I have difficulty getting up every day to teach! A great sin was done to me but I can't say out loud who did it to me. My goal is to be able to say all of it. I'm so ashamed." Ayda starts crying in earnest, her shoulders shaking.

Yvette passes her the tissue box. Ayda doesn't take the tissues so Yvette places the box on the floor next to Ayda's chair.

Ayda doesn't seem to be aware of anything happening around her. She is back to that night, long ago when she was betrayed by someone she admired and abandoned by the God she serves.

Dawn leans toward Ayda and tries to comfort her.

Internal dialogue...

Holly...What in the world happened to her? She seems like she had more than a sex thing happen to her.

Karen...OMG this is gonna be some fucked up shit right here.

Dawn...poor thing I wonder what happened to her and how could a man molest his daughter? Poor Imani...

Yvette...nasty bastards live in people's families.

Penny...I know how you feel Ayda.

Denise looks around the group and catches Karen's eye, "Karen its' ok if you want to speak. We will give Ayda space to process her feelings and then come back to check in with her.

Karen says, "I didn't want to appear insensitive toward Ayda."

Ayda looks up and smiles a little while dabbing at her nose. "It's ok, thank you...go on."

"Well, I'm Karen, and like I said earlier, I'm still on active duty with the Navy."

The group murmurs, "Thank you for your service."

Penny doesn't reveal she, too, was in the Navy. She's too self-conscience as it is. Most of the time when she tells people about her work history, she comes away feeling like they think she's a big mouth...always talking about herself. So she stays quiet.

Karen says, "Thanks. Well anyway I'm stationed at the recruiting office and I was sexually assaulted about three weeks ago by another sailor. We went out on a date, to the movies and on the way back to my car, that was parked at my office, he pulls over near Walnut St, you know the area I'm talking about; that old warehouse district where homeless people go to live?"

Some members of the group shake their heads that they know this area.

"Well anyway, he pulled in there…long story short he went up my dress and put his fingers inside me, pulled them out and licked them. I punched him in his fucking face and got out the car. I walked back to my car and went home.

I was afraid to report it cause people say it'll be harder on me than on him. You know that shit about men sticking together. Well now I have a guy I'm seeing and I don't know if I should tell him what happened to me. I guess that's my goal for being here."

Internal dialogue…

Lynn…that wasn't very smart she should've told someone!

Yvette…stuck his finger where? And did what? Did she say he was a sailor? Nasty ass!

Cheryl…nasty muther fucker!

Karen…I'm also wondering if I'm gay. Some of the guys think that if a girl doesn't like sexual things they do, then they must be gay.

Holly misses most of Karen's disclosure because she is scared she'll be the last person to speak so she raises her hand.

Denise, "Ok, Holly you ready to go up next?"

"Umm…my umm…name is Holly. I'm not married and I don't have kids." She looks at Imani, "I was in college years ago but I quit…umm…well I don't want to go into it a lot but…"

Picks at her nails…

34

"I quit school cause I was…ummm…well something happened to me after hours at my internship by…ummm…he was cleaning and I should have left on time but…umm I guess my goal is to…not be so nervous." Holly looks down and realizes her cuticles are bleeding.

Internal dialogue…

Penny…so is that what I look like when I'm biting my nails?

Yvette…girl needs some Xanax.

"Well to piggy back off Holly," says Lynn, "I'm nervous a lot too. I kinda feel stupid for being here because, well as I look around the room it's obvious I'm the oldest, yet here I am still letting this old wound continue to hurt me.

I'm 60 years old…anyway when I was 35 years old, which seems like a 100 years ago yet hurts like it happened this morning; anyway, I was 35 years old and living in Maryland. I was a foster care social worker and got myself raped by one of the foster kid's biological fathers. I went to his home to complete an assessment prior to his daughter's first unsupervised visit."

Lynn looks at the sign-in table and she goes back in time…and continues to speak…

"Of course he was nice and friendly. He even offered me a soda which I declined. So anyway, we sat down and started the assessment.

When I started asking him about his parenting skills, he became defensive and yelled at me. I naturally ended the assessment and as I stood to leave he hit me in the head with a lamp.

When I woke up he was raping me. I managed to reach out and found some kind of wood thing, which turned out to be the same lamp he hit me with. I hit him on the side of his face. It was enough for me to get him off me.

35

I got up, pulled up my panties and pants. I ran outta there and got into my ugly white state car and took off. Thankfully my car keys were in my jacket which I still had on. My purse was in the trunk of the car.

I drove straight to the emergency room where I was given a forensic examination to collect evidence of the rape.

Internal dialogue…

Lynn…they found his pubic hair inside me! I've never felt clean down there since.

He was subsequently arrested, convicted and sentenced to 25 years. He's getting out now but I don't know where he will live. I hope he stays in Maryland. Anyway my goal for being here is to work through his getting out and the fear I'm feeling because of it."

Lynn takes a long sip of her coffee and looks around the group with a soft smile.

The group is jolted out of Lynn's story by the inappropriateness of Dani's bubbly voice, "Well hi everyone! My name is Dani and I'm a personal trainer. Exercise has really helped me heal. Maybe ya'll should come on down and work out with me sometime! Lynn and Ayda, I can tailor my workouts to fit older women so don't worry…ok?"

Dani is dressed in pink yoga pants and a tight white tee shirt. Her curvaceous body is well toned and its clear Dani is very comfortable in her skin.

She has her bleached blond hair pulled into a bun on top of her head. Her blue eyes are natural, but she wears non-prescription blue contacts to make her eyes really "pop!"

Cheryl and Dawn look at each other with wide eyes and start laughing.

Ayda, looks up and says, "Oh, ok, thank you."

Lynn looks at Dani but for once doesn't say anything; she just continues to sip her coffee. Thinking to herself; shut the hell up you little rude blow-up doll!

Dani, smiling continues, "So I'm engaged for three months but this will be my second marriage. My first husband or I guess I can call him my ex-husband now!" She laughs looking around the group.

Everyone is just looking at her with various expressions.

Internal dialogue…

Yvette…Bitch please!

Holly…she's so pretty it might not have been anyone's fault they wanted to have sex with her! I sure hope they don't know what I'm thinking!

Ayda…sometimes we are punished by God for being more than he has called us to be.

"Well he got drunk one night after his stocks tanked on-line and decided that having sex with me would make him feel better. He didn't seem to care that I didn't want to have sex with him.

If I were as healthy and strong as I am now I could've set him on his drunken ass but I was 195lbs then and no muscle to speak of. So he wrestled me down and had un-consensual sex with me. I think that's what the judge called it. When we went to court, my attorney showed the judge pictures taken of me at the hospital. My nose was broken and I had bruises and bite marks all over my upper body. If not for those pictures, I'm not sure if the judge would've ruled in my favor. My attorney had warned me that it would be he said versus she said without the photos. Anyway he got some time and I got everything else!"

She starts laughing and even snorting! She sounded like a horse!
Hard to believe such a sound could come from such a small person.

"Sorry ya'll…but that shit is funny when I think of him having to
move back in with his momma and the only job he could get was to
work at the A-Z Emporium on Fayette Street!

I see him sometimes, you know I go there for my exercise clothes,
not much else cause it's always too crowded with people and their
loud kids!

Internal dialogue…

*Imani…Dani better watch herself cause some of these women look
like they want to slap her bun off her simple head!*

*Denise…Keep your face still and don't start laughing! Poor thing
doesn't see the change in body language since she started talking.
Look at Cheryl, Yvette, Dawn and Karen…they want her to shut
up…they might even want to shut her up!*

Anyway my goal for being here is to make sure I don't have any
stuff lingering before I get married to the most wonderful man
EVER!!!

I've been listening to these mindfulness audio-books and I just want
to be "in the present" of my life…I want to live my "true" self and
not be something fake just because it's easy. Can ya'll feel me on
that?" Dani looks expectedly around the room.

Internal dialogue…

*Dani…But what if Pete betrays me even though I'm learning to be
present? I mean the books are good and make sense but it's hard to
trust when I have proof bad things can happen.*

Most of the group is dumbfounded by how she sounds like a stuck
up airhead but she might have some, a little, but some depth beneath
it all.

Dawn says, "Wow Dani I didn't see you coming! You seem to have some insight."

Holly smiles and says a little too fast, "Dani I want to come and workout with you after the groups are over. I really would like to be around someone like you. You seem to really want to move forward but, be what did you say? Be "present." I like that."

She turns to Denise, "Is it alright to be around one another outside of group? Sorry I should've asked before opening my big fat mouth." She looks at Denise with tears starting.

Internal dialogue…

Yvette, Cheryl and Karen all think…Stalker!!

Dani…Awww isn't she sweet to want to be around me! But that's only because she thinks I have my act together, which I don't.

Ayda…be careful who you want to be your friend…you can't trust women.

"Well this group has norms but outside of the time we are together, formally, what you do with your time and your life is your own. Sometimes it's good for healthy survivors to become each other's support system as your family and friends may not understand what you're going through.

Just be careful that you don't feed into the past and the negative that it can bring. That leads to very destructive behavior."

Internal dialogue…

Yvette…Yeah like getting together and talking about killing some mutha fuckers! That would solve all these bitches' problems but none of them look like they could kill…'cept maybe Cheryl.

Holly smiles and looks at Dani who gives her a wink while drinking from her water bottle.

"Ok looks like I'm the last one to share, my name is Yvette and I'm a nurse at Morganville Memorial Hospital. I was molested by my grandmother's brother when I was 7 years old. My family never talked about it to me.

Of course the family, to this day, continues to gossip about it. I'm 41 years old now and he's dead. So I'm at a peaceful place but I know there are some unresolved anger issues that need attending to.

Internal dialogue:

Yvette...Cause I'm getting fucking tired of replacing broken mirrors! My husband, I'm sure is tired of fixing the walls after I kick them in!

My goal for being here is to identify my anger "nuggets" and find a way to deal with them."

Yvette nibbles on a cookie and Cheryl leans in and says, "Girl I know 'bout that anger shit. Hell most days I got a whole mountain of anger nuggets!"

Denise clears her throat and speaks, "Thank you ladies for your honesty and courage. I'm sure talking so openly to strangers was not easy. Hearing your own voice say your trauma, your fears and goals is a very strong therapeutic moment. Please don't lose sight of that. You have a voice and you can't expect others to hear you when you don't hear yourself. Now we have 15 minutes left does anyone have further comments or questions?"

The group is silent...

"Ok," says Denise, let's call the first meeting a success and give ourselves a hand clap for surviving it!"

Everyone claps, Dani the most enthusiastically.

"Now it's important to leave here in a safe frame of mind, so let's check in...what can you do to help yourself manage the stress you

40

may be feeling as a result of your first group disclosures?" Denise looks around the group…

Karen, "Reading."

Dawn, "Journaling."

Yvette, "Knitting."

Dani, "Exercise and meditation."

Imani, "Eating the rest of the chocolate cake at my house."

Ayda, "Sewing."

Lynn, "Watching British TV murder mysteries."

Penny, "Work."

Cheryl, "Cleaning my kitchen and bathroom, I love the smell of bleach."

Holly, "I like to do on-line shopping."

"Those are all wonderful de-stressors if everything is done in moderation. As our group moves forward it's my goal to help you learn techniques to recognize and manage your stress triggers and therefore lessen the stressful feelings.

So let's try one of those techniques now, we did it at the start of the group…palms flat on your thighs, breath in through your nose, hold it…and release. Ok, let's do that one more time only this time try to close your eyes. If you don't feel like it you can leave your eyes open.

Breathe in through your nose, hold it…and release. Great job, now let's do those shoulder shrugs. With your palms still on your thighs, lift your shoulders up toward your ears, hold it…and release.

One more time but let's add in the breathing part. Just listen for my instructions. Palms on thighs, as you lift your shoulders toward your ears, breath in deeply…hold it…and release."

Denise looks around the group one more time and says, "Ok, ladies thank you for coming and have a healthy week. If you find yourself in crisis please call 911, your therapist or our crisis hotline, 1-888-649-3336. Our hotline is available to you 24/7. Enjoy life and good night."

There are murmurs of "good night and thank you."

Lynn said, "I like it when things end on time." Imani and Holly agreed.

Cheryl, Dawn and Yvette are the first to leave.

Ayda asks, "Denise do you need any help cleaning up?"

"Thanks, Ayda, but no, that's my responsibility. Besides it gives me time to process the night and prepare for the next week. But really, thanks for offering."

Ayda smiles and gathers her belongings, then leaves.

Penny is the last one to leave; Denise can tell she was stalling so she could be alone with her.

"Hey Denise, are you from this area? I'm just wondering because you seem familiar to me, but I just can't place it."

"Well I've lived in a lot of places, but I was not born here. I have lived here only a few months. What about me is familiar?"

"I don't know something about your mannerisms, but maybe it's just the cop in me being nosey! Sometimes when I follow my nose it leads me down some really crazy paths!"

"Consider this," says Denise, "Maybe you feel uncomfortable in the group and you're looking for a connection to help put you at ease.

It's natural for a police officer to gravitate toward someone they perceive as their equal, the other leader in the situation. But Penny this time, we are not equals. Your equals are the other ladies in the group and I think you might be afraid to recognize yourself in them. Just consider that, as Yvette said, "a nugget" to think on.

Smiling, Denise turns and starts to fold up the chairs.

Penny stares at her back, chews her lower lip, turns and walks out.

Denise turns and stares at the empty doorway…this is going to be an interesting eight weeks.

See what we can find…

Next day Ruth and Penny meet at their usual café.

Ruth, "You want to talk about your meeting last night?"

"Well if you must know it was fine." says Penny.

"Fine…that's it?" asks Ruth incredulously.

Penny looks up from her cup, "You know Ruth what happens in group stays in group ok? You and the, she uses her fingers to make quotation marks; "leadership" are getting what you want. Crazy Penny is in a support group so it's done, but nobody said I had to talk about what it's like or what goes on in there. Go to one yourself if you're so interested."

Ruth's eyes are bulging out her head and she looks like she wants to slap Penny.

"Fuck you ok, Penny! I was just asking because I care about your stupid crazy ass alright! Fuck me, my bad!"

Ruth stands and leaves the café. Penny stands and then rushes after her.

"No you didn't just throw my stuff in my damn face. Ruth, see that's why I'm never gonna share my secrets with you ever again. People claim to be a friend and then smack you right in the face with a secret pie!"

Ruth grins, "What the fuck is a secret pie?"

Penny glares at her over the roof of their car, "Oh so now shit is funny?"

"Look ok, I'm sorry I am way out of line."

Penny rolls her eyes and snorts, "Yeah, sure you are sorry."

"For real girl I am sorry. Ok, I respect where you're coming from so let's just focus on the case at hand and leave your personal stuff on the sideline, unless, and I mean this Penny, unless it becomes a job issue. You feel me?"

Penny continues to glare at Ruth.

"Ok, so know this, girl I love you and I want the best for you. Hell that's why I'm your partner, cause I want you to have the best! Now come on and smile so we can move the hell on with investigating this crazy ass murder."

Penny finally softens her look at Ruth, "Yeah ok, and the case at hand." She reaches down and opens the car door and gets in.

Ruth drops her smile and a frown replaces it. She wonders what is going on with her partner and whether they will survive the outcome.

Ruth and Penny drive over to the bar where Raymond Jones was murdered. Once out of the car they begin the grueling work of canvassing the neighborhood. Each will take a side of High Street and meet back at the car.

Penny has the misfortune of running into Miss Stephanie and her dog Roxie. Miss Stephanie has lived on this street for over 20 years.

She's almost 70; at least that's what she tells people…all the time! She'll say, "You know I'm near 70 so you should help this old lady out." Then she'll ask for anything from paying her bills to buying her dog some food. Once she asked the mayor when he came a calling for votes to give her his watch because it was pretty and she was near 70!

She is quite the character to see. She wears those silky caftans and sandals in the summer. In the winter you don't see her as much, but when she does venture out she wears a ratty fur hat, scarf tied around her hair, and the ugliest chinchilla coat you will ever see. She loves those fake Uggs boots and somehow finds orange glittery ones!

To top it off, Miss. Stephanie has the thickest eye glasses you'll ever see! No pun intended. She refuses the simple surgery to remove the cataracts because, as she says, "If you poke me in the eye, you'll take out my mind."

No one understands much of what she says. She has difficulty telling real life from the soaps she watches all day and her over active imagination. Then there's her dog Roxie…

"Officer, you an officer right?" asks Miss Stephanie in her nasally slow way of talking.

Penny takes a calming breath, "Miss Stephanie you know me, and I'm Det. Darling."

"Yeah I know, but I love the way you say yo own name. It sounds all sweet and sugary…Dar-leng! Roxie look its officer, my bad, Dee-tec-tive Dar-leng" as she strokes Roxie's head.

Penny breathes in again, this time more deeply than the last one, "Hey Miss Stephanie, what can I do for you today?"

"Well you wanna know who kilt that Mr. Jones don't you?"

"Yes, we are investigating his murder," says Penny.

"I heard his (takes her hand and covers Roxie's ears) stuff was cut clean off! Is that true?"

Penny shakes her head and really wishes she were back in bed, "I can't go into specifics about the case with you. Do you know something about Mr. Jones that you want to tell me that might help us catch his killer?"

"Well, let me see…Mr. Jones and what I know…" Miss Stephanie closes her eyes and sways from side to side humming.

Penny silently screams, Oh have mercy crazy lady get away from me!!!!

Miss Stephanie stops swaying, opens her eyes and says, "Well I saw somebody coming down the alley from his backdoor the other night. I think it was the same night he was kilt."

Penny's eyebrows raise and she says "Are you serious? Can you identify the person?"

Miss Stephanie slowly says, "Well see Roxie and I were watching TV.

Roxie loves those dancing shows. The women are half naked and the men with their chest hairs out! What a sight, so that night was the elimination round and …"

"Oh my gosh Miss Stephanie please tell me what you saw and stop this other foolishness about some stupid dancing show!"

Penny all but jumps out her shoes she so exasperated by this tangential conversation.

"You mean what did me and Roxie see?" Asks Miss Stephanie who appears to have lost some of her connection to the conversation. Seems she was remembering those dancers with the chest hair out.

Penny tries but fails to keep the frustration out of her voice, "No I mean what did YOU see? Roxie is a friggin stuffed animal for Pete's sake! Now tell me what you think you saw or stop wasting my time!"

Miss Stephanie starts stamping her feet up and down likes she's marching in place. She digs her nails into the "fur" behind Roxie's ears.

Then she stops marching and angrily says, "Well a fine fuck to you!"

Miss Stephanie walks off in a huff all the while stroking Roxie. Over her shoulder she yells, "I ain't talking to her 'bout nothing she so damn disrespectful to you. It'll be a cold day in Hawaii before I tell her anything! Call you "stuffed," I'm sorry baby, she's just jealous you aren't her little doggie."

Penny looks up to the sky, closes her eyes and takes a long deep breath and is disappointed that it didn't work as well as at the end of the group session.

Penny continues to walk down the street and has the misfortune of seeing another staple of the neighborhood, Gene the Pimp as he gets out of his Oldsmobile.

How that car continues to move is a miracle of modern science. The car's color is a dark reddish hue that gets its look from the rust all over it. Seriously, if you didn't know any better you would think the car was actually brown!

Gene has been a pimp since dirt was dust. It's amazing that he can still pull girls into his nasty little stable. He's 6'5", broad shouldered, skin the color of coffee with just a little too much cream and he has his hair processed straight. He keeps it dyed black, slick on the sides, and wait for it...the top is in a pompadour!

He looks like a caricature of the zoot suit guys from back in the day! Sometimes the top of his hair is curled in layers and he walks around like an old lady who doesn't want to comb her hair out till Sunday-go-to-meeting.

Today, finishing off his look is a black polyester shirt that has red fake leather tips on the collar and the sleeve cuffs. His pants are red fake leather with a black seam going down the legs...front and back!

OMG, what is on his feet? Fake Louis Vutton wedge heeled tennis shoes!!!! What in the world is up with this man?

Maybe I should turn around and wait for him to go into his liquor store. Gene doesn't own it, but he calls it his anyway. He calls all the establishments on High Street "his."

But before Penny can make up her mind, Gene turns so he can survey "his street."

He adjusts the big black square glasses he's known for wearing. He can still find the frames but unlike his original pair from back in the day, they don't come with rhinestones anymore. So he has one of his women hot glue some on the handles.

Gene has a reputation to keep up and his glasses are his signature look. Like all the pimps from the Blacksploitation era…he's gotta have a look to let everyone know he's the man with the plan!

Gene has been operating whores on High Street since his mentor, Bubby passed away 23 years ago. He and Bubby were like father and son. Not a day goes by that Gene does not have a drink to honor his "street father."

Shit, he sees me and breaks into one of his leering grins. I might as well get this over with so I walk up to him.

"Hey Penelo-pie Dawlin! Girl you looking good." He gives me that oily, nasty up and down look as only a street rat could.

I put my hands on my hips and glare at him with my head cocked to the side.

"I mean "officer," see ole Gene don't want to be charged with being disrespectful to an officer of the law even if she's the finest thing on this block right this very moment!!

Hope I'm not being too familiar and all." He tries to look apologetic, but it comes off looking like he's trying not to fart.

Oh, did I mention Gene has a gold tooth, and if you can believe it, a diamond or most likely a glued on rhinestone chip in its center.

Even though he disgusts me I always smile at the son-of-a-bitch. Truth be told I like Gene cause he's honest about who he is and what he does, at least to a certain point. I've never busted him for beating up his girls or johns. Not sure if he does and nobody tells. But to me, as pimps go, he's a stand up guy.

Shit, what is wrong with me? Oh yeah, according to Ruth I'm crazy.

"Good morning Pimp Gene, how are you today?

He looks at me sheepishly, "Now officer Dawlin, you know ole Gene is just a hard working man trying to make a dollar and help everyone he can."

"Yeah, ok Gene, look, I'm investigating a murder and I don't have time to play with you today. I just want to tell you that I'm interested in any information you or your girls might have about the murder at Jones' Bar the other night. You don't have to say now and out in the open but call me if you have anything that would help us catch whoever did it."

I hand him my card.

"Well officer Dawlin I sure will give you a call." He looks me up and down again then adds a lick to his nasty big fleshy lips. Yuck!!

"Now is this yo personal number or work one?"

"It's my work number," I say trying to hold my "cop face."

Pimp Gene asks, "How 'bout adding yo personal number on the back?"

I turn and walk away throwing over my shoulder, "Thanks Count Chocula!"

Gene drops his smile and frowns, "See that ain't right! Who told you to call me that shit? I ain't no damn Count Chocula! When I find out who started that shit…"

Penny crosses the street and sees Ruth at the end of her block talking to a prostitute.

"Ok, thanks Squidget, look girl, be careful on these streets, you hear?"

"Yeah, yeah, yeah Officer Ruth I hear you. I got almost enough money so I can get me some of that all you can eat shrimp at Fisherman's Shrimp & Lobster tonight!

I'll be able to lay low for a few days cause my welfare check will be here in about two days. So see, ain't nuthin to worry about. Squidget gonna take care of Squidget!

I ain't gonna ever end up working for no Count Chocula! I keeps my money!"

Squidget punctuates "my" by poking herself in her small bird frame chest.

Ruth says, "Don't get caught on Pimp Gene's turf, ok? Just be careful of him and the "somebody" who killed Mr. Jones."

Squidget says laughing, "That tall old ass Count Choc-ugly mutha fucker don't scare me! Knock that fake diamond out his mouth!

"Yeah, you bad while he ain't around, and we here to protect you!" Ruth starts laughing too. "Girl you go on and keep it real!"

"Yeah, I'll keep it real nasty, officer Ruth." She says as she turns and sashays down the street.

Penny asks Ruth, "Anything?"

Ruth, "Naw just handed out cards. You know how this lot works, someone will call later and ask about a reward. "How 'bout you?"

"Well I spoke with Miss Stephanie, she claims they saw something, but then she got all pissy because I had no time to hear "Roxie's" version of events."

51

"Penny you could've blown the case wide open and you messed it up! Roxie probably did see the killer!"

They both laugh as they walk toward their vehicle.

Miss Stephanie and Roxie sit on the couch watching "Let's Talk Live Morganville" a local news and entertainment show.

Roxie says to Miss Stephanie, "Mommy you should've told the police lady what we saw the other night."

"No, baby, she was mean about you and we don't help mean people."

"But mommy," says Miss Stephanie in the light sing song voice she adopts when Roxie is speaking to her. "We saw someone walking out of the bar. We saw them from behind, shouldn't we tell what we saw."

"No baby, we're gonna keep our mouths shut till that police Penny learns some manners." Miss Stephanie continues to stroke Roxie's head as she starts talking along with the hosts of the TV show.

Penny and Ruth arrive at the office and go through their email and phone messages. Nothing relevant to their current case so Penny gets up and stretches.

"Hey let's go back to the crime scene. There's nothing for us to do here at the office and we may see something we missed."

Ruth looks up and asks, "Why when we just left the neighborhood without going into the crime scene. That makes no sense…why didn't you mention going into the place when we were over there, like seriously Penny WTF?"

"I know, but I thought that if we put our faces on the street that when we got back someone would've reached out to us. Since that didn't happen, I'd like to take another look around the entire bar, this time not just the room where he was found."

"Penny, I ain't got time for that super sleuth shit today. I have a deposition in the Perry case to prepare for. Do you really need me to go with you?"

"Nope partner, I'm on it…besides, I "see" better alone. I can focus and feel the crime when your negative vibes aren't there to distract me."

Penny picks up her purse and winks at Ruth as she walks away from her desk.

Ruth says, "Yeah well I'd shoot myself if I *saw* life through your crazy ass eyes!"

Penny stops dead in her tracks and slowly turns back to Ruth.

"Aww shit Penny, I can't even joke with you because…" Ruth stands and walks over to her partner.

"Sorry for being so insensitive, I just want you to be well enough so one day I can talk shit to you. Seriously though Penn please don't hurt yourself today, can you promise me that?"

"Thanks Ruth, you're all heart and yes, I can promise that I won't kill myself today. I haven't had time to properly plan it. You know these things aren't worth it without the proper plans." She sticks her tongue out and walks away from her stunned and very worried partner.

Ruth's ordeal...

Ruth is meeting with one of the city's State's Attorney to prepare for her deposition. The Perry case just walked into Ruth's life one day. She was having lunch at the Pita Palace when a man comes over to her table.

"Excuse me, I hate to bother you during lunch but I just got this new phone and I'm having trouble sending a text message. Could you please help me for just a second?"

Ruth frowns, but puts down her sandwich and looks over at the man's phone.

"Ok, what is going on...what the fuck is this?!" Ruth jumps up and grabs his phone. There is a picture, up close and personal of his penis!

The little pervert says, "Hey give me back my phone I just wanted to see if you'd be interested in having me for dessert. You know after you eat that sandwich."

He starts laughing and licking his lips. "You sitting here all alone and looking finer than a hot fudge sundae! You wanna get with me?

While you got my phone why don't you put your name and number in it baby and we can plan a hook-up, if you're too busy for a quickie right now."

Again he licks his lips and has the nerve to do a little spin turn so Ruth can take in the fullness of him!

Ruth says through gritted teeth, "You little shit, I'm Det. Ruth mutha fuckin Hill and your stupid ass is under arrest. It's illegal to show pictures of your dick to women who don't give their permission!"

Then before he knows what hit him, he's thrown to the ground and cuffed.

The prosecutor on the case, Will Covington says, "Det. Hill I think they will take a plea so this deposition should be all you'll have to do. I know it sucks to have to spend your valuable time dealing with this shit when there are other things you could be doing."

"Yeah well sex perverts really get under my skin. Before we go on record, let me say this, if it was another place and time I might have hacked his shit off and fed it to him as his own dessert."

Ruth looks so fiercely into Will's eyes that he turns away feeling uncomfortable and confident that Det. Hill would have done just what she said.

"Well ok, here comes the stenographer…let's get ourselves ready to start."

Denise arrives early for setup; her assistant had to leave early for a doctor's appointment. But it's all good because Denise will have quiet time to replay last week's group conversations.

She sets the chairs up in a circle like last time, posts the norms on the wall and proceeds to make coffee and finally sets out the snacks. Almost forgetting the sign-in sheet she goes back and places it on a small table in near the entrance. Looking around she is satisfied and takes a seat against the wall to wait for the ladies to start arriving.

I haven't had a moment to think about the group since the last meeting. It's been pretty hectic at the rape crisis center which is in so many ways very unfortunate. So many near rapes, sexual assaults on and around the college campus as a result of alcohol, drugs and immature young adults; can make for a lot of referrals.

Holly arrives first. After signing in she gets coffee and some cookies. She looks around but doesn't see Denise who is still sitting against the wall but in shadow. Denise only turned on the overhead lights directly above the group. The rest of the conference room is dark.

Holly makes two attempts to sit down and finally decides on a seat. Denise watches a nervous Holly trying to make herself comfortable.

The other group members come, sign-in, decide on refreshments, and then take their seats.

Denise joins them by taking the last seat in the circle. "Welcome back ladies! So glad to see you all decided to join us again. As you can see I've posted the group norms on the wall. If we need to revisit any of them, for clarification, just let us know."

No one says anything so Denise moves on, "Now anything from last week you would like to talk about?"

Again no one responds, however Denise notices that Holly looks like she's processing data like a robot!

Her eyes are moving rapidly from side to side and her face is flushed. Even her lips are parted like she's gonna speak but nothing comes out. Who is this woman? Is she a ball of nervous energy or is something else going on with her?

Internal dialogue...

Holly...I don't think I should've sat here...what did they say last week? I can't remember anything and I bet somebody is gonna ask me what I think about something that was said. How much longer before this group is over?

To keep the group moving forward Denise proposes, "I'm going to put out to the group a simple or straight forward question to get us going.

You've made a fantastic start last week. There was 100 percent participation; this is telling me that we aren't here to waste eight weeks. Push yourselves…is everyone ready?"

Everyone nods and murmurs okay as they look at their laps or at Denise.

What is this bitch up to now wonders Cheryl.

Denise clears her throat and asks, "So what did you do to *provoke* the sexual act you experienced?"

Cheryl's head snaps up and she looks across the circle to Denise, "I didn't do a damn thing to provoke that mutha fucker!

What you mean what did I do?" She was caught off guard by the question.

Internal dialogue...

Yvette...Yeah it's on now!

57

Lynn...Cheryl is a scary person.

Ayda...Mary, mother of my Lord Jesus...please give me strength to be honest.

Dawn, who is sitting directly across from Cheryl interjects, "I think Denise is trying to get us to acknowledge any guilt we may be feeling. Like are we still in our feelings about it being our fault?"

Dawn looks pass Ayda, who is sitting between Dawn and Denise and asks, "Is that right?"

Looking around the group Denise says, "Let's see what comes of my question. It's not for me to discuss, but for the group."

Cheryl fidgets in her chair and turns to look around the group. She points herself in the chest as she says, "Well I can tell you I didn't do any damned thing to cause that fool to fuck with me. He blamed it on the drugs, but he was a fool all his life. He was always messing around with his own cousins when they were small.

I heard his mother was letting him suck her titties 'til he was six years old. What kind of shit was that? Mothers will fuck up their boys for sure, that's why I ain't got none."

Internal dialogue...

Karen...Did she say someone let their son breastfeed until they were six years old? WTF?

Imani...That's really gross!

Ayda...God is in this place and He will carry our burdens.

Cheryl...Why did I just say all that?

She takes a breath and before she can say anything else Lynn speaks.

"Cheryl can I ask you a question? Of course, you don't have to answer if you don't want to."

58

Cheryl looks at Lynn who is sitting right next to her, "Sure but you'd better be prepared for my answer."

Lynn nervously laughs and says, "Ok, but you seem like a very strong woman…so I'm wondering what you did after the assault?

"What do you mean what did I do? You mean did I go to the ER like you and have evidence collected, call the cops, did I tell anyone…what exactly are you asking me?"

"No, sorry I wasn't clear; I mean what did you do to your brother-in-law after you got raped?" Lynn looks at Cheryl with such intensity that Cheryl has to take a sip of water before answering.

"Well Lynn and company, you wouldn't believe it, but bad ass Cheryl just cried. I didn't do anything.

I was a weak fool then but let that shit happen now. I'll kill any punk ass bitch who fucks with me!"

She takes a hard bite of her cookie…poor cookie.

Ayda asks, "Dawn you said this might be to see if we had any guilt about what happened."

Dawn nods, "Yeah I've worked on guilt with my therapist for a long time."

Internal dialogue…

Yvette…La-de-da! Who gives a fuck what you've done? You're not our therapist!

"Ok, well then Cheryl do you feel guilty for not doing more to stop him? Is that why you're so angry all the time?

Denise steps in, "Well Ayda let's not assign anger to Cheryl as an "all the time" response.

"I'm sorry Cheryl, I don't know you and that wasn't fair."

Cheryl says, "No Ayda...you're Ayda right?"

"Oh yeah that's right I forgot to say I was Ayda."

"No Ayda you...I don't know...this is too much focus on me right now. Let me think about it...I'll talk later."

Denise says, "Let's respect Cheryl's request and keep our discussion moving; Cheryl you join when you like."

Internal dialogue...

Ayda...Why doesn't God have mercy for me? He allowed this to happen! Will He also allow me to get into heaven? I want to pray for my old girl scout leader but I just can't! If I don't forgive Censeria for what she did to me I will go to hell! Matthew 6:14 says, "If you forgive men when they sin you, your heavenly Father will also forgive you." But what if Censeria doesn't want my forgiveness and she has no remorse for what she did to me? Do I still have to forgive her?

"I just want to say I wasn't trying to make Cheryl feel bad." Ayda dabs at her eyes and continues, "I don't know what I did to provoke what happened to me. I feel like I should've realized it was wrong before it actually happened to me. I feel guilty that I was 12 years old and knew right from wrong but I didn't do anything to stop it from happening." Ayda begins to cry in earnest.

She continues, "I still feel like some kind of nasty person. Why did it happen to me and no one else? What did the person see in me that no one else saw?"

Internal dialogue:

Ayda...Please God don't let my mouth slip and I say "she" out loud! Then they will really know my horror!

Ayda continues to cry and the group is silent for a few moments then Yvette speaks up.

"Well I was seven years old when my great-uncle molested me. I was home alone with him and he had just gotten out of prison for robbing a local liquor store. The store owner was shot by the other guy with my uncle but both were sentenced for the shooting.

"Anyway, Ayda I was wracked for years with the questions about why did he chose me, why was I left alone with him, why didn't anyone prosecute him and send him back to jail, why had God left me so this bad thing could happen to me?

It was like I was emotionally stuck at seven years old but I realized something bad had happened to me. Then I just stopped thinking about it.

It wasn't until I was 18 years old that the memory of that day came rushing back to me. It hit me one night while I was up studying for finals my freshman year at college.

Even though I finished school and tried to make a career for myself, by the time I was 27 years old I realized I was a wreck." Yvette stops to take a sip of coffee.

Imani raises her hand…"Yvette, right? I was a child as well when I was molested by my father." She lowers her head as if all the strength has left her.

"I'm sorry, what was your name again?" asks Yvette.

Denise interjects, until we get familiar with each other let's start our statements or questions with our name…should I add that to our norms?

Everyone agrees and Denise stands and adds, "Before speaking please say your name." Then she sits back down. This was a needed break for the group as most of them were crying or near tears.

Yvette looks at Imani, "I'm Yvette, why are you looking down after saying you were molested by your father? What are you feeling? I

61

promise you the worst is over…this is your beginning to the rest of your life…just trust in you."

Imani looks up at Karen, not Yvette as she feels more of a connection with Karen since they are close in age.

"So, ok, I'm Imani and I feel like I'm a fraud, like my life has been a lie and that makes me a liar. I do feel guilty because if I didn't do something my daddy wouldn't have been confused and do that to me." Imani balls her fists up and hits her thighs.

Karen and Lynn lean in on each side of her and whisper support.

Lynn gives Imani some fresh tissues and sits back. She would like to hug Imani but isn't sure if she would welcome it. It would be so embarrassing if she tried to hug her and the girl slapped her or something. So she just sat back and sipped her coffee.

"Does anyone ever feel guilty for wanting to kill the bastard that hurt you?"

Everyone looks up astonished cause no one expected that question to be spoken out loud and certainly not from Dani!

Internal dialogue…

Denise…Shit, I've got to assess for a real threat this early in the process! Shit! I know I have a legal obligation to assess the risk for harm to self or others but I didn't expect this!

Penny…What if I hear something about a murder? Should I tell them I've tried to kill myself?

Karen…Shit's getting real! Go doll baby!

Imani…I've thought of killing my parents

Holly…I think of someone killing me all the time!

"Sorry I forgot our new rule, I'm Dani…I'm gonna be honest, it's hard to say my name every time I want to talk! Denise why don't you make us some name tags or something? Well don't look at me like I got three heads or something!" Dani frowns and looks around.

Internal dialogue…

Denise…bossy much!

"I mean aren't ya'll ever tired of beating yourselves up over somebody else's craziness? I don't feel guilty cause I didn't do anything to my ex-husband and every time I see Michael at the A-Z Emporium I laugh and honestly I get a little turned on from the irony of it all!

Internal dialogue…

Yvette…I can understand that!

Ayda…Holy Mother what is she talking about?

Denise…That is so inappropriate!

Dani continues, "Now Ayda, don't go praying or passing out! It's my true feelings in this present moment and I'm feeling like ya'll are alright for me to express myself."

She looks across the circle at Ayda and gives her a point with her index finger. "Ayda honey, I don't know what happened to you or why you feel so responsible but ya'll, you, Imani and Yvette were little girls and little girls don't know nuthin 'bout the world."

Karen speaks up, "Dani you may be in another phase of recovery or whatever but not all of us have moved as far as you have.

I mean you got actual justice for what your ex-husband did to you. I don't have that satisfaction…sorry my name is Karen."

Dani responds, "Karen you are right, I did get justice, but satisfaction is another thing all together. I'll never be satisfied that he got his just for thinking he could take my body and make it his whipping post or sex post or whatever.

Don't get me the least bit wrong or twisted when it comes to my anger and negative stuff; I'm pissed off every time I think of my inability back then to physically fight for myself.

Once the court stuff was over I immediately began to work on me. I decided my take away from the incident would be that my body would never be so out of shape and weak that I couldn't fight for myself!"

Internal dialogue…

Denise…Did she just say "don't get it twisted"?

Cheryl…Country Barbie got it going on!

Yvette…Did she just say "twisted"?

Ayda…Get what twisted…her hair?

Lynn…I don't like it when white girls talk like trash or try to sound black.

Holly asks, "I'm Holly…but how Dani did you move on? I mean what were the steps you took that put you in the frame of mind to even have a "take away" from it?"

Dani says, "Holly, I have no idea, it's just who I am or who I chose to be. I didn't go to therapy, read books, like I do now, or anything there was just something inside me that said, "Do this and keep doing it." I don't have a magic solution but stewing in it wasn't going to work for me…no offense."

Internal dialogue…

Yvette, Karen, Cheryl and Lynn…then why are you here?

Denise…Dani you are full of shit! Something brought you here.

64

Penny speaks up, "I'm Penny and I am a police officer. I know first-hand that justice and satisfaction aren't the same for everyone. I think I became a cop in order to help others find justice thinking it would make their hardships better but over the years I just found more and more injustice and I became more depressed about my choice to be a cop.

So guess what I did? Well I became a Detective because I thought I needed to be more involved in cases and perhaps really make changes. Well that too was a fairy tale because the robberies, assaults and murders keep right on happening. What can I really do or the "system" do to give you ladies and other victims their lives back? Nothing…my life changed the moment my cousin took advantage of my love for him. I looked up to him like he was my big brother. I trusted him and he betrayed me. I have not received any satisfaction from my job that fills that hole."

Penny looks at Dani and starts to say, no I don't want to kill them I want to kill myself but she stops short. She just can't say those words out loud.

Denise speaks up, "We have 15 mins left in the group."

Dawn asks, "Cheryl, Ayda, Imani…you guys okay?"

Cheryl says, "Yeah thanks for checking back with me. I've heard some very powerful things tonight and I have a lot to think about. Thanks all of you for sharing…appreciate it." She offers a smile but it doesn't reach her eyes.

Ayda says, "I'm Ayda…I would like to discuss this more next week if we can. I'm glad to hear more people encourage me to think about my situation in another way. It means more when people have been through it tell me it's not my fault. I pray to the Holy Mother that my heart can receive what my ears have heard. Thank you all."

Everyone looks at Imani who has kept her head down after speaking earlier. She doesn't look up or say anything.

Denise draws the group back to her. "Okay we have had some very powerful discussions tonight. Let me remind you to call 911, your therapist or our crisis line if you find yourself in crisis. Ok, let's try the relaxation technique I introduced last meeting.

Palms flat on your thighs, eyes closed or open if you want, deep breath in...hold it...release. Let's do that again...deep breath in...hold it...release. Good now let's add the shoulder shrugs...while taking a deep breath in bring your shoulders up toward your ears...hold it...release. One more time...deep breathe in while pulling shoulders up...hold it...release.

Excellent...have a healthy week...see you all next week."

Once home, Penny snuggles on her couch, turns on a movie; she likes to have background noise when she is thinking through a case. Tonight though, her attention isn't as focused on the Jones' case, she keeps thinking about the group tonight. The amount of pain and anger was almost too much to bear.

How come she didn't hate her cousin? How come she decided to hate herself more than him? How come she wants justice for everyone except herself?

Ok, Penelopie stop it! Focus on this case for at least an hour then come back to the group stuff. This discipline has always worked for her. Penny has always been able to compartmentalize her life; it has been the key to her success.

Maybe I'll share that with the group next week, put things in their place and deal with the most important first, and right now that is this case…who killed Mr. Raymond Jones and why?

Penny pulls open the file and looks at the photos she took earlier today of the bar putting them in order as if she's walking through the front door. From this vantage point she can see the bar, stools and take in the floor.

There are six tables with four chairs each and 10 stools at the bar…so she thinks there were at least 34 people in the bar plus the two people who helped Ray behind the bar.

Let me see, ok, yeah a guy named Devenious Wilbox, an ex-con and now a church Deacon who works in the bar washing dishes.

Truly you can't make this stuff up!

And a waitress named Hope Jones, but no relation to the deceased. Miss Jones is a student at the college, getting her second Master's Degree, this one in Astronomy, because having one in Geophysics and Planetary Science wasn't enough!

She lives with her sister, goes to school, works at the bar and is an online professor teaching Earth Science and Geology.

She could be an astronaut or something; instead she's a cat lady living with her sister! So much talent going to waste…alright Penns stop being so judgmental.

When interviewed, she said she was working at the bar that night though she didn't express any real emotion.

She did however, un-flatten her affect when she was told how Mr. Jones was murdered. Then she got a little green…I wonder if it's the same shade as the little green men she might have studied!

Penny actually laughs out loud and guiltily puts her hand over her mouth and looks around.

Ok, focus…so I really don't get the feeling either of them had anything to do with Mr. Jones' death.

Alright Mr. Jones, let's open your file and see what National Crime Information Center (NCIC) has to say about you.

Raymond Jones, 6'1" African American born April 7, 1943; previous record includes 3 misdemeanors for peeping at women showering at a recreation center in the 90's since then nothing.

Place of birth Morganville, West Virginia; parents deceased; only sibling a sister died last year (Candace Collins age 70). No known children; extended family in Brookhaven.

Well I guess tomorrow I better talk to Ruth about interviewing his next of kin. Nothing more on Mr. Jones…now let me look at the crime scene photos one more time…there might be something.

But as Penny looked at the photos she didn't see anything out of the ordinary. The forensic team said it was a difficult scene to process because there were fingerprints all over the place. Probably delivery people, staff, and customers, but we have to try so I'll just have to wait to see if there are any unusual hits that come back.

Penny closes the file and places everything in her book bag. She's never outgrown her love for her book bag.

When I decide that I might be a grown up I'll buy a real briefcase.

She makes herself a gin and tonic with ice. She sits back on her couch and while looking at the TV, she thinks of the group.

So much pain, misery and anger…how have we all made it this far? Can we help each other?

Some of the ladies have men in their lives, what's wrong with me? Ruth is always telling me I need to get laid! But Ruth thinks sex and food are the answer to EVERY question.

Maybe if I decide to live I'll think about getting a man. Ok, let's put that in a compartment for later…ohhhh is that "*John Wick*" on again? I l-o-v-e this movie!

By the time the credits roll Penny is fast asleep.

She has no idea someone else was watching the movie with her and now watches her sleep.

Good and Plenty...

Good and Plenty are hookers for Pimp Gene and they *really* like their jobs.

Good, aka Wendy Browne and Plenty, aka Tina Johnson had been best friends since they met at a corner store on Prospect Street.

They were both caught by Mr. Iswara for stealing bubblegum when they were six years old. Wendy started crying really loud and her mother came down the aisle to see what happened. Tina said Mr. Iswara was fussing at them for stealing, but they didn't steal anything.

Tina said they "found" the bubblegum on the floor and tried to put it back.

Wendy cried even louder! Mr. Iswara apologized for the mistake, and gave each girl two pieces of bubblegum for being so honest.

Wendy immediately stopped crying and took her mother's hand.

As they walked down the aisle and before Tina found her mom, they made eye contact and were friends ever since. Of course they were stealing the bubblegum but "goody" Wendy got scared and dropped hers so Tina was whispering really loud to pick it up. That's when old man Iswara heard them and came from behind the counter to catch them red handed.

Wendy and Tina got the working names of Good and Plenty because they only wear pink and black clothes. Wendy always wore pink clothes because her mom said she looked like an angel in pink. Thank God her mother died when she was 11 years old because she wouldn't think Wendy was an angel now.

Tina was known for having too much mouth by her father. "You talk too much...you got plenty mouth don't you..." then he'd smack some of that mouth outta her. When Tina turned 15 years old, she ran away and Pimp Gene found her. Gene insisted go back home and stay in school and while there, they could screw some money outta the male teachers.

Tina was a natural, and soon Wendy was following her friend's lead. When they turned 18 and had their high school diplomas, they moved in with Gene and became his full-time hookers.

Standing on the corner starts for them at 6pm each day and ends when "our cootchies get dry," says Tina.

Gene lives like he owns the two streets just south of the college.

He says, "All roads lead to my pussies…you can't get to the grocery store, drug store or bookstore without passing one of my girls...money and mo money!"

Besides Good & Plenty Gene has two more girls working for him but they aren't on the street cause they need to be protected because of who they are. One is a Judge's daughter and the other is the Mayor's cousin!

Yeah ole Pimp Gene can pull 'em that's for sure. See what drugs will make you do! Both are coke heads and need to make money that can't be traced.

Ole Gene just making a way for those who ain't got no other way.

Good and Plenty are walking down the street, after a long night of hooking, talking about the murder of Raymond Jones.

"You think they gonna open the bar back up? I liked those pepper poppers old Mr. Ray used to make," says Plenty.

"Probably not, I mean who gonna run it?" asks Good.

"I wonder why somebody fucked Mr. Ray up like that? He was a quiet and nice old dude. You don't think Count Chocula did it do you?" whispers Good.

"Who knows," says Plenty. "Gene still got a nasty streak, but why would he do it?"

"I don't know…shit here come that damned crazy Miss Stephanie," says Tina rolling her eyes.

"Good morning night ladies," smiles Miss Stephanie.

Well if we were night ladies we wouldn't be out this morning would we?" taunts Wendy.

"Roxie says good morning too, even though she warns me to be mindful around ya'll night women." Miss Stephanie has Roxie in a dog carrier today.

Good & Plenty bend down and look in at the stuffed dog. They look at each other and burst out laughing!

"Well ok, funny uhh, piss on the both of you," yells Miss Stephanie as she walks away. Piss on them Roxie…right in their face until they drown!

Somewhere in Maryland...

"Authorities have found a man's body in the Nanjemoy Creek; authorities have identified him as Donavan Tate, recently released from prison, convicted of raping a state employee over 25 years ago.

They have also found the remains of another human body, but, as of this time, no identification has been made…...more information to follow as we get it…back to you Leon in the studio."

Squidget is adjusting her clothes after servicing her last john for the month. Her check will be here soon and since she heard there was a mix up with the restaurant getting shrimp…I mean really who messes up an order for shrimp when it's all-you-can-eat shrimp week!!!!

Man you can't trust anybody these days. Now I gotta make alternate plans!

So Squidget is going to go to the A-Z Emporium and treat herself to a new lunch box. The one she has is getting worn out, and in her business, a lunchbox comes in handy.

She uses it to hold her bottled water, mouth wash, gum, mace, razor, and fruit snacks.

There ain't nothing like being in between blow jobs and being hungry or thirsty. So Squidget likes to plan ahead.

I may buy myself one of those expensive ones for $20 so it will really keep my shit cool on those hot days.

One time my candy bar looked like chocolate pudding. Hell candy too expensive to be melting!

I better get another blue ice pack too…can't ever have too many of those things. Hell I need one just to cool off my "who-haw" after a long day of work.

Squidget is in the camping section when a store employee, walks up to her.

"Are you finding everything you need alright miss?"

"Uh yeah, but I can't reach that yellow and fuchsia lunchbox up there on the top shelf. See it?" Squidget points to the only yellow and fuchsia lunchbox in the universe!

"Sure I see it, who couldn't, that thing is loud!"

"Well can you get it or do you want to stand here looking at it?" says Squidget putting her hands on her hips, that, today, are covered by red and gray striped yoga pants. Her shirt is a sleeveless purplish tunic.

The salesman takes her all in and says, "Sure I'll get it for you, be right back."

He returns with a grabber and lifts it off the shelf.

"Here you go. Is there anything else I can do for you?"

Looking around he leans in and says, "I mean I got a break coming in 30 minutes if you've got the time, I've got a little money." Michael Bauer, Dani's ex-husband, smirks.

Squidget walks close into Michael and says in her best sexy whisper, "Honey you better enjoy that break you got coming, cause that's the only *coming* you're going to be doing today."

She kisses his cheek and walks away.

The A-Z Emporium security chief watches the entire episode and makes a note in the security log. "Employee M. Bauer seen kissing while on duty; tell his supervisor."

What comes out of my mouth…

Ruth and Penny meet for coffee the next day…sitting at a table outside the café…

"Hey Ruth, I think one of us should talk to Mr. Jones' extended family. His file says there is a niece living in Brookhaven." Penny says, as she scarves down her second Boston cream donut.

"How can you eat two of the same donuts? If you're going to eat all those empty calories shouldn't you eat two different flavors?" Ruth says with the same seriousness as if she's interviewing a perp.

"Are you kidding me right now? Mind your business about my donuts okay? You're just mad you didn't order them before me!

Now the family of the man that was killed and had a finger stuck in his ass…please?"

"Sometimes Penny…ok, I'll go see the niece. What are you going to be doing?"

"I'm going to see Dr. Ellis, our wonder boy medical examiner and see if he's found out anything more. See you in the office around," she checks her cell phone, "2 pm ok?"

"Yeah that's fine…later gator." Ruth gets up and heads toward her car. She drives away and Penny realizes she'll have to walk to the medical examiner's office because she didn't drive! Ruth picked her up from home…shit there goes my donut high.

While walking through the downtown area, Penny sees Denise Wallace, their support group facilitator, going into a coffee shop.

Should she go in and speak or would that be bad? Well, she told us what we do on our time is our business so I'm going to speak.

Penny enters the shop and Denise sees her right away.

"Good morning Penny how are you today?" Denise says reaching forward to shake Penny's hand.

"I'm doing great, just finished off two donuts and now I'm walking them off as I'm headed to the medical examiner's office."

"Oh, you're working…sorry guess I should say Det. Darling instead of your first name," says Denise looking worried and apologetic.

Laughing, Penny says, "Not everyone in the world has to call me that! I do have friends and random people who call me Penny!

Actually no I don't, cause I don't have friends only co-workers and my mom who really doesn't want to call me at all."

Penny slaps her hand over her mouth and her eyes grow large.

"Oh my God Denise I am so sorry, I don't know why all that popped out my mouth! Sometimes I can be so impulsive and filter-less and all kinds of shit comes out my mouth!

I am so embarrassed, really I'm…"

"Take a breath and let's sit," says Denise.

She leads Penny to a table in the back of the shop.

"Now sit here and I'll be right back."

Denise returns with a cup of hot water and a tea bag that she places in front of Penny.

"Here make yourself a cup of herbal tea it will calm you down a little.

I'm the only one at this table that can have a coffee…you've had enough sugar, and I suspect, caffeine already this morning."

Then Denise reaches out and touches Penny's hand, "Really Penny, it's ok you didn't say anything that will cause the world to stop so please relax and let's just start over okay?" Denise squeezes her hand and leans back sipping her coffee.

"Now what's up with you today," she asks Penny.

Penny closes her eyes, takes in a deep breath and says…"Okay I'm good," she opens her eyes and says, "Well, I'm investigating a murder, you probably heard about it, Mr. Jones owns the bar on High street.

He was found murdered a few weeks ago and I've still got nothing to go on." Penny dunks her tea bag in the hot water wondering how many packs of sugar she should use to make this taste good. Penny hates tea and is trying not to eye Denise's coffee which smells AMAZING! Girl focus!

"Yeah, I heard about that killing. OMG, I've never met someone who investigates murders! I'm impressed Penny, you must be good at what you do."

"Yeah I guess so but most of the time it just feels like luck, you know; being in the right place to put the right piece of the puzzle in place."

"And what do you do while you're waiting for the right piece and the right time to come along," asks Denise, pausing to take a long sip of her coffee.

Penny can almost taste it and plans to as soon as Denise leaves…she's gonna buy a large cup of that!

"My partner and I interview people, pass around our cards and wait for the forensics to get back to us with anything they find at the crime scene." Penny looks up from her tea bag dunking at Denise who is staring at her.

"I'm sorry was I boring you? I forget how to talk to regular people." Penny looks down at her tea and takes a sip. Shit I forgot the sugar; she starts ripping open two at a time until she has opened six packs.

78

Denise asks, "Do you always put yourself down Penny? I mean I asked and you answered my question. What was wrong with that exchange?"

Penny is taken aback by the forwardness of Denise's feedback.

"I hear so many self negative vibes coming off you…how can you do the work you do and still carry around such negativity?"

"Ummm, I don't know honestly Denise I just don't know anymore." Penny feels her eyes well up but she manages to pull herself together before she embarrasses herself further.

"Well, look thanks for the tea and for…I gotta get to the medical examiner before he gets too busy.

I'm gonna hit the head then go on." Penny abruptly stands and holds her shaking hand out to Denise.

Denise stands and shakes Penny's hand, but doesn't let it go.

"Ok, I can't let you go right now…"says Denise looking worried.

"Why not?" asks Penny, looking from their still shaking hands to Denise's face.

"Well not until you tell me what a "head" is!"

Letting go of Penny's hand Denise laughs and Penny explains, "Sorry I was in the Navy and that's what we call the restroom. I guess old habits are hard to break."

"You've never mentioned that in group, is there a reason for that?"

"No I guess it seems like a lifetime ago and not important to what brought me to the meetings. Will you tell Karen and the others?"

Internal dialogue…

Penny…I don't want them to think I'm a show off.

"No, it's your life story and it's your decision what and how much to tell. I will have to tell the group we saw each other today…just to keep everything transparent…that's the only way to build trust. Do you understand?"

"Of course and that's fine. Ok, see you in a couple of days and have a good one." Penny leaves the tea on the table and walks into the restroom.

Denise leaves the coffee shop.

When Penny comes out of the restroom she makes a beeline to the counter and says, "Hey what kind of coffee did that lady I was talking to have? It smelled AMAZING!"

Ruth meets the family…

"Ms. Graves, Marsha Graves? I'm Det. Hill from the Morganville Police Department…may I come in please?"

"Why what's wrong? Has something happened to my daughter or son-in-law? Jesus, what is going on?"

"No ma'am nothing has happened to either of them as far as I know. I'm here about your Uncle Raymond Jones; he was found murdered."

Pushing out a sigh of relief, "Oh well there isn't nothing to talk about, but you can come in if you like." She goes back in the house fanning with a dish towel she had in her hand.

"Have a seat, you want something to drink?"

They sit at the kitchen table.

"No thank you," says Ruth.

"I am curious about why you seem not to care about your uncle's passing."

"Well that old man ain't no uncle to me. When my momma died I stopped even thinking about him." She says with disgust, and balls up the dish towel.

"What can you tell me about Mr. Jones, did he have any enemies that would want to harm him or other family or friends I can speak with?"

"I don't want to be rude, but I'm probably gonna be. Let me see…" she closes her eyes and counts out loud…"'bout 30 some years ago, Ray Jones raped my daughter after he got out of jail for robbing some white man who got shot while they were robbing him."

"There isn't anything in his record about a rape."

81

"No there wouldn't be cause my momma and daddy didn't let it leave the family. My daddy and uncles beat the shit outta Ray and left him for dead on the side of the road one night. They never mentioned it again.

We took Lil Momma, that's what we call my daughter because she's been bossy since the day she was born; well anyway we took her to the doctor and he said nothing was broken in her and she could have kids later.

When my daughter got older, she said she wanted to see somebody about what happened to her so she went over to Pittsburgh to see a therapist and it really helped her to heal.

She's been doing real good all these years. She's married to a good church going man and both have good jobs."

I don't mean to continue to upset you Mrs. Graves, but when was the last time you or your daughter saw Mr. Jones?"

"I last saw him about four years ago when I went to Morganville to meet my daughter for lunch. I knew who he was but he didn't recognize me and Lil Momma didn't recognize him either. I left it that way.

So I guess the last time my daughter saw Ray was after he finished raping her."

Ruth stayed a little while longer and thanked Mrs. Graves for her time. She found out that both she and her husband had been away at a church retreat around the time Ray Jones was murdered.

She also found out they don't want anything to do with his body or his business. Seems old Ray won't be missed at all.

But as Ruth is backing out the driveway she knows that no matter how difficult it will be, she has to interview Lil Momma…aka Yvette Dyson.

82

Ruth's cell phone rings and she answers it through her Bluetooth connection her car radio.

"Yes, this is Det. Hill may I help you?"

"Det. Hill this is Yvette Dyson, I understand from my mother you want to speak to me about my great-uncle's death."

Ruth and Yvette agree to meet in the park behind the hospital.

Yvette is already there, sitting with her legs crossed eating out of a container of yogurt. She's wearing yellow scrub pants and a multi-colored scrubs top she described over the phone. She has on the requisite tennis shoes that nurses wear now instead of the throw-back white shoes.

"Mrs. Dyson?" Ruth asks, and takes a seat next to her on the bench.

"Yes, you must be Det. Hill…right?"

"Yes ma'am I am."

"Well before we start can you please show me some identification? You can't be too cautious these days."

Ruth agrees and shows Yvette her badge and picture ID.

"Ok, so ask your questions, I've gotta get back to my floor."

"So your mother told me your great…"

"Please just call him Ray, I don't want to ever think of him as my family…okay?" Yvette holds the spoon in front of her mouth as she speaks, then slowly places the spoon in her mouth.

"Sorry, of course, as you wish. I understand Ray sexually assaulted you when you were seven years old."

"Well that's right, why are you asking about that now?"

"Well, we are investigating his murder and found out about the assault. When was the last time you saw Ray?"

"I last saw Ray when he rolled off me, sweating and panting. I don't know where he went or what happened after that. My next memory is me waking up freshly scrubbed and in my bed."

"So you have no idea who would've wanted to kill Ray or do anything to mutilate his body in the process?" Ruth watches Yvette closely.

"No, I don't know anything about it. I didn't know he was dead until my mom called. I don't want to be rude, but I'm not available to rehash my trauma because Ray is dead. That just doesn't seem fair does it? I should have to re-live the worst time of my life like he's still raping me all over again?

Det. Hill is there anything else?"

Yvette stands and throws the yogurt container and spoon in the trash can next to the bench.

"Mrs. Dyson, one last question, does your husband know what Ray did to you?"

"Yes, I told him when we went through pre-marriage counseling with our pastor. He's never mentioned Ray to me since those sessions. He respects my decision to move on with our lives. Anything else you want to know?"

"One last question, where were you and your husband two weeks ago?"

Yvette looks toward a patient being pushed by a volunteer enter the park…"I was working the 3 pm -7 am shift to cover for a friend who got married. My husband stopped by for dinner and then he went to a card game with some college friends. They have a standing game at the Retro Game Shop."

"You won't be surprised that I will have to check that out?"

Turning to leave, Yvette says, "Det., you do you and I'll go back to doing me okay? And thanks for fucking up my day."

Internal dialogue…

Ruth…she is a suspect

Yvette…I'm glad his ass is dead! Look as hard as you want Det. Hill…you won't find anything tying me to old Ray's murder.

Ruth watches her walk away then puts on rubber gloves and reaches into the trash bin to retrieve the spoon and yogurt container.

Ruth stops by the lab before heading home, "Please process these prints and see if there is a match to any we found on case #175908843Jones. Send me the report by email please."

"Ok, Det. Hill," says the technician.

Once Ruth leaves the office, the technician places the bag in the refrigerator and goes back to watching the game. He thinks, to himself, that shit can wait 'til half-time then I'll fill everything out and get it processed. I got too much riding on this game…come on ya'll!

Ruth and Penny meet at the office and each give a brief overview of their day.

Ruth just says, "Yeah, nobody is gonna claim ole Ray's body. His family hates his ass for molesting a niece over 30 years ago. The niece hasn't seen him since the rape. I did get her prints and alibi, she could be involved."

"Well, I saw Dr. Wayne Ellis and he was in rare form today! He was eating an egg salad sandwich, drinking a Coke Zero and finished off three oatmeal raisin cookies while going over the autopsy photos of Ray with me.

Oh, and then he started prepping another body for cut up! The man is a machine! The smells alone almost caused me to throw up!"

"Ok, ok, ok, you and Dr. Ellis are too graphic," says Ruth with a disgusted look on her face.

"Sorry…anyway, he says Ray was definitely alive when his finger was cut off and the way the anus was gripping the finger he thinks Ray was alive when it was stuck in too. He did some digging to see if anyone out there has experience with is type of signature killing, but nothing came of it. So no serial killer out there doing this shit to people, I guess that's a plus."

"Anything else?" asks Ruth.

"Naw nothing else really turned up from the autopsy. Since no family is claiming the body, the city will cremate Mr. Jones and place his ashes in the state cemetery. Seems wrong though…"

Ruth asks, "How so?"

Looking out the window, Penny says, "To live a long and full life only to have no one miss you. Nobody to cry for you…nothing to prove you were ever alive."

Ruth looks at Penny and fresh worry bubbles up inside her.

Holly arrives first, as usual, but tonight she waits to pick her seat. She stands by the coffee pot and slowly makes herself a cup.

Then she pretends to check her phone for messages until Dani arrives. Holly immediately grabs the seat next to Dani.

Dani starts talking to Holly about the new exercise routine she's teaching at the gym.

"Talking" is a loose description of what's going on because Holly just smiles while she sips her coffee and drinking in every word Dani says.

Holly has thought of nothing else all week except how strong and funny Dani is. Holly is determined to discover Dani's secret to moving forward and having a full life.

She's even tried to start drinking more water, at home, like she sees Dani do during the group. But tonight she's so nervous so she picked coffee to drink…she needs the caffeine.

Internal dialogue…

Holly…maybe I will start exercising with Dani. I hope Denise doesn't ask me if I've started yet 'cause that would be embarrassing!

If I go to the gym and I'm around other people they would be looking at me and judging me! No, I'm not ready for that yet. There must be some other things Dani learned first before she got to where she is now.

OMG! What did she just say? I missed it 'cause I'm listening to myself again!

The rest of the group members arrive…

Denise smiles and says, "Hello ladies and welcome to our third group meeting. I hope everyone had a healthy week."

She looks around and is greeted with a variety of smiles, from bright to waning.

Everyone nods hello…

"I think after we make our first comments of the night it will be ok not to say our names again. So let's try, and if there is still some unfamiliarity, we'll go back to identifying ourselves…now any follow-up from last week?"

Lynn clears her throat, "I'm not sure how much I want to say about my week, except I found out the guy that raped me was murdered!"

There are audible gasps and …"what"…"when"…"WTF"…

Denise quiets the group, "Ok, let's give Lynn some space to tell what she is willing to share."

"Thanks Denise…this seems so weird since I was just talking about him…well anyway, seems he was released from prison."

Cheryl asks, "Y'all know by now I'm Cheryl right?"

Not waiting for an answer, "I'm a parole officer so I gotta ask, Lynn were you signed up for VINE so you would get notifications about him?"

"What's bine?" asks Karen.

Cheryl looks at Karen and spells out, "V-I-N-E…stands for Victim Information and Notification. You can get information about an offender's court date, protective order status, probation and parole information too."

"Well what's the "E" stand for?" asks a perplexed Dani.

Penny laughs out loud in spite of herself.

Cheryl looks annoyed and says, "Does it matter; if so, Google it!"

Then Cheryl turns back to Lynn leaving Dani embarrassed.

Holly is embarrassed for Dani and mad at Cheryl.

Lynn says, "Yes, I knew he was getting out, but I guess I was too numb to do anything or to feel anything. At least I told myself I was numb, but looking at it now, I think I was just terrified to deal with my feelings." She wipes a tear from her cheek.

Denise asks Lynn, "Are you comfortable expounding on that feeling of being terrified?"

"Maybe," says Lynn.

"Just give me a few moments to get myself together."

Denise, who is sitting to the right of Lynn, reaches over and pats her on the hand.

"Take your time and jump back in when you're ready.

Anyone else want to follow-up with anything from last week?

Silence…

Ayda looks away from Lynn but continues to clutch her rosary. She clears her throat and says, "I was really bothered by Dani asking if we ever wanted to kill them. I just felt that was an inappropriate question for her to ask us."

Ayda turns and looks defiantly at Dani.

Dani sputters water out her mouth, "WTF Ayda, next time you know what, say your first name, Miss Holier than thou!"

Ayda tears up again and says, "I…forgot to say my name…you're right…my name is Ayda…and I should forgive Dani…" She starts to cry in earnest now into her tissue.

Dawn is sitting two chairs from Ayda; they are separated by Dani and Holly.

Dawn leans toward Ayda and says, "Ayda, honey it's me Dawn…honey why are you crying?"

Ayda cries out, "Because I feel I'm being attacked for my religious beliefs!"

"What?" yells Dani…"No one, especially me, even mentioned your religion! You are the one attacking me for what I said, which was just to ask an honest question!

So tell me then Ayda, what should be done to the people who hurt us? Go on tell us what your religion has to say about it? This is a place to speak our minds, so have at it!" blasts Dani.

Ayda looks around the group and says, "Proverbs 3:7 says, "Don't consider you to be wise, fear the Lord and turn away from evil.""

Before anyone can respond, Denise asks Ayda, "What does that scripture mean to you Ayda? And let me remind the group of your own norm, no judgments…let Ayda educate us on the importance of that particular verse to her."

Denise leans over toward Ayda, "Are you up to discussing this?"

Crying but speaking confidently, Ayda says, "Well it speaks to my heart and I tell my mind there is nothing I can do to figure bad things out because God is smarter than me.

Every time I think of that awful day I get through it by reminding myself that God doesn't want me thinking evil thoughts and He will punish me again if I let myself think them."

Imani asks, "Ayda you said God would punish you again…do you feel like it happened to you because you were bad and you needed to be punished?"

90

"Yes, something in a past life must have caused God to punish me in this life. If that is not the case, then I have been chosen by God for a purpose, but I am too unworthy to recognize what the purpose is."

Internal dialogue…

Lynn…Christianity doesn't ascribe to past lives; but not my business to question Ayda's beliefs.

Dani looks around Holly so she can see Ayda and says, "Well you might not believe me Ayda, but I can relate to feeling like being punished for being wrong somehow. I used to think my ex-husband was financially destroyed because he was so in love with money that the universe was teaching him a lesson.

Then I started not having all the material things I was used to. Well, I started thinking I was getting what I deserved too. 'Cause truth be told, I didn't love him. I just wanted to be with him so we could live large!

I guess he treated me like he owned me because he paid for me. Ayda the only difference with you and I is I know why God is mad at me. I was an idolater of money!"

Internal dialogue…

Karen…is this church?

Yvette…Lawd have mercy…shut the fuck up!

Denise…I wonder if Dani can spell "idolater."

Holly is shocked and before she can stop herself she blurts out, "But Dani you don't feel that way about things now do you? I mean you're stronger now and you know you aren't wrong or being punished…right?"

Holly looks at Dani with the intensity of a thousand suns and Dani is almost burned!

Dani, smiling says, "Physically I'm stronger yes, but emotionally I have to work at staying present or I may slip back into thinking the wrong stuff. I do believe our Higher Power punishes us when we are not doing right by him and others."

Denise says, "Sounds like you are talking about faith, guilt, self-anger and pain. Let's follow this exploration of emotions tonight because until you acknowledge, label and accept your true feelings, your goals will remain only goals and never realized.

Don't feel pressured to talk anymore than you feel comfortable, but please take these precious opportunities to find your voice."

The group is silent and Denise allows the group to work through the silence.

Penny clears her throat and speaks, "I feel sad and lonely most of the time. I feel like I'm a shell of a person, just moving through life.

Lynn, I understand what numb feels like, at least what I call numb. It's a place where I can't tell what I feel or if I feel anything at all.

Ayda, I have often wondered where God was that night and all the days since then. I used to think I was hurt so it would make me a better policewoman.

That if I try to help people right the wrongs done to them, I thought it would make me feel better, but it doesn't. I thought it would be enough to fill the dark cold space left by the rape, but it doesn't come near fixing it.

I mean it does at the moment, but there's always someone else ready to take something else from me.

My cousin, Rory…oh my God, I've never said his name out loud since the night of the rape…"

Penny starts breathing fast, she has a film of sweat over her top lip and her hands are beginning to shake.

92

Denise quickly rises and walks over to Penny. She kneels in front of Penny and says, "Penny take your time and breathe slowly and deeply. Focus on my voice…you are safe, you are safe, *you* are safe."

Cupping Penny's hands into hers, Denise continues, "Penny repeat after me…I am safe."

Penny looks into Denise's eyes and stutters out, "I'm sssafe."

Denise says, "Say it once more Penny."

Penny brings her focus to Denise again and this time looks more deeply into her eyes. For some strange reason she feels instantly safe.

Penny never noticed before but Denise has the same brown eyes as her father; a soft brown with just a splash of greenish gold throughout. Her mother used to say her father had angel dust blown in his eyes just before he was born.

Penny forces her mind to come back to this moment and she hears Denise's voice telling her she is safe.

Penny says, "Thank you Denise, I know I'm safe."

Internal dialogue…

Penny…of course I'm safe now…I saw my daddy in your eyes! It was a sign from him that he's still with me!

Denise says, "Penny take a sip of your coffee, continue to breathe deeply and just relax. You can join us when you're ready."

Denise rises and returns to her seat.

Penny is still reeling and while everyone is in their own thoughts, she's having flashes of Rory's face close to hers.

She closes her eyes to stop the images. It takes all her compartmentalizing practice to maintain her composure. Inside her mind she puts the word "Rory" back inside the black box she has constructed for all those things that are too awful for her to process.

She opens her eyes and looks down into the milky coffee and thinks, I'd rather die once than re-live this memory all my life.

Silence...

Internal dialogue...

Karen...Penny looks like she's having a melt down! Sweet, I wonder if we will need to call 911.

Yvette...She better not pass out! I'm not doing CPR on her without a face shield.

Ayda...Forgive me Father, but I'm glad she has distracted them from me. I maybe too weak to continue hiding my shame; being raped by a woman! Oh Father please...please take this pill from my lips!

Holly looks over at Dani and gives her a little smile. She's not rewarded with a return smile but a question...

"Holly what are you feeling? You don't say a lot about your feelings."

Holly pees a little in her panty liner.

"Ummm...well I guess, wait, what words do I pick from?" She asks looking anxiously at Denise.

Denise smiles and says, "We don't have a list to chose from so just take your time and try to notice what you're feeling right now."

Holly blurts out, "Embarrassed, I feel embarrassed right now."

Denise asks, "Can you expound on that? Why do you feel embarrassed?"

"Cause I don't know the answer" Holly takes a gulp of coffee and coughs.

Internal dialogue…

Holly…Of course everyone is looking at your dumb ass and you start to choke! Holly Chism you are by far the stupidest girl ever to be born!

Cheryl speaks up, "What you mean you don't know the answer? You don't know what you're feeling right now? How can that be?"

Holly looks at the carpet and wonders, has the carpet always been this shade of bluish green? It's really ugly! Bet it was on the clearance side of the furniture store. OMG Holly! They are looking at you!

"Ummm, I just feel embarrassed right now. That's all I can think to call it…sorry."

Daini says, "Hey Holly don't be sorry for how you feel darling, we are all in this together. So let me ask you this way, does the rape still embarrass you?"

Holly screams inside her head *I KNOW IT'S MY TURN TO TALK BUT I'M NOT READY!*

As calmly as she can, Holly says, "Well I guess so." She starts to pick at her cuticles. Penny notices the habit again and cringes because she does it too.

I guess I feel embarrassed all the time 'cause I think people know about me."

Imani joins the discussion by asking, "What do they know about you? I'm asking because I think people know I'm a fraud.

Here I am walking round like I'm all together. How all together can someone be when their Dad has molested them?"

Imani takes a deep breath and continues, "I mean not a stranger or someone stupid raped me…it was my father! Of course, now we're just acting like one big happy family, like nothing has ever happened."

Holly looks at Imani, like for the first time and says something she's never said out loud before, "No Imani you're not the fraud I am."

The group members all look up in shock. Even Denise does a "whack-a-mole" head snap.

Holly continues, "Danny, ummm, he's the janitor, he didn't put his thing in me all the way. I don't think. So see I'm the fraud, going around talking about being a rape victim when all of you have actually been raped. I'm sorry ladies, maybe I shouldn't be here."

Holly lowers her head in shame and begins to cry.

Internal dialogue…

Holly…Why did I just tell that big fat lie? I'm a crazy person! I gotta get out of here! I'm not ready to tell anyone what happened!

Before Denise can reflect, Penny says, "Holly, as a police officer; believe me when I tell you Danny sexually assaulted you and you are indeed a victim since it was against your will."

Holly doesn't look convinced and she isn't able to look at Dani.

Denise says, "Go at your own pace Holly…you are doing great."

Holly doesn't look up and continues to cry.

Silence…

Denise says to Imani, "You mentioned fraud as well…expound a little more on the significance of the relationship title of the offender."

Yvette swallows the last of her water and speaks before Imani, "I can relate to what Imani said about knowing the person who raped her. I was raped by my mother's uncle. He's dead now too…"

Yvette looks at Lynn who appears to have regained her composure.

"My parents respected my decision to go to a therapist once I was an adult. But they didn't talk about it with me EVER! I guess they felt they were supportive just by being silent.

Truth be told all I remember about the incident is seeing his back reflected in my grandmother's bedroom mirror and the smell of his cologne. Sometimes when I'm walking down a store aisle and someone goes by smelling like him, I get nauseous then I get angry 'cause I have that smell in my memory.

Seriously, I can't even walk in the store to get some friggin candy or tampons or whatever without him being an active memory?

Ok, that's all I got for now." Yvette crosses her legs and munches on a cookie.

Imani, shaking her head says, "I don't even have memories of anything just a scar. See my Dad had gonorrhea when he molested me. Seems I contracted it, but my parents wouldn't take me to the doctor's office for treatment. That is until one day my ankle got swollen and an aunt noticed it."

"Sweet Jesus," murmurs Ayda clutching her rosary.

Internal dialogue…

Cheryl…Ayda please shut up!

Lynn…Jesus please protect your child.

*Imani...where was sweet Jesus when I needed him? Maybe I
shouldn't say anymore...*

Imani wants to finish so she rushes to say, "So they finally got sober
enough to notice I was really sick and they listened to my aunt when
she told them to take me to the ER. Once I was checked out by a
doctor, he told my parents I would need surgery to have a sizeable
chunk of my ankle removed in an effort to save my entire foot.

I had the gonorrhea for so long it had traveled down, or something.
Anyway my foot was in jeopardy of being amputated."

Imani pulls up her right pants leg and shows a flat concave scar on
her right ankle.

Internal dialogue...

*Holly...Oh my please don't show us! But, yeah show us, so it will
keep them on you and not back to me.*

Yvette...nasty bastard and his wife stayed with him...stupid bitch!

*Imani...Yeah look at it! See what I've lost and tell me everything
will be alright. I hate my parents!*

Cheryl...back then the docs didn't even report that shit!

Karen asks, "How do you feel about your Dad Imani."

"I feel like both my parents spend their lives trying to make it up to
me. They buy me stuff whether I ask for it or not. It's like they are
trying to buy me.

But to answer your question truthfully, and I'll apologize up front if
it offends Ayda, but I hate them! I wish they were dead! No, I wish
they died before they even had me!"

Imani takes in a deep breath. Denise might be on to something with
this talking and breathing crap...I feel amazing right now.

98

Imani smiles as she bites into her chocolate chip cookie.

Ayda's head pops up and she clutches her rosary. Her lips move in a silent prayer.

Ayda says to Imani, "Sweetheart you can't mean that. Our God says we must honor our mother and father. It is a sin against God to hate them and wish them dead."

Yvette sits up straighter in her chair and turns to look at Ayda, "Now look Ayda we are here to talk about our true feeling not listen to you preach to us. How do you know what Imani's God says to her?

I'm sorry Denise or anyone else but…well no I'm not really sorry. Ayda your beliefs are your own but don't you sit here and tell this young lady that she's gonna go to hell or something because she's been hurt by her parents. She's here trying to deal with it which is more than I say about you.

All you do is just sit there crying, praying, and judging everyone else. We've been coming here for three weeks and you don't really talk about anything!

Ya'll excuse me…I gotta go pee." Yvette storms out of the room and slams the door shut.

Denise decides to let the group flow without interruption from her.

Silence…

Internal dialogue…

Karen…Well alright Yvette! You are one bad bitch!

Holly…I feel sorry for Ayda.

Lynn…Oh my goodness, Ayda did it now, but I understand what she's saying. I just wouldn't say it!

Cheryl...I knew someone was gonna say something to Ayda to shut her up.

Imani, talking really fast says, "I don't care what anyone thinks; this is the place to say stuff and I'm saying I hate my parents more now for how they treat me than before. At least before they were being truthful, no pretense just honest fucked up assholes.

Now they are so respectful with their government jobs, dog, house, cars, and they take two vacations a year!

Plus...here comes the big bonus! They get to brag about how smart I am and how proud they are of me to all their friends!

Yep, I really hate them."

Imani starts laughing and eating one cookie after another, laughing to herself.

Yvette returns from the restroom and sits down. She makes it a point not to look in Ayda's direction.

Internal dialogue...

Yvette...we can't process a damn thing while Ayda's ass is sitting up here making us feel guilty all the damn time!

Karen...These people are really fucked up! What if I end up like them; still dealing with this shit for years? I gotta decide what's what now! Maybe Dani is on to something when she suggested fucking somebody up might be the answer to our problems.

Holly...What time is it? Yeah, we are outta time!

Denise shuts down the group the same as previous sessions. Next week she hopes Lynn will provide more information about the death of her offender. Also, let's hope Ayda brings more than a sermon or Yvette might shoot her with a holy-ghost gun!

100

Let's mind our own business...

Miss Stephanie and Roxie take a bus to the Mall of Morganville. The Mall of Morganville has three levels with one level being all restaurants, one has all the clothing shops and the top level has movie theaters. There is a skywalk from the top level to the parking garage.

Miss Stephanie is looking for a pair of polka-dot read and black capri pants to wear under her pink caftan. She wants to wear her new pants to the annual block party in a few weeks.

She has a black tunic to wear as well, but she only plans to wear it in her home. She won't actually put it on for outside.

She feels comfortable wearing moo-moos but doesn't want those nasty men to see through it so she wears capri pants underneath.

Roxie will need a red and black polka dot bow to wear as well.

Just as Miss Stephanie and Roxie start looking at the clearance rack of capris, Stephanie stops dead in her search.

Did I just see that same back I saw coming out of Jones' bar?

She leaves the rack of clothes and follows "the back."

Roxie starts barking, "Shhhhh Roxie," whispers Stephanie, loud enough that "the back" stops walking and turns slightly, recognizing Stephanie's voice.

They both stand completely still...just feet from each other.

Stephanie leans down and whispers into Roxie's carrier, "We better leave it alone Roxie." Stephanie and Roxie turn around and head back to the clearance rack of capris.

"We've got a lot of shopping to do Roxie before the afternoon bus comes back for us."

"The back" listens as Stephanie moves away and thinks I'm going to have to take care of that crazy woman…and her little dog too.

Three days after the group...

Ayda Espina is brought into the ER by ambulance. Her neighbor was in the back yard cutting hedges and saw Ayda floating face down in her pool. It's unclear how long she'd been there.

Yvette Dyson is in the ER when Ayda arrives. She can't believe it's Ayda from her support group. She's momentarily stunned and unable to move.

The other medical team members are running a Code Blue...Yvette finally snaps out of it and responds to the emergency.

Unfortunately after 27 minutes of CPR and medication, Ayda Espina is pronounced dead.

Her death is attributed to respiratory impairment or in layman's terms; Ayda Espina drowned.

When a person drowns, water enters the trachea and that causes muscle spasms that seal the airway and prevents air and water from passing through. A formal autopsy will give the actual cause of death and try to determine if this was an accident or homicide.

That same day...

Penny meets with Lt. Brogan, "Sir, I'd like to request some time off please."

Lt. Brogan is surprised because Det. Darling NEVER asks for time off, especially with an unsolved murder lingering.

"What's up Det.?"

"Well, sir I thought I could attend the support group meetings and continue to work but I'm finding the groups very helpful, which means I am distracted by my thoughts and feelings.

Sir, I wouldn't ask if I didn't think it was better for me to take some sick leave during this time.

Ruth has the Jones murder investigation covered since there doesn't seem to be any breaks at this time anyway.

We've canvassed the neighborhood and she's made contact with his family."

Leaning in Penny says, "Sir, I'm in a weird place right now and honestly I wouldn't be good on the street right now."

Lt. Brogan sits back in his chair and puts his index fingers together, rubbing the tip of his nose across them.

Internal dialogue…

Lt. Brogan…Shit! I knew it; she is crazy! Ok, how do I handle this? I can't say no or that could be a lawsuit in the making. Hell I'm the one who showed Det. Hill the flyer for the rape group. What would it look like if I didn't support her? I really respect Penny when she's on her game and I sure hope she gets back in the saddle. Ok, let me just go with it and I'll talk to the Chief later.

"Look Penny, you are the best when you're at your best. I can't imagine how bad assed you'll be when you come out of the other side of whatever the shit that haunts you. How much time are you asking for?"

"Sir we have five more groups…I'm asking for my sick leave to start today and end in a month." Penny looks pleadingly at Lt. Brogan.

"Ok, I'll authorize it with one condition."

"Yes sir what's that?"

"You have to check in with Det. Hill everyday…just to say hi and let us know you're ok. Can you agree to that?"

104

Smiling Penny says, "Yes sir I sure can! You know if I don't keep in touch she will come find me!"

They shake hands and Lt. Brogan watches Det. Darling leave the office. He's worried that this might be the last time he sees his officer. What if she decides she no longer wants to be a cop, then what?

Hell what if she finally kills herself while on leave! Will they have any legal liability? Should I have acted sooner when Det. Hill first brought her concerns about Det. Darling's depression?

Well at least I'll have her official request for leave in her file…just in case. Hell I've only got three years left and I gotta take care of myself too.

Lt. Brogan picks up the phone and calls Chief Ritchie.

Penny calls Ruth on her cell phone and they arrange lunch later that day.

Penny plans to tell her partner about her extended leave. In the meantime Penny goes shopping for food and goodies for her self-imposed sabbatical.

Funny she doesn't feel funny about not being a cop for the next 5 weeks. What does that mean?

Maybe I'll bring it up to the group this week and see what they think.

Lessons of the street...

Squidget is cleaning her face with a moist toilette. She's trying to fix herself up before getting breakfast at Iswara's coffee shop.

But before she can turn around and leave the alley, where she's been cleaning herself up, someone snatches her by the hair and jerks her backwards.

She looks up into the face of Pimp Gene!

Pimp Gene is pissed and he snarls, "Bitch I told you to stay away from my damn streets didn't I?

Squidget is squirming to get away but he has his hands securely wound in her weave. For once that damn Mousey put the tracks in real tight and no matter how hard she tries to get away her hair is firmly attached to her scalp!

Stuttering, she says, "Hey man you want half the duckets?"

Pimp Gene is even more enraged and spits out, "Half! Bitch I'm taking it all! Who the fuck you think you are trying to settle some terms with me? I'm a fuckin pimp and you are a nasty ho!"

If possible he tightens his grip on her hair even more.

 This is one good weave and worth the $45 I paid Mousey to do it but damn if this shit don't hurt!

"You gonna give me all the money now or I'll fuck yo ass up royally!"

Squidget reaches in her bra and gives Pimp Gene the $20 she just made off one of the professors from the college by giving him a before class blowjob.

"Pimp Gene continues to hold Squidget's hair while he pockets the money and says, "I believe I said *all* the money! Bitches always think they can run a game. Don't make me strip search yo ass right here on the mutha fuckin street!"

Squidget reaches in her bra and pulls out $150 and reluctantly hands it over to Pimp Gene.

Smiling while tucking the money in his pocket, Pimp Gene says, "Look you eeva come work for me or keep yo skinny, nasty ass out of my way.

So now you know I gotta teach you a street lesson since you don't want to listen to my words.

Get yo ass in my car and suck my dick or take an ass whipping right here and now!

Your choice bitch!"

Squidget says through gritted teeth, "Hey, you know me Pimp Gene! My mouth is yo mouth baby!"

Once Squidget has learned her lesson from Pimp Gene, he gives her $5 of her money back because he says he's a "righteous dude." Then he pushes her out of his car and peels off…singing a Luther Prince song.

Squidget cleans her face with another moist toilette and takes a swig from the mouthwash bottle she carries in her purse. She spits it out on the street corner.

Muttering all the way down the sidewalk toward the coffee shop about how she's gonna kill Pimp Gene.

After Squidget orders a large coffee and bagel slathered with butter and chocolate cream cheese, she sits down at the only empty table in the shop.

Last night was a rough one for her but she rationalizes that she's gotta lay down, stand up, bend over and blow whatever comes her way to have enough money to get off the streets by winter. Today's setback didn't help. It beat a fat lip and an ass whipping though.

Nobody wants you slobbering his knob with a busted lip.

Squidget is lost in thought until she hears, "Excuse me may I sit at your table Miss? All the other tables are full."

Squidget looks up and sees a well dressed woman.

"Sure if you want to be seen sitting with a ho, go on and sit down."

The woman sits down and places her coffee cup on the table.

"Well I'm ok sitting with a ho if you're ok being one!" The woman says and then flashes a dazzling white smile.

Squidget laughs out loud and everyone in the little coffee shop looks at her.

She calms down and says very loudly, "Apologies everybody she just said some funny shit!"

The coffee shop owner comes over; he's the first cousin of Mr. Iswara, the corner store owner. His name is Mr. Iswara too. Even though their family has lived in West Virginia for over 25 years, both still have significant accents.

"Iz everything alright at the table?

Miss Squidject I ask that you watch your language in here. Maybe you want to take your coffee and bagel to go?"

The woman sitting with Squidget says, "No sir, she doesn't want it to go, all is well here...thank you."

Mr. Iswara nods and walks away, but he plans to keep an eye on that randi (Hindi for whore) of a girl.

He's also going to spray her chair with a disinfectant when she leaves…nasty randi!

Squidget looks suspiciously at the woman and asks, "So you want something from me or you just really cool like that?"

"Well it looked to me you already gave someone something earlier. I saw you getting out of that rusty car a few blocks down the street."

Frowning Squidget says, "That fucking Count Chocula stole my fucking money and made me suck him off!

Then the bastard had the nerve to give me $5, 'cause he wanted to show me he wasn't such a bad guy."

The woman sits wide eyed and then looks around to see if anyone overheard Squidget.

The woman leans in and whispers, while appearing to take a sip of her coffee, "Good God girl! OMG and TMI! I wasn't expecting you to be so graphic!"

"Sorry, I'm not used to talking to someone who ain't from the street…my bad."

The woman rises, "Well…ummm…have a nice day...I've got to run an errand."

The woman stands and reaches for her coffee cup, turns and all but runs from the coffee shop and Squidget.

Good, aka Wendy Browne, is still pretty but lord help you when she breathes on you! A doctor once told her there was something wrong with her insides and that's why her breath smelled like shit all the time.

She chews gum constantly and her purse is always filled with little mints. She once asked Pimp Gene if he would pay for her to see a gastro doctor, but he said he couldn't smell a thing and to get her ass back out on the street.

Wendy is 5'9", about the color of light milky caramel. She wears a yellow wig with pink accents at the tips. Gene used to call her high yellow back in the day and likes for her to have yellow hair.

Wendy is reed thin with little to no tits or ass but she has a regular list of local men who like her pre-pubescent body.

Also, she's well versed in literature and poems so it makes her a favorite of some of the older and widowed professors. With them, she just sits jerking them off while they read her poetry. Easiest $50 bucks EVER!

Wendy stopped thinking about leaving Pimp Gene after her attempt during their first year together. He put her in the bed for three weeks. He had beat her so bad she thought she was going to die.

One of Gene's long-time customers was a physician and he stopped in to check on her. After she was healed, Gene made her service the doctor anyway he wanted, for three weeks as a way to pay him back.

She never thought of leaving Pimp Gene ever again. Besides, it really wasn't so bad just as long as she and Plenty bought home the money and gave it to Pimp Gene.

Plenty, aka Tina Johnson, is tall about 5'11", a brown skinned afro-centric chick. At least that's how she describes herself.

Tina has made herself believe she's working, "under the radar of the man," and doing what she wants to do.

Tina is a fighter and has many facial scars to prove it. She says Wendy is the pretty bitch, but I'm the fighting bitch!

Tina and Squidget have had quite a few run-ins over the years. Tina doesn't like anyone near her street. She and Wendy have an understanding laid out by Pimp Gene...they work like a well oiled machine.

They have each other's back and are for the most part loyal to Pimp Gene. Tina and Gene have been lovers over the years even though he's nicer to Wendy. Fucker always did like a light skinned bitch over brown sugar.

Pimp Gene says the fact that we came to him with the name "Good & Plenty" was cool, since all we wear is pink and black all the time. He also said, I give him plenty mouth, but he likes the way I think and he knows I have his back. I remember when my Dad used to say that just before slapping the shit outta me. At least Pimp Gene don't hit us anymore and shit.

She's also been savvy enough to hide a little money along the way. She wants to be ready for the day when she can get the fuck outta dodge!

Will she take Wendy with her? Probably not...she's seen enough of that girl's ass along the way; probably more than I've seen my own.

One day it'll be time to cut that bitch loose.

Off the streets...

Good & Plenty take turns in the bathroom getting ready for bed.

They are allowed to come home from the streets at 6am every morning.

Pimp Gene won't bother them until about 3pm. Then they get ready to hit the streets again at 6pm sharp.

Pimp Gene used to tell them "Gotta catch those dudes and their money, as they're on their way home."

Wendy goes into her bedroom and closes the door. She likes to read from the little book of poetry she keeps on her nightstand.

I really wish I could go to that college up on the hill. I would take classes and learn how to really write poetry. Maybe when I come back in a next life, I'll be in a better situation.

Maybe I'll atone in this life for whatever I did in the last one because I must have pissed God off. Otherwise why did he make me a whore?

Tears stream down her cheeks as she reads another poem by Wendy Pitts, a well known African American poet. One of Good's regulars gave it to her because he saw they had the same first name. He's the only one who knows her real name.

Brian is really a sweet guy. He lives alone and has never been married. He's a medical technician at the hospital and is studying to be a pulmonary doctor.

His mother and father both passed away from complications associated with Chronic Obstructive Pulmonary Disease (COPD). They were heavy smokers and worked in one of the factories on the outskirts of town.

They died very young, both in their late 50s and Bri, as I like to call him, is doing everything he can to ensure he's not a statistic too. He exercises, eats well and stays away from second hand smoke. He always wears a rubber when we have sex too. He says it's nothing disrespectful to me, but he has to be careful.

I understand and don't blame him. I did tell him I make all my johns wear rubbers but you can't be too careful these days.

I've learned so much from him and he says there is treatment for my stomach issues but he understands that I can't do anything right now so he gets me samples from the hospital to help with the severity of the smell coming from my guts.

Bri is so good to me! I don't deserve him.

Pimp Gene would pitch a bitch if he knew how emotionally close Brian and I are.

In her room, Tina drinks herbal tea with a splash of cognac while watching the news. Still no word on what happened to that old guy who owned the bar across the street.

Stretching, Tina wonders when somebody is gonna take that place over. It's in a great location to those college kids, which means its prime money for us! I hope they open it soon.

Wendy is the first to wake up and begin moving about.

She takes a shower, lotions her body and brushes her teeth.

She doesn't hear Pimp Gene moving about the apartment. Maybe he's still out doing some business or something. Surely, he's not still asleep.

Pimp Gene keeps different hours from the girls so he leaves them sleeping, but he always comes back to make sure they are ready for the street on time.

Wendy tip toes down the hall to make some coffee and boil some eggs. She doesn't dare turn on the TV since Pimp Gene might be asleep.

His bedroom door is closed so he must be in there. Strange though, because he usually doesn't sleep past noon and it's now 2:45 pm.

She hears Tina moving about her bedroom too. Soon Tina pads down the hall toward the kitchen.

"Morning girl, you heard from Pimp Daddy?"

That's their affectionate name for Pimp Gene.

"Morning, naw, I haven't heard a peep from him and his door is still closed."

Tina walks over to the only window in the shabby apartment and looks down to the alley.

"Well his car is still parked down there. What you think is going on?"

"I don't know," says Wendy. "You can set your watch by Pimp Daddy so this is some strange shit. Should we check his room?"

Tina says, "Girl you crazy or sumthin? You know we can't go messin round his room! He'd shoot us for sure!"

"No, I mean just knock at the door a little. He might be sick or something."

Wendy and Tina think on it for a few minutes.

Wendy takes her eggs out of the boiling water and transfers them to a bowl of cold water.

114

Tina says, "Ok, let's just knock a little and if he yells, just say sorry that we were scared here alone or something…ok?"

"Yeah that's good we were scared alone…Pimp Daddy will like that."

They ease down the hall arm-in-arm and stand outside Pimp Gene's bedroom door. His bedroom is the largest in the apartment and he has his own bathroom. No tub, just a shower, sink and toilet.

They each make a fist, Tina whispers, "1, 2, 3."

They both knock then jump back a little. But Pimp Gene doesn't yell out at them. They wait a few minutes and after giving each other significant silent looks, they move as one to the door again and knock.

This time they hear a soft moan so they wait for Pimp Gene to yell at them, but he doesn't.

Wendy clears her throat and says, "Pimp Daddy you alright in there?"

They hear another moan and what sounds like chains rattling. What is really going on in there?

Tina says, "Something's wrong in there…what you wanna do?"

Whispering, Wendy says, I think we should try the knob."

Tina puts her hands behind her back as a sign it won't be her.

Wendy takes an exasperated deep breath and reaches for the door knob.

She slowly turns the door knob and is met by a sight she would never have expected to see.

Pimp Gene is lying on his bed but certainly not the way he's used to being in his bed!

Pimp Gene is lying flat on his back, naked and shackled.

Each wrist was down toward his side and chained to the bed frame. He had something weird in his mouth and a sleep mask over his eyes. A pink and black fuzzy sleep mask, but it wasn't one of theirs!

His torso was shiny like someone rubbed oil or something all over him.

Down by his dick…wait…where is his dick?!

Internal dialogue…

Tina…This is it; today is the day we go free!

Wendy & Tina eased into Pimp Gene's room and turned on the light for a better view of what was going on. Pimp Gene was stirring a little and making pitiful little moaning noises. Now with the light on, they could see his dick was stuck to his leg by something thick and white.

Internal dialogue:

Tina…What the fuck was going on?!

Wendy…He's gonna be mad as hell! I bet he blames us!

Pimp Gene's head was on the mattress and his chin was in one of those S&M leather chin straps with a black plastic ball in his mouth.

Next to him, on the pillow was a portable DVD player with a post-it that says, *"play me before helping Pimp Gene."*

Wendy and Tina look at each other and both of them are stunned, scared, but nosey so they remove the post-it and push play.

Tina immediately pushes down the volume cause Pimp Gene doesn't' seem fully awake yet and she doesn't want him to wake up until they see what's what.

116

They don't really need the volume because watching the DVD was enough. They see Pimp Gene already shackled down like they found him but there is someone dressed all in black, totally covered so you can't even make out the body type. You can't even see the eyes cause of the black sunglasses over a ski mask.

The person is seen taking out a bottle and holds it in front of the camera. Awww, hell it's glue! The kind in the brown bottle with the brush attached to the top.

They rub a really large amount on the shaft of Gene's dick.

He's just laying there like he doesn't know what's happening to him!

Wendy whispers, "Let's take it out so we can hear too."

Wendy picks up the DVD player and they both tip back out of the bedroom.

Moving quickly to the kitchen table where they rewind the DVD and turn up the volume…but only a little.

This time when the DVD starts they hear a distorted voice say, "So Gene you have been a bad boy for far too long. It's time for you to retire! Come on now…are you awake yet?"

Groggily Pimp Gene says, "What…what's going on?"

"Awww, sorry Gene you got set-up and now it's just me that's going to have a good time. I'm here to help you retire from pimping and treating woman like shit! You've gotten your last piece of change off the backs of those four women you have whoring for you. Yeah I know about the "secret" whores you have too.

You are a misogynistic prick who thinks women are not worth anything but tits and ass. You think you can take from women and they will never push back.

You are an embarrassment to real men who treat women like they are supposed to be treated…loved and respected…people, not objects or the means to your financial end.

Now first things first…I'm going to glue your little pecker to the side of your leg so all you can do with it is piss. People are tired of you walking around the streets, adjusting your dick or rubbing it as a way to say "hello."

You think you "Big dick swinging Willie," but you really are not…your time is over old man.

Oh…I almost forgot…full disclosure…I'm recording this little embarrassing moment. Yep I'm going to leave a copy for your girls with the hope they see it and get their courage up to leave your nasty ass for good.

Ok, what's next? Well I paid this girl a few streets over to give me a personal gift. She didn't know it was for you personally; just thought she was helping someone pass a drug test."

There is some movement and then the person holds a clear plastic funnel to the camera and a small baby juice bottle. They then move toward Pimp Gene and yells, "Hey Gene you up baby?"

Gene clears his throat and says, "Look I don't know what the fuck you playing at ok, mutha fucker! But I know you better take this sit off me and wipe whatever the fuck you put on my dick off!"

"Gene such bravado from such a small man…and looking down at your prick I really mean a small man!"

"I'm gonna kill your fucking ass when I get loose and what the fuck is wrong with your voice anyway? You got some kina speech fucking thing or what? You don't sound right."

"Seriously, you want to talk about my voice at a time like this?

I don't have a lot of time to fuck around with a piece of shit like you...so smell this ok?"

Gene has no choice but to sniff the contents of the baby juice bottle...he starts to cuss. But before he can get too much filth out...a plastic funnel is shoved in his mouth.

"Yep Pimp Gene ole boy, it's not apple juice it's piss! Nasty fucker like you needs a golden shower to symbolically move you into the golden years of retirement!"

Wendy and Tina are spellbound as they watch the figure pour half the bottle's contents down Gene's throat and then pour the remainder all over his face.

Gene is going bat shit crazy! But no matter how much he struggles, he can't get free.

The figure takes out some kind of pills and puts some down the funnel which is still in Gene's mouth.

"Now, Gene I'm going to take the funnel out of your mouth if you promise to swallow the pills on your own ok?"

As soon as the funnel is out of his mouth, Gene spits the pills out. They land on his chest and the mattress. He starts coughing and cussing.

The figure moves off camera and comes back with the juice bottle half full of what looks like water.

"Ok, let's try this again asshole."

Gene, not being very bright, opens his mouth to cuss and the funnel is shoved back in place.

"So since you wanted to be an asshole, I've gotta do this again.

119

Just relax…the pills will help you to have a good night's rest…and I've even gotten you some water…toilet water to help you wash them down."

"Shit," whispers Tina.

After Gene swallows the pills, the figure looks around, as if to check the room…then the DVD ends.

Wendy and Tina look at each other and smile.

Good gone…Plenty no more…

Wendy and Tina watch the DVD four times before finally stopping.

Wendy made herself a cup of coffee and peels the boiled eggs. She sat down at the kitchen table and added salt and pepper to the eggs.

Tina goes to the refrigerator and comes back with a beer.

Tina speaks first, "What in the fuck we gonna do now?"

"What you mean, what we gonna do now?" asks Wendy with huge brown saucer eyes.

"Well shit if we cut him loose he might kill us to make sure we keep quiet about this shit…right?"

"Oh I dunno…I mean you probably right cause Pimp Daddy can be real mean…but Tina we can't just leave him locked up like that with his junk glued to his leg!"

"Why the hell not? asks Tina.

"You know what this is right? It's a sign for us girl! We can stop being hos and do something else with our lives!" Tina says and then takes a deep drink of her beer.

Wendy takes a sip of coffee and looks over the rim of the cup at Tina, "What lives, we ain't never done nuthin but whoring. I'm too scared to try something new now.

I'm almost middle aged! That's way too old to start something new in life!"

Tina rolls her eyes and says, "Is it too old to die? Cause if you sit yo skinny high yella ass here with Pimp Daddy he's gonna kill you 'cause you will know his shame. You'll, for once, have something over his head…understand?"

"Somewhere in me I know you're right Tina but I'm scared," cries Wendy. Then straightening she asks, "Can I go witch you?"

"Hell naw girl I'm getting my shit and the dollar duckets I've hidden away so I can get the hell outta dodge…you feel me?

If so, you better do the same! I mean like right fucking now while he's still groggy from whatever shit that he got put in his mouth."

Tina gulps down the rest of her beer, throws the bottle in the trash and runs to her bedroom. She does stop on the way and listen in at Pimp Gene's bedroom door…he's snoring.

Wendy continues to sip her coffee and thinks about her next steps. She can't just leave him alone to die all chained up like some kind of animal. Pimp Daddy has taken care of her and she can't just do him any kind of way.

Wendy always knew Tina was keeping cash somewhere and so was she…for that day when Pimp Gene would tell her she was too old to ho for him.

OMG! I've gotta call Brian. He'll know what she should do.

Wendy tip toes to her bedroom and retrieves her cell phone. She calls Brian and asks him to meet her downstairs in the alley.

He says he'll be there in 20 minutes.

While Wendy waits, she starts packing only the things she can't live without; one of them being her book of poetry and her collection of Luther Prince CDs.

Brian calls Wendy once he's arrived in the alley.

She asks Tina to wait till she gets back and runs down the stairs to the alley. Once there she gives Brian the highlights and asks for his guidance.

"Yes!" says Brian throwing a fist into the air. "Honey you are free! Ok, go back and get your stuff together. I'll come right back with some of my stuff. We'll go to a hotel so we can talk about long-term plans."

"What about Pimp Daddy? I can't just leave him in there all shackled up!"

"Why not leave that fool tied up? And stop calling his ass Pimp Daddy…he's a leach."

"Oh Brian please don't…when you talk bad about him you're talking bad about me too." Wendy lowers her head and bites her bottom lip in an effort not to cry.

Brian reaches for her and holds her until he can feel her body relax.

"I'm sorry my love, I would never mean to say or do anything that would hurt you. You're right, we can't just leave him there, but we have to be smart about how we get him some help. We have to do it in a way that doesn't implicate you or your roommate.

So go and get your stuff together and bring it to the alley. When I get back, I'll pull my car up to the entrance of the alley and we'll load you up. Call me when you're ready to come down."

Brian kisses Wendy tenderly and she turns to go back into the apartment building.

They never notice Squidget standing behind a dumpster. She had just finished giving a scrawny freshman a blowjob when she saw Brian walking up the alley.

Something told her not to approach him and just wait; way to go listening to her inner Squid!

So Good is gonna fly the coop with Mr. Goody Two Shoes!

Well fuckin alright girl, do yo thang!

123

Wonder what that nasty fighting bitch Plenty gonna do?

Well when Miss Good comes out to meet her man…Squidget is gonna sneak in and find out the deal-e-o!

Good and Plenty hug one last time…now they are Wendy and Tina…

They peek in on Pimp Gene…who technically isn't *their* Pimp Gene anymore since they quit being his hos.

He is stirring a little and making some groaning noises. He sounds like he's more awake than before. They don't make a sound and close the door.

They've agreed to leave him as he is and once they are safely away, they will call the cops, unanimously, and tell them that something happened to Pimp Gene…or the man formally known as Pimp Gene!

A brief reflection...

Imani McCollin is 22 years old and by all accounts has had a wonderful life. She was doted on by her parents and extended family.

She was an All American track star in the 400 x 4 relay. Imani was a straight "A" student all through-out as an underclassman. Now she's working on her Master's degree at WVSAU.

Even though her parents live about 45 minutes from the campus, her parents have provided her with a furnished apartment and a car.

Yeah her life is wonderful...'cept that she can't forget her father molested her when she was four years old.

Imani started therapy when she was six years old. Her mother felt it was necessary because Imani would go up to any man she met and grab his crotch or try to sit on his lap.

At first her parents would laugh it off, but when she grabbed her father's crotch at her sixth birthday party and said, "Daddy can I play with your thing?"

As fate would have it she did it when there was no one else in the room.

Her Dad had been keeping her busy so her mom could sneak in a woman they hired to be a princess for the party.

Imani's dad, Anthony or Tony as everyone called him, took her by the shoulders and shook her. "Imani you've got to stop doing that to people what is wrong with you?"

Imani's eyes filled with tears and she said, "But daddy you used to like me to play with it. You said good little girls play with their daddy's things."

Imani began to cry in earnest now. "I'm not a good girl anymore daddy?"

Tony hugged his daughter close to him and he whispered in her hair, "Honey you are the best little girl ever and daddy is so, so, so very sorry."

His wife came in and closed the door. "What's going on in here? Is the birthday girl getting anxious for her party to start?"

Tony, still holding Imani looks at his wife and says, "Rosie, we gotta get this child some help."

Tony sat and continued to rock Imani until Rosie said they have to go on with the party 'cause everyone is waiting.

Imani's parents took her to a therapist and she worked with the counselor for over five years. Imani learned to say all the right things and continued to be a "good little girl." Her counselor discharged her from therapy saying she had achieved all her goals and she was no longer a victim but a survivor.

Imani didn't feel like she had achieved anything but maintaining a lie. Almost every night since she was 10 years old and realized her father was a monster and her mother was something just as bad for staying married to him after what he did, Imani imagined her parents dead.

Her latest thought is about them asleep in bed and she sneaks in and shoots them both in the head. Honestly, this has become a common theme of her dreams. But she could never kill anyone. Besides what would her life be like without their money? Does that make me a whore for even caring about the money?

Imani closes her eyes and thinks about all the stuff she's missed out on because she was daddy's little good girl. No sleepovers were permitted at her home or she at someone else's.

No boyfriends, no un-chaperoned school activities, hell I couldn't even attend the prom without my mom being there to volunteer! My dad had say over everything I wore and who I became friends with.

They have had me by the throat "for my own good" for far too long.

The group members arrive…all but Ayda.

The first person to mention her absence is Lynn, "I wonder where little Miss Ayda is? She's never late…did she quit?" She directs her gaze in Denise's direction.

Denise, who is sitting one seat down from Lynn, looks around the circle of women and says, "Your group norms allows for a member to miss up to two meetings without worry of being discharged. So let's give Ayda the courtesy to miss her first meeting without it distracting us too much."

She looks around and Yvette looks down into her coffee cup.

Internal dialogue…

Yvette…Shut the fuck up Yvette! It's none of your business and besides medical information is privileged information. You aren't losing your job over this shit.

Holly and Dani nod their heads in agreement to what Denise said.

Karen, Dawn, Cheryl just shrug their shoulders as if to say, "whatever."

Lynn, feeling like she's been admonished says coldly, "I was just looking out for Ayda; I didn't mean to break one of our rules!" She folds her arms and sits back in her chair.

Internal dialogue…

Lynn…I think Denise is harder on me because I'm white!

Denise looks around Imani, who is sitting next to Lynn and asks, "Lynn you appear to be feeling something, would you like to share it with the group?"

Lynn, looking deflated now, says, "Sorry everyone, I just have been holding my feelings in for so long, about that God-damned man, that affects everything that comes out my mouth!"

Denise, "Well you're in a safe place here…so talk to us."

Lynn takes a deep breath and lets it out. Then, with shaking hands, she brings the coffee cup to her lips, but it doesn't look as if she is able to take a sip.

"Well everyone knows Donovan Tate was found murdered some days back." She looks around the group and everyone nods their heads. She's never noticed them being so attentive to her before. She's not sure how to feel about that right now so she'll just ignore that nagging sensation of embarrassment and move forward.

"I'm still so angry and I feel guilty about feeling angry. So many people don't get justice when they've been raped or molested or anything. Here I am with not only justice, but the man is dead. Why aren't I happy about it? Why can't I still find peace? I mean what am I looking for?"

Karen asks, "What are you angry about?"

"I'm angry that I wanted to do good things in the world and he took it from me. I wanted to keep children from being in bad situations and he took that from me!"

Penny, "So Lynn are you saying that you stopped working after you were assaulted?"

Cheryl grunts her frustration, "Penny please, you are so nice…assaulted…girl she was fucking raped by a nasty sick in the head pervert!

She was trying to help him get the child out of foster care and he fucking killed her insides for her effort. I think that's what happened? Lynn…?"

Lynn sideways smiling, "Yes Cheryl that's more in line with what happened, but I think Penny was just being kind."

Penny who's sitting next to Cheryl just looks at Cheryl and rolls her eyes. She's embarrassed by Cheryl calling her out.

Internal dialogue...

Penny...OMG, no she didn't just call me out like that! What in the hell is wrong with these people? Somebody is always pointing a finger at me; even when I'm just being appropriate. I hate my life...it's so unfair...I didn't do anything wrong.

Cheryl...Fucking Penny...cop sitting in here trying to make shit sound good...ain't no way to make shit sound good...rape is rape damn it!

"Well anyway," says Lynn, "I just thought I'd feel better when he was arrested. Then I thought I'd feel relief when he was convicted, but I didn't feel anything. Or at least not what I'd expected to feel."

Karen, "What did you expect to feel?"

"I thought I'd be happy, feel all powerful and vindicated somehow.

Now he's dead and I feel just sad and blank like, now what do I feel...what do I really think? What do I feel about him? I've wanted it to be over but..."

Karen says, "I kinda know that feeling of *thinking I'll feel a certain way,* but finding out I don't. I know I should be angry at the guy who assaulted me but I just don't feel anything. I'm so scared of what will happen if people in my command find out that I guess it's stopping me from feeling anything else."

Lynn says, "I can understand that, I was afraid to say anything at first but the blow to the back of my head needed medical attention, otherwise, I'm not sure if I would've told anyone. I was so ashamed and scared. I know when I first told my story it sounded like I was "all together" when I got out of there, but I wasn't. I was in pain and my head was bleeding really bad.

I mean there wasn't anything in the social services orientation that prepared me for that. I didn't really know how my supervisors or co-workers would react…so who could I trust?"

"Did you think to call the police yourself or did the hospital staff?" asks Dawn.

"The hospital called the police and my parents for me. I had absolutely no clear thought to do anything.

My Dad took it pretty hard and until the day he died he hated all black men. I know it's wrong and I don't support his views but that was the consequence of the rape.

Internal dialogue…

Yvette…Bet his ass hated black people before the rape.

Cheryl…no offense but Tate must've been hard up to rape a case worker; guess he didn't think about what to do after he finished. He could've killed her!

Holly…I wonder if Lynn has a problem trusting men or black men since the rape. I don't trust anyone, but I do want to be included in stuff.

Dani…Poor thing…

Denise…I hope race isn't a discussion point tonight.

Lynn continues, "My mother was amazing and she helped me to heal physically and mentally. I was able to continue helping people but I worked with the vulnerable adult population after that."

Lynn takes a sip of coffee and says, I'd like to take a break now please."

131

Karen raises her hand, "I'd like to ask what people think I should do and why. I'm not sure it's worth reporting it anymore."

"Girl what do you think will happen if you tell your superiors?" asks Cheryl.

"I don't know, I guess they will investigate," says Karen.

Imani asks, "What can happen to him? I've never been in the service before so I have no idea what the consequences can be."

"Well it's an Article 120 of the Uniform Code of Military Justice (UCMJ) for rape that's clear but I'm not sure what the punishment would be," says Karen.

"Before you start talking about punishment," says Cheryl. "What about the investigation phase? What do you think will happen then?

They will ask questions of you, all your friends, him and whomever else they want. Are you prepared for that shit?"

Karen looks down at her hands.

Internal dialogue…

Holly…Say something that is not stupid please!

Holly clears her throat, "Ummm…I just want to say I wouldn't tell if I were you. I would find another way to get even with him…like find out who his parents are and send them a letter or something. That's my thought…thanks."

Denise smiles, "Good job Holly for joining in and expressing yourself."

Internal dialogue…

Denise…What? This girl right here…

Karen…Did she just say tell his parents?

132

Yvette...Holly, don't open your stupid mouth for the rest of the night! Damn!

Cheryl...Tell his mommy like we're in fucking second grade!

Imani...Poor Holly is dumb! I hope Yvette and Cheryl give her a break!

Holly blushes and says, "I've been working out with Dani and I feel stronger physically so maybe that's why I can say a little more tonight." She smiles and continues to blush.

Dani beams at her new found friend. While exercising, they have found they have more in common than they thought. Both believe that the justice system is one thing, but personal satisfaction, not revenge, is something totally better! They have promised to keep this thought to themselves and not share it with the group.

Dawn says, "I don't disagree with Holly about getting some measure of satisfaction, but there are consequences to that as well. What do you know about this man and how will he react to threats made against his professional and personal life?"

Karen looks at Penny, "Hey Penny you're a cop right?"

Penny lost in her own thoughts, abruptly focuses back on Karen's question, "Yeah I am, but I'm on extended leave."

"Well do I have to report it?"

Shaking her head, "No, if you don't want to report it that's completely up to you, but I would encourage you to do so. Don't you want him punished for what he did to you?"

Karen says, "Yeah I do want him punished but I just think it might cost me more than it cost him. I've been talking to other female sailors about how the military handles sexual harassment and I've found it's not really beneficial to the victim.

Most said they felt "black balled" by their shipmates. All of a sudden people stopped talking when they walked in the room or some sort of "hint" was dropped to let them know what people were saying about them.

One woman said her car was keyed after she told a guy she would tell on him for saying inappropriate things. When she went to the Command Master Chief, he's the senior enlisted person in her squadron, and told him what was going on he said, "Oh they keyed your car to warn you not to say anything. I wouldn't take this any further if I was you."

"Oh my GOD," gasped an angry Imani. "This day and time and that's all he said?"

"Yeah that's what he said," says Karen.

"See all those men stick together…fuckers!" says a disgusted Cheryl.

"Well to be fair, you didn't actually hear him say it right?" questioned Yvette. "I mean you are repeating something that someone told you right? So he might have said it another way or said more. You can't know right?"

Karen, looking angry says, "Yeah so what's your point Yvette?"

Internal dialogue…

Karen…This bitch is getting on my nerves!

"My point is things get turned around, if we base our feelings and actions on what someone else said. Their words, actions and feelings become a part of our narrative and it muddies the waters. What I'm saying is do what *you* know you want to do.

You already know you're not gonna turn him in 'cause you're scared of the unknown. Am I right?"

Everyone just stares at Yvette because she actually said what most of them were thinking, and she said it calmly!

Cheryl breaks the silence, "Well I think Yvette is on to something," she mumbles more to herself.

You're not going to get any justice on this. I have offenders on my caseload that get around the system all the time. Yeah sometimes there is a long sentence given in rape cases, like Lynn's, but most times the district attorney offers a plea bargain and the nasty mutha fucker takes it. Most victims authorize the DA to make a deal so the victim doesn't have to go through the rape publically."

Dani says, "Well what about your future honey?"

Karen asks, "What do you mean my future?"

Dani responds, "Well I was watching CSPAN one day while working out at the gym. Those ass holes won't let you turn the TV to something that has moisture to it! Those dry programs are the worse but they make me spin faster so I can get outta there!" She starts laughing and snorting.

Internal dialogue...

Imani...For real she watches CSPAN?

Holly...What's Cspin?

Yvette...Someone please shoot me! Her voice is sooo annoying!

Dani continues, "OMG sorry ya'll! I got so tickled...anyway on CSPAN they were talking about veterans getting some kind of money and stuff for being hurt while on active duty. Does this count as something you can get some money from when you get out?"

Karen looks at her like she's never seen the woman before.

"I have no idea what you're talking about, but thank you Dani, I'll check into it tomorrow. I hadn't thought about my future...thanks."

Dani beams and Holly grins at her. Holly thinks maybe they can celebrate how brilliant Dani is by having a little ice-cream after the group. They usually have herbal tea and gluten free cookies but that's getting a little old!

Damn, Dani is smarter than I first thought, thinks Denise.

Karen says, "Well everyone has given me something to think about, thanks ladies, I appreciate all of your comments and suggestions."

After a few minutes of silence, Denise asks, "Ok, this has been another great meeting. Now, I'd like to ask a question for discussion."

Cheryl groans, "Seriously Denise, every time you ask one of your "thought provoking questions," I get pissed off."

"Well, sorry Cheryl my questions are not meant to piss you off but to make you think, identify your feelings and begin to honestly process them." She smiles and looks around the group.

"So, my question tonight is, what do you all do to manage these intense feelings you carry around all day? What helps you cope?"

Cheryl starts laughing, "Yeah, now Denise that's a question I can readily answer! I fuck my husband's brains out every chance I get!"

Dani howls with laughter and spills some of the water she was about to drink.

Dani says, "Honey child I know that's right! Sex is a great exercise routine!"

Lynn, laughing says, "Cheryl I love your candidness! Unfortunately, no sex for me, I just drink coffee and put puzzles together. I'm working on a 1,000 piece puzzle that, once finished, will be a picture of the cutest little bunch of bunnies you've ever seen!"

"Well, I don't know about that as a stress reliever for me,." says Cheryl. "All those little pieces would drive me crazy!"

Holly raises her hands and asks Denise, "What if the thing you do isn't something you do like a project, but something you do to yourself. Can I say that, even though it's not a good thing to do, but when I'm nervous I do it anyway?"

Internal dialogue…

Denise…If she says she masturbates, I'm leaving the room!

Yvette…what is this fool gonna say now?

Cheryl…OMG girl don't say what I think you're gonna say!

Lynn…I knew it! She's on drugs.

Imani…I wonder if she's a cutter or something.

Denise clears her throat and says, "Holly and all of you, this is not a judgment group remember. Just be as honest as you feel comfortable."

Holly says, "Ok, well, I bite my nails and pick the skin around my nails." She lowers her head and places her hands underneath her thighs to hide them.

Internal dialogue…

Denise…Oh thank GOD!

Yvette…Is that all!

Penny looks over at her and holds up her index and middle finger, "See the discoloration of these two fingers?"

Holly nods her head.

"Well it's that way because I've picked at the skin all the way up just past the first joint. I've tried everything to stop like putting that

137

nasty stuff on that is supposed to keep people from biting their nails but it didn't work. I've tried band aids, gauze, tape everything and I still do it when I'm stressing about something that I don't want to think about.

It's embarrassing as hell but without it, I feel like I can't possibly cope with what I am feeling. Most times I don't even acknowledge what I'm feeling or notice I'm doing it.

I know people notice, it but they are kind enough not to say anything. Holly, you're not alone."

Holly smiles at Penny and mouths, "Thank you."

Dawn raises her hand, "I like to knit as a hobby, but I find that I over shop for yarn when I'm stressed and the projects get started, but never finished."

Denise asks, "Stressed how? Let's explore stress for a few minutes… it seems to be a common emotion shared tonight."

Dawn replies, "Well, as a principal, when I hear one of my students has been hurt by a family member or another classmate, it makes me stressed. I do all I can to help all my students, but sometimes things are out of my control.

I guess when I feel out of control it actualizes in my life by me shopping for things I don't really need. I tell myself I'm going to do a project for someone and that makes me feel better because I'm helping someone. I guess like, Lynn said, I want to make a difference by helping someone else. Knitting isn't a big deal, but it's all I know to offer. I can't do much else."

Holly says, "I guess I also like to read. I can lose myself in another world then. I like reading this author who combines romance and the supernatural together. She describes the main female character so well. I feel like I know her! I like reading about her 'cause she's in trouble a lot, likes to drink coffee and eats whatever she wants.

She's kinda like Lynn, Penny and Dawn all rolled into one person. She's a bounty hunter who is trying to help people!"

Internal dialogue...

Denise...Is she delusional?

Karen...Who is this chick? Maybe Ayda will be here next week and pray for Holly...she needs it!

Denise asks, "When you're reading do you pick your cuticles or bite your nails?"

"No, I do that mostly when I'm driving home from work. Hey come to think of it, I do it driving to work too."

Dani says, "Maybe you're feeling something scary about work?"

Holly blushes and says, "Well I was raped by the janitor, but not at the courthouse. I mean I was sexually assaulted by the janitor. Dani and I looked up rape after our last meeting and I saw that what he did to me was "sexual contact" which under the West Virginia law is..." She reaches in her purse and removes a small yellow piece of paper, like a large sticky note.

"Article 8B...Sexual Offenses are sexual contact by intentional touching, either directly or through clothing of the breasts, buttocks or any part of the sex organs of another person, or intentional touching of any part of another person's body for the purpose of gratifying the sexual desire of either party."

Holly folds the paper and places it back in her purse. She looks up to the astonished faces in the group.

Internal dialogue...

Holly...Dani will be so proud of me! I'm going to hell for lying! Shit!

Focusing back on the group, Holly says, "What?"

Karen says, "Damn you did something I've never done."

"What did I do?"

Imani speaks before Karen can respond, "You actually looked it up. I mean I've always just said what happened, but I never thought to look it up to see exactly what the law had to say about it. I never had the guts, honestly, to look it up and see it in black and white."

Karen said, "Yeah reading it will make it real…like more real than it already is."

Internal dialogue…

Yvette…These ladies run from a lot of things! I mean I'd be like Cheryl said, "bat shit crazy" if I hadn't gone to therapy and dealt with my feelings. I'm not sure what they've been doing. Seems like they are just discovering things about themselves that seriously shouldn't they have figured out a long time ago? In this age of Apps for everything why hasn't anyone looked up the statutes regarding their case?

If not for my parents I would've sued the hell outta old Ray. Hell I could own that fucking bar of his by now. Well I guess I'll find comfort in his death since that's all I could get from him.

Lynn over there freaking out about "what she should feel" well I feel great that he's dead and I can go downtown without worrying about running into him. I do wonder if he would have recognized me. Well nothing to concern myself over now. He's gone and I'm still here. Maybe the others would feel a little better if their offenders were gone too; but then again, maybe not, judging by Lynn's reaction to the death of her rapist. Wait, what did I just miss?

Denise has asked if anyone else would like to share their hobbies or coping technique before the group ends.

Karen says, "I like to watch British TV shows!"

Some start laughing…

"I know but seriously some of those shows are excellent! I love the ones with the Det. inspectors and their trusty sergeants. I mean it's well acted and there are no commercials."

Karen starts laughing and Dani leans in and says, "Girl I love me some Maryland Housewives so I know what you mean. You like what you like!"

Denise, "Well on that note lets end our group…breathe in…"

Sleuthing time…

Ruth, on her own and determined to find out who killed Raymond Jones. She has her work cut out for her since there are no witnesses, no forensic evidence and up to this point no one that can tell her if Mr. Jones had any enemies.

This is some fucked up shit, she thinks. I may have to put this in the cold case file if I don't come up with something soon. Of course, Penny will think I couldn't crack the case because she wasn't here with me.

I would never admit this to another living soul but I have to solve this without her. I'm tired of being Det. Penelopie Darling's partner. Like I can't do clean police work without holding on to her coattails.

So at 11 pm Ruth heads down to High Street to interview the night crowd. Maybe there will be someone who saw something or can give her a sliver of a lead. Someone knows something, I just need to find that someone!

Ruth parked her car two blocks up from the street where the bar was located. She locked her car and started walking down High Street. She was dressed in jeans and a tee shirt with sneakers. Ruth thought people would be more apt to talk to her if she looked like everyone else.

The first person who agreed to speak with her about Mr. Jones was a woman named Shayla who said she was coming from a nearby restaurant the night Mr. Jones was killed, but she didn't see anything out of the ordinary.

"See I don't go into bars like that. I have drinks at a restaurant, but not at one of those smoke smelling bars. Cause that smoke will get in my clothes and in my hair and girl you know I can't afford to have my wig cleaned that often!" She laughs and puts her fist out for a fist bump. Ruth gives it to her.

"So anyway I was walking past the bar and keeping my head straight ahead because that nasty 1970's looking man was leaning against his rusty ass car."

Ruth laughs and says, "Ok, go on…I know the guy you're talking about."

"Well that wanna be pimp makes some nasty ass remark about my booty being just the right size for him to eat his dinner off! Can you believe that old ass line? So I told him to back the fuck up and stop being disrespectful. Then…"

"Miss," interjects Ruth, "Can we please return to if you saw something suspicious at the bar?"

"Oh yeah, well the only thing I saw was regular people walking around. Like I said I kept my head forward. Wait! Someone strange passed me on the sidewalk heading in that direction."

"Who was that?" asks Ruth.

"Some old woman wearing one of those big caftan looking dresses. You know the ones they sell in the wig magazines? And she was carrying a dog carrier."

Ruth shakes her head up and down, "Yes I know the woman you're describing. Thank you for your time today Miss…"

"Ms. Shayla Mullins and Det., I sure hope that you all down at the police station start doing something to really clean up these streets or one day you're gonna look around and there will be more dead bodies around here."

She turns and sashays her "eat off my ass" down the street.

Ruth looks after her and thinks, Lord give me strength, I've got to interview Miss Stephanie and Roxie. Thankfully, it's late and I won't have to talk to her without the benefit of a good night's rest and some strong coffee.

The next day around 10 am, Ruth knocks on Miss Stephanie's door.

"Miss Stephanie are you in there? I'm Det. Ruth Hill and I want to question you about Mr. Jones' death."

Miss Stephanie turned down the TV show she was watching, "*Murder She Said*" and got off the couch. She slowly walked to the door and shouted, "What you want with me?"

"Well Miss Stephanie I understand you were on High street the night Mr. Jones was killed and I just want to ask if you saw anyone you thought looked suspicious."

Ruth heard two dead bolt locks turn and then the lock on the door knob turned as well.

Miss Stephanie peeped out, but there was a door chain still in place.

"Look I got nuthin to say about nuthin. I tried to tell that other dee-tic-tive what I saw, but she made fun of Roxie so I ain't saying nuthin else."

She slams the door in Ruth's face.

Ruth tries another tactic, "Wait Miss Stephanie, does Roxie have anything to say about that night?"

Suicide is an option…isn't it?

Penny woke to a wet pillow, she had been crying in her sleep again. The nightmare is always the same…because it really happened…

"Mom, I'm going to the library with Jenny ok?"

"Sure honey who is driving you?"

"Rory's picking me up along with Jayson. Then we're picking up Jenny and heading to the library at the college. What time do you want me back home?"

"Well, said her mom, "It is a school night so come back no later than 10 tonight."

"Ok, mom I love you and see you soon."

Penny bound down the steps before Rory's car could come to a halt. Rory was her grandmother's brother's youngest son & that made them cousins.

Penny and Rory were almost the same age and went to school together. This year they were juniors and their parents were giving them a little more freedom.

Jenny was Penny's best friend and she had a crush on Rory for the past two years, but he didn't seem to notice. Every conversation between Penny and Jenny always found its way to her cousin Rory. Penny could understand why all the girls had a crush on Rory, but, still he was just her silly old cousin.

Rory was 6'5" tall, lean and muscular. He wasn't classically handsome, but he had charisma and a great sense of humor. He was also the star of the high school basketball team and the leader of the "cool guys" at school.

For the most part Rory was cool and not a show off, but, at times, he could be mean. For instance, the way he treated Jayson Ellison.

145

Jayson is another cousin, but for the life of me, I have no idea how we are related. Anyway, Jayson became the butt of the jokes within Rory's little clique. But, I guess, for Jayson, it was better to be the jester than to be a fool without the light that shone from Rory.

Penny stretches down to touch her toes. She does this when she feels light headed and thinking in such detail always makes her feel light headed. Once she stands up straight, she walks to the living room and plops down on the couch. Penny closes her eyes and relaxes her body…and continues to remember that night…

Jayson pushes up the passenger seat and gets in the back so Penny can get into the front seat of Rory's 2-door Celica.

"Hey you could've stayed up here Jay," I said.

"Naw, that's ok, ladies should sit up front." Jayson smiles and looks all embarrassed.

"You sure know how to treat your cuz! Thanks honey."

The rest of the memory is lost until we are all riding toward the college library. At some point we picked up Jennifer Bradshaw and now she's in the front seat and I'm in the back with Jay. I'm sitting behind Rory because his legs are so long and if Jay sat there he would be uncomfortable since he's 6'3".

Rory says, "Hey why don't we check out the haunted house on the way to the library?"

Jayson sits up straight and yells "Why would we do that? Man that place is haunted for real!"

Jennifer laughs…a little too loud, but she acts weird when she's around Rory so I'm kind of used to it.

Jennifer says, "Rory I'm game if you're game…you know what I'm saying?"

146

I see her reach over and touch his thigh.

Rory looks in the rear view mirror at me and says, "Well cuz, what you think? Are you chicken too?"

"Hell yeah I am Rory Johansen! You better not drive us up to that haunted house in the pitch black! Are you crazy?! I'll tell if you do!"

"Alright, alright then," Rory says and looks over at Jennifer. "You and I are the only ones brave tonight."

Jayson says, "You can take me and Penny to the library and you can come back here with Jenny if you want."

Jennifer's head snaps around, "I don't like being called Jenny thank you Jay! Jenny is such a little girl's name and I'm almost a woman, so please call me by my full proper name."

"Ummm…yeah…ok…Jennifer, sorry," mumbles Jayson. "But I don't mind if you call me Jay or Jayson ok?"

Jennifer smiles and turns to flash, not only her smile, but her very adult tits his way. Jayson is star struck by the melon moons and even Rory takes a quick peek which is exactly what Jennifer wanted.

Penny, in the here and now, squeezes her eyes tighter. She is beginning to cry, but she doesn't care. Crying has never changed the past so she continues on.

Rory drives past the turn-off to the haunted house, but doesn't drive to the library.

"Hey Jennifer and Jay, do ya'll mind standing outside the car for a minute? I just really need to talk to Penny for a sec."

"Sure Rory," says Jayson.

147

"Why do we have to get out the car Rory? It's dark out there and a little cold this time of night." Jennifer asks, while looking out the windshield and her side window.

"Yeah Rory what's so important that you can't talk once we get to the library," I ask him.

"Well it's something personal and I need to ask it before we all separate. I can't explain it, just trust me, it's important and I need to speak with my cuz. Ok?"

Without another word, Jennifer pushes open the door and pulls the seat lift so Jayson can get out. I scramble to get out too and pull Jennifer by the arm and whisper to her.

"Girl I bet this is it! He's gonna ask me if you will sleep with him!"

Jennifer grins and says, "You really think so? I mean I was hoping he would since he invited me to go to the library. He's never even looked at me twice! So embarrassing that I didn't pick up on his signs toward me! Ok, how does my breath smell?"

She blows a breath in my face.

"Your breath smells like grape kool-aid."

"Yummy right? I found some grape bubble gum at the market. After tonight it's gonna become my lucky bubble gum!"

Jennifer gives me a quick hug and I get back in the car and close the door.

"Rory what's this about are you thinking of having sex with Jennifer? If so she's gonna say yeah...and yes she's on the pill...and no she's not on her period. Anything else you wanna know?"

Rory takes the car out of park and drives up a little. I look at the shocked faces of Jayson and Jennifer. Their faces are red from the *glow of the brake lights. I see Jayson take off his athletic jacket and place it around Jennifer's shoulders.*

Rory turns off the car and pulls up the parking break. His car is a 4-speed so the gear shift is sitting right between us.

Rory says, "I can't fuck Jennifer because I'm in love with someone else."

Shocked I say, "Well I don't mean no harm Rory, but forget who ever she is for tonight, cause if you don't do it with Jennifer she's gonna try and kill herself again! You know she's tried to overdose on pain medication before!"

"Penny taking aspirin isn't really trying to kill yourself! She just wanted attention. She wants something I don't want to give her I want to give it to someone else."

He looks like he's in pain. I've never seen my cousin look like this.

"Ok, so what do you want me to do? Tell Jennifer for you?"

"No I want to tell you something. I'm in love with you Penny. I want to make love to you Penny...tonight."

I hear Rory say he's been parking his car in my driveway every night for the past three weeks and just watch my bedroom.

I hear him tell me he can't focus in the classes we have together because he's thinking about me.

The last thing I hear him say is that he can't help it and he's sorry.

Then he rips down my zipper; almost separating it from my pants. He grabs me by the shoulders and pulls my upper torso to the back seat while the rest of me is in the front of the car.

I'm fighting, but it's no use, he's too big and strong. The round gear shift is sticking in my back and I'm crying.

Then I look to the side window and I see Jayson and Jennifer pounding on the windows and trying to get the car door open.

Suddenly they stop...just as Rory penetrates me.

Jayson puts his arms around Jennifer and they walk away.

I stop fighting and lay still while the cousin I loved like a brother raped me.

Afterward, I crawled to the back seat where Jayson was. I don't know what happened...how did he get there?

Jayson was crying and I reached out to him and said, "Don't cry Jayson, it's not your fault." Jayson looked at me and pulled my shirt closed. During the struggle I guess the buttons came off my shirt. Jayson put his athletic jacket over my shoulders and continued to weep.

Jennifer never said anything and I'm not sure if she was crying or not. Rory took her home first and even walked her to the door.

I gave Jayson his jacket back and thanked him.

Then he took Jayson home. Rory didn't walk Jayson to the door. He just pulled into the driveway and Jayson hurriedly got out of the car and never looked back.

Rory told me to get up front with him, but I refused.

Once at my house, Rory got out and put his jacket over my shoulders. All the lights were on in my house so I knew mother would be in her sewing room and my father would be watching TV.

I was wrong, seems mom had gone to visit a sick relative but daddy was playing checkers with one of the neighbors at the dining room table.

No one noticed my shame or the state of my clothing.

Rory had the nerve to come in the house and even talk with my dad about his strategy to win the checker game.

I sat in the living room unsure what to do next. Rory sat next to me and took back his jacket.

"Penny I know you think that what just happened was a sin and all, but it's no worse of a sin than when you screw someone."

"I'm a virgin Rory. I've never screwed anyone." My flat voice told him.

"Oh, well I'm sorry Penny. It's your own fault this happened...yeah I tried to not think about you, but there is something you did that made this thing happen.

Now it's over I won't bother you again ok?

Remember, a sin is a sin and God doesn't care about what we did for one sin anymore than any other sin you do."

Rory got up and walked out, saying goodnight and left me to contemplate my death for the first time.

I woke the next day to a huge bruise on my lower back, bleeding from my vagina and a massive headache. My eyes were dry and sore from all the crying I'd done the night before. My lids were swollen almost shut from so much crying.

For some reason I didn't tell my parents. We were going away for the holidays and I just didn't want to ruin it for them or for me. I only had a few weeks of school before the winter break.

I hid from Rory and Jayson by taking different hallways to class and getting to class last so they couldn't talk to me.

We had three classes together, so if I couldn't think of a reason to leave early, I would stay behind to talk with the teacher.

As for Jennifer, well she cursed at me that I stole her man and I was a slut. She said she never wanted to speak to me again and if I came near her she would tell everyone what a freaking whore I was.

I'd lost my whole life.

What if I told my parents and they reacted like Jennifer? Maybe they would blame me or not even believe me.

What about my grandmother? Rory is her nephew...son of her favorite brother.

I started having headaches, stomach aches, and wouldn't it happen this way, right before our trip to the mountains I got pneumonia!

Shit on top of shit!

My parents called my grandparents to come stay with me and they went on anyway.

Penny opens her wet eyes. She sits up and cries out loud…like the wounded animal she is inside.

Penny grabs a couch pillow and stuffs portions of it in her mouth and yells louder, cries harder until she has nothing left.

She curls into the fetal position and falls asleep thinking…Rory was right, God made me pay for the sin…He took my parents from me because I made my cousin covet me and I didn't tell what he did.

While on vacation, my father had some kind of accident and died. Her mother came back from the trip but she never came back to Penny.

God knew I was bad so he took my wonderful father from me.

Penny's grandparents took her to live with them until her mother's grieving subsided and Penny could return home.

152

It never did…Penny's mother became withdrawn, cold and refused to care for Penny.

Penny falls into a deep and much needed sleep.

Tina takes on the world...

Tina takes Pimp Gene's car to the airport. She's headed to San Diego with the $5k she had stashed in the hidey-hole she made by hollowing out the legs of her wooden bed frame. She saw someone in a movie hide their money that way and Tina decided that was going to be how she made her ticket out of the life.

Every chance she got, Tina used a mini hand drill that she purchased from A-Z Emporium to hollow out the bed posts.

The hand drill looked like an old fashioned egg beater but with a drill bit on the end. It took some time but Tina was a patient woman once her mind was determined to do something. She knew one day she would get the chance to get away from Pimp Daddy, but not in a million years did she think it would end like this.

Tina parked the car on the street several blocks from the airport, on Bismark Street, where it was sure to be picked apart. Ole Gene didn't hang in this part of the city so folks won't be scared to jack up his car.

Here comes Squidget...

Squidget snuck in through the back door to the apartment building. She was able to catch the door before it shut after that damn Good ran outta there like the devil was after her.

Squidget made her way, undetected up to Pimp Gene's apartment. She listened at the door and didn't hear anything. She knocked and called, "Yo anybody in there?" She didn't hear anyone speak so she decided to go in the unlocked apartment.

Squidget tiptoed into the apartment and whispering, "Is anybody in here?" There wasn't anyone in the kitchen or the living room so she crept down the hall. The first door, what she assumed was a bedroom, was closed, so she listened at the door. She could hear someone moving on the bed. But it sounded like chains clanking too.

What the hell is going on in there? Well only one way to find out...

No more sleuthing today…

After a disastrous attempt at interviewing Miss Stephanie, Ruth went back to the office. This case is cold as a freezer! You know it's bad when you gotta ask a crazy lady if her stuffed dog saw anything! Shit…sometimes I hate my job.

A cop in vice gets a call from someone who says Pimp Gene is tied up in his bedroom and somebody needs to come over and untie him.

The police officer says, "Sure I'll stop what I'm doing and go right over to help that scum bag!" He hangs up the phone and writes, "check on P.G. after shift."

If that asshole is tied up maybe this will teach him a lesson and he'll stop whoring girls. Guess one of them made the knots too tight! The officer continues typing his reports while listening to the radio.

The ladies are all present except for Ayda.

Denise remarks on Ayda's absence and informs the group that Ayda was found dead in her backyard swimming pool last week. The newspapers say it was an accidental drowning due to Ayda falling asleep and falling off the floating lounge into the water.

The autopsy showed Ayda had taken Zanax with wine.

Yvette still doesn't say anything; she just can't get involved with this.

Denise continues, "I want to focus on what we're feeling right now."

Lynn says, "I read about that but wasn't sure what to think or feel. Now I think Ayda was a lovely person, but she seemed to need more than our group could give her."

Denise asks, "How do you mean?"

Lynn says, "Well she cried ALL the time and even though her trauma happened several years ago she couldn't say it out loud. I get the feeling it was same sex assault from something she said to me walking to the car after the second meeting. I didn't want to push, but I was worried about her."

"She was a downer to me if you want my honest response. I felt like I was being judged for being honest" said Dani. "I really try to like everyone but she was really made my spider senses tingle in a bad way. But I'm real sorry she's dead."

Karen said, "I felt sorry for her but she scared me really…you know the thought of being her age and still so messed up was really scary to me and the way she acted really made me want to move on with my life and not dwell on this one moment of time."

The group is silent and it seems like a cold has crept into the room.

157

But one person is very happy that Ayda is gone for good…

Internal dialogue…

Ayda couldn't be helped anymore. I knew her death would benefit someone! Ayda was able to do some good out of what happened to her.

Knocking everyone over the head with her "holy stick" was getting old fast! Sometimes you just have to put your religion on the shelf and take matters into your own hands…Ayda was going to keep the group from expressing their true feelings. She was, like most crazy and religious people, just too overbearing. Always trying to appear humble when they were just feeling superior because, in their minds, they got picked for a special project by God and you didn't!

Well all of us have been picked sweetie…just you, for now, paid the ultimate price for being such a pain in the ass about it!

Penny is stunned she didn't know about Ayda's death. I guess it's none of my business since I'm on a leave of absence, and since it was an accident, Ruth wouldn't have been involved in the case.

Penny says, "I'm sorry Ayda is gone but I wonder if it was an accident or suicide. Sometimes it's hard to tell. I mean you can think you want to die so much that you'll do risky things with the hope it will happen.

Not today, but other days, I would've felt jealous of Ayda for being able to get out of this never ending misery."

Denise asks, "Why is today so different Penny?"

"Some days I can be more hopeful than others that I will stop reliving the nightmare and I'll feel good about myself again. I used to be a really happy person before I was raped by my cousin…then my dad died and my mom just stopped living. I just can't find anything to be happy about.

Thanks…I'm done for now."

"Penny, I can't imagine how hard that was for you." says Denise.

Denise asks if anyone has any feedback for Penny.

She allows the silence to sit.

Cheryl says, "Some deep shit happening tonight…"

Karen says, "Yeah…ummm…hello everyone, this might not be the right time but…I really appreciated all the support I got last week. You were right when you said I knew what I was going to do. I've decided not to tell anyone about what happened.

So much time has gone by, I mean like over a month and I haven't said anything so it will really look bad on me if I say something now.

Dani, I followed up on what you said about getting some type of compensation but since I'm not saying anything then I can't claim disability for military sexual trauma. But it's all good though…sometimes you've gotta let the universe handle the situation.

I wish Ayda was here so I could tell her that I believe God will make a way for me outta this. Also, I've learned that just because a man screws you over it doesn't mean you should become gay as a result!

All eyes stare at her…

Yeah, everyone looking at me like I'm nuts, but, for weeks I was wondering if I should start dating women! I've got nothing against being gay but you know…"

Karen stops talking and looks around the circle. "Ok, give it to me! Bring on the feedback ladies! I can take it!"

Dani raises her hand and speaks, "Honey I applaud your decision if it's the best one for you, but I would've told on his ass! He needs to pay and you need to get paid; like Denise is always reminding us, no judgment, just my thoughts honey!"

Lynn raises her hand the same time as Imani. Lynn says, "Imani you go right ahead, my comments can keep."

Imani smiles and then turns to Karen, "Are you forfeiting your right to compensation because it will make you feel some kind of way?"

Karen asks, "What do you mean?"

"Will you feel like a whore for taking money? Sorry for being so blunt...I think my inner Cheryl is coming out!" She looks at Cheryl and smiles.

Cheryl says, "Yeah well nuthin wrong with that!"

Karen says, "Imani no worries about your delivery. I appreciate your honest question but the answer is no that's not the reason. I just believe my life is better off just putting this behind me and moving forward with my life.

I've also broken up with my boyfriend. He wasn't right for me and I was with him for all the wrong reasons. I have a lot of work to do on me right now so that's where my focus is gonna be.

I've heard women who experienced sexual assault while on active duty have a hard way to go and I'm sorry, but, I just don't want that in my life right now. I wasn't actually raped and I'm still alive so that's a big plus."

Penny raises her hand, "But what quality of life will you have? How will you move forward when you are constantly dreaming of the past?"

"Well for starters I've never had dreams of the assault. The guy and I were friends and I did flirt with him some time. Did I ask for it or deserve it HELL NO!

But do I want to ruin our lives and our family's lives over this? Naw not me, but thanks to all of you for being here and helping me make up my mind."

Lynn raises her hand and says, "I think you're making a brave decision and I send you blessing of peace as you move forward. I did decide to tell and let me say it wasn't all I thought it would be."

Penny raises her hand, "But, Karen isn't not telling what happened, like condoning the act...the rape?

I didn't tell either and I've spent most of my life... sorry, never mind."

Denise, "Let's take a moment to connect to what we're feeling about Karen's decision. Let's take in the fact that Karen wants to move forward...have any of you thought about how your life would be different if the assault never happened?"

Internal dialogue...

Yvette...What's up with Penny tonight? She seems weird...

Karen...Damn I wish they would leave me alone! They've forgotten all about Ayda dying.

Dawn...I think Penny is going to kill herself. Denise better do something fast!

Holly...Do I have to say anything? I don't know how to fit in the conversation.

Dani...I want to join another support group! I really like the way we challenge each other.

The group is quiet until Denise asks, "Now does anyone have anything else to offer?"

161

Imani raises her hand, "Yeah I do wonder what my life would be like. I mean what would it look like when my parents don't have to buy my love?

How would their love really feel and how would they express it?

I think I would've been allowed to do stuff with my friends instead of feeling like a fragile secret that needed to be kept safe.

Ayda's not here so I can say it again, I hate my parents and I can't imagine not."

Yvette clears her throat and raises her hand, "Well I don't say much, but I take it all in, everything I hear.

Internal dialogue…

Dawn…I know she didn't just say she doesn't say much!

Denise…She's delusional too!

Lynn…She doesn't say much! What she's never bit her tongue in any of the groups!

Yvette…I'm so full of shit! I've never found an opportunity when I didn't express my opinion!

I guess I am feeling positive about the way Karen made her decision no matter if it was popular amongst us or not.

I will say, Karen, you have the right to report when you are ready and if you chose not to then peace to you. I didn't have a choice to tell or not to tell. My family made the decision for me.

I don't know if there would be anything different in my life if that sick bastard hadn't happened to me. My family has so many skeletons lurking round the house so one more didn't seem to be a big deal to them.

Hell, my grandmother's first son was the product of incest with her father. She ran away from home and returned four months later pregnant.

The family never officially spoke of it, only gossiped about it. Grandma got married and kept on keeping on. Seems this is the way my family moves forward…by never looking back.

Now my great-uncle is dead, murdered to be exact; he's dead and I'm still living."

Looking over at Penny, "Hey Penny, this shit ain't a good reason to die over.

I believe I've got too much to live for."

Holly raises her hand, "I agree with everything I've heard. I just want to put out to the group that I've been feeling angry and I want satisfaction for what happened to me, but I have no idea what will make me feel better."

Internal dialogue…

Holly…Ok, so I said something! Was it the right time? Maybe I sounded like a killer or something! Shit Penny is still a cop right?

She starts picking at her cuticles.

Holly takes a deep breath and continues, "Also I'm not sure how to answer Denise's question about what my life would look like if…Well I think I'd be attending college and getting ready to get married."

Cheryl asks, "Then why aren't you…attending class? Your brain didn't die when he tried to stick his dick in you right?"

Holly's mouth flies open and she's speechless.

Internal dialogue…

Karen…Wait till I repeat that line!

Lynn…Good God she is crass!

Denise…I hope my face is fixed appropriately! That shit was funny!

"Damn! Cheryl you know how to put it out there don't you?" asks Dawn laughing nervously.

"Well I'm just saying…if you want something why are you making excuses?"

Holly, sounding angrier than she has ever allowed herself to express says, "Well if you must know, I just feel like I'm gonna get hurt worse than before. I mean I have knives all around my house 'cause I'm scared something is gonna happen to me.

I feel like there will be someone out there who has been waiting for me to let my guard down by living like everything is normal. I don't feel normal."

She takes a big bite of her cookie and gets up and goes to the snack table for more. Not even caring if they are looking at the cellulite on her thighs.

"Yeah, I feel you on that," says Cheryl, I have a baseball bat at every door. I carry mace and a pocket knife in my purse. But that doesn't stop me from living my life. I just live it like I'm ready for the next fucker to step outta line!"

"Ok, ladies, let's pump our brakes a little," laughs Denise, "I'd like to go back to what Penny expressed earlier…living or dying. We can revisit safety if Holly is comfortable, a little later. How do you decide to live or die?"

Penny, "Sometimes you decide to die and the universe has other plans so you *have to* keep living whether you want to or not."

Dawn says, "Honey, I'm sorry but life is so much better when you learn to accept your circumstances and make the best of them. There are strengths to come outta every situation; you just have to be healthy enough to see them."

Cheryl looks between Denise and Penny, "I ain't gonna let nuthin kill me but the good Lord! I'll kill a mutha fucker before I let them fuck me up so bad I want to kill me.

Lynn you asked me in an earlier group what I did after the rape…well I didn't kill him because I wasn't as strong and determined as I am now. Now I would be the one fucking him up for the rest of his life.

I think about how I would fuck him up and I think a cattle prod up his ass for starters! Then I'd slice his balls, but not cut them clean off. I want him to think of me every time he tries to piss or come! Mutha fucking crack head!"

Cheryl stops talking and wipes away the lone tear streaming down her face.

"Naw Penny…any of you…don't ever give into this shit. It happened but it's not still happening…life is out there happening for you go live it!"

Silence…

"Well I tried to kill myself once," says Imani. She looks down at her hands, but takes a deep breath and continues. I stole my mom's valium pills and hid them until I had at least 10. Then I took them with a large gulp of my dad's best bourbon. Of course, my doting parents found me and took me to the hospital.

One time drinking charcoal as an antidote was enough for me! After that, I did what Penny said might have happened with Ayda, I put myself in positions to get hurt by accident, but as you can see I wasn't successful."

165

"I see living and dying every day," interrupts Yvette. "Your body is so complicated, yet fragile…it's really amazing and should be treasured.

I don't know if suicide is an answer to our problem but yes it can be an option, but so can homicide."

Some in the group stiffen but don't say anything.

Internal dialogue…

Yvette…I wouldn't really kill anyone but it's fun to say and will keep these women away from me!

Holly…I'm scared of Yvette.

Yvette continues, "Why would you choose to hurt yourself and not the person who hurt you? That's the question I'm just asking.

You are all so wonderful in your own uniqueness…seriously…fuck 'em and move on. Or go ahead and kill yourselves and end your suffering!

Kill them and see if you feel better! But damn do something besides moan about it!"

Internal dialogue…

Denise…Shit! Yvette is out of control! I gotta shut her down immediately!

Denise says, "Yvette, let's stay with the non-criminal theme of moving on…so imagine you did move on…what would that look like?"

"I wouldn't go to therapy or come to support groups!" laughs Cheryl.

After laughing the group grows silent once more.

Dani speaks up, "I would own a gym and give free classes to women who were sexually assaulted. I would want them to feel strong and sexy. I used to think my fat ass was sexy, but I was just hiding my unhappiness underneath the fat."

Karen asks, "So Dani do you equate your happiness to your weight?"

"No, but I was hiding a lot of insecurities by dressing up in expensive clothes no matter what size I was wearing. There had to be something going on with me for me to marry my ex.

I was always a little chubby and wanted to be in with the cool kids. It's cliché, but true. So when Mike picked me just the way I was, well it felt good. I ignored everything else including myself."

Penny says, "I would take a long trip and just do whatever I wanted. I would try to discover myself all over again."

"Why would you waste your time like that?" asks Yvette.

"Seriously, you already know who you are, it's the person you've become minus the fall back memories of the rape. Step outside of that moment and look at all the stuff you've done!"

"Well that's easy for you to say Yvette. You were supported by your family or at least you were raised by your parents.

My parents weren't there for me." says Penny.

"You were raised by what your grandparents? So you had support too. Are they still alive?"

"No."

"So do you think they would want you to waste the opportunity at life that they gave you? For real, I imagine my life, moving forward to be this...my husband and I work, live our normal lives and retire.

Once we retire, we can travel once a year, shop a little, decorate the house, take care of our parents and die peacefully.

167

I don't want or need a lot and I don't expect that my life would've been something magical if great-uncle Raymond Jones had kept his hands to himself."

It takes a moment but recognition dawns…

Penny and Cheryl gasps and look bugged eyed at Yvette.

"Yeah, yeah, yeah, the guy who was killed a few weeks back was my great-uncle and the man that molested me."

Holly is the first to speak, "What and you didn't tell us?"

"Why would I have to tell you anything?"

"Well we are in group together…"

"Yeah, but that doesn't mean I have to give all of myself to it. I don't have to come in here and open my mouth on all my life."

Dani says, "Holly she's right. Yvette and all of us only say what we feel comfortable saying…Denise reminds us of that all the time."

"Well I'm not the only one who has had her abuser die," says Lynn. "How does it feel Yvette to know he is dead?"

"I'm glad he's dead so now I can walk downtown without wondering if I'll see him. My family thinks I don't know who he is or rather was but I did.

 I heard my mom and auntie talking about how old Ray was trying to make something of himself by running a bar down on High Street.

I even walked by there a few times. Once he was sweeping the sidewalk and looked me right in the eye. He smiled and told me to have a good day. He had no idea who I was and I didn't tell him. I just kept on walking."

Holly asks, "Do you wish you had told him so he would look at you and feel bad about what he did to you?"

168

Yvette snorts, "Naw I don't need him to show me he felt bad. I wanted him to feel bad in that deep dark place of his soul."

Yvette closes her eyes and says, "That place where our secrets come out of their boxes and torment us.

Internal dialogue…

Lynn…I'm impressed by her use of examples!

Karen…I'm glad I came tonight; this shit is deep.

Dawn…Go girl…process that shit!

Denise…Yvette is a complex woman and I think I like her!

I just shut off all my feelings toward Ray and kept it moving. Besides, if I dwell on Ray I'd have to take a long hard look at the rest of the family too. I decided Ray wasn't worth me shutting out all my family.

They all played a part in the cover up, but they also played a part in my recovery."

Karen asks, "How do you mean, if you don't mind me asking."

"Well, family will come together the best they know how and try to make it seem like bad things don't always happen.

I was loved, the best they knew how to love, and cared for. All my comforts were met and I was given every opportunity to succeed. My family's history is a dysfunctional one, but they are united none the less, and I accept the choices they made to protect me from the police, neighborhood gossips, and, most importantly, from Ray.

My family taught me to be strong and never apologize for doing whatever I got to do to keep on keeping on!"

"But didn't you ever want Ray dead for what happened to you and how did you feel about your parents?" asks Imani.

"No Imani I didn't ever want my parents dead!

My relationship with them is nothing like your relationship with your parents. My parents are simple working people. They go to church and try to do the best they can.

I don't hold them responsible for the choice Ray made that day.

As for Ray, well my grandma said it best, "Honey don't waste your precious prayers wishing for the bad people to die…they ain't never gonna really die 'til the good Lawd say so. The bad people will die, just like the good people, no denying that for sure, so pray for something else more worthy."

Holly fidgets in her chair but doesn't speak for fear they will think she's crazy.

Internal dialogue…

Holly…I just think we should stop talking about death and hating people…it makes me uncomfortable. Penny, Yvette and Imani are really scary women.

After a few minutes of silence Denise says, "Well this has been a very dynamic group session. Our time tonight is almost up.

We only have three more sessions so consider this…if you want any psycho-educational materials about depression, suicide prevention, managing stress, etc., let me know and I'll bring it.

Also, some groups like to have a potluck after the last meeting so it's up to you all.

Now I'd like to check in with everyone before leaving. Tonight was a tough one…I'll pick the first person and they will pick the next person until we've checked in with the entire group…Lynn."

"Well, I'm feeling more than before. I'm really noticing my ambivalence toward Donovan Tate…I can say his name and not

170

explode! Well it was more about how I see myself or how I thought I saw myself. I do know how I feel about him, I hate his black ass!"

"Well alright sista; show your true colors!" says Cheryl.

"I'm saying that without it meaning the same thing as my Dad. I don't hate all black people because only Donovan Tate raped me and hit me over my durn head with a friggin lamp! I'm sorry for being so descriptive! I've never allowed myself to say that out loud.

I'm glad I came tonight and I look forward to thinking about tonight for the rest of the week. Thanks ladies!"

Internal dialogue…

Yvette…Wow somebody is getting too comfortable!

Dawn…Shit! Yvette is gonna eat her alive!

Holly…Wait, so the guy who raped her was black? Is that worse than if he were white?

Denise says, "Lynn who's going next?"

"Sorry Denise…I pick Imani next."

"Ummm…well I'm thinking a lot of things, but not sure what to say. Just that I'm ok and I've got a lot to think about. I pick Karen to go next."

"Thanks Imani! I knew you would pick me for next. No for real, I'm feeling like a weight has been lifted off me. I feel really good about my decision not to make this moment in my life the lens that I see my entire life through.

Internal dialogue…

Karen…Got that line from Dawn the other night! It really sounds like I got my shit together…but do I?

171

I pick…Yvette cause she really kicked ass tonight!"

"I don't know about that, but I haven't expressed myself like this before. Seriously, I'm usually quiet and I just sit back watching folks. But I felt free tonight to talk so thanks. Oh, I pick Cheryl."

Internal dialogue…

Denise…Yvette is delusional! She really believes she hasn't expressed herself before tonight!

Dani…When has Yvette not felt comfortable to express herself?

Imani…Yvette! I just can't deal with her. She's so confusing.

Cheryl says, "I'm doing good…taking it all in and finding I'm really proud of myself for hanging in there. My life is good in spite of what happened…maybe even because of it.

I fought to make sure I accomplished all my goals so I could prove that Gerald, yeah that's my brother-in-law's name, didn't break me. But I'm realizing my determination came with a side of kick ass anger.

Now I'm seriously gonna look at why I'm so angry…thanks ya'll…Dawn you know you next!"

"Of course I am! See, Cheryl and I have become buds and I think I've found a life-long friend. I'm in a good place tonight so much so I'm wondering why I keep going to therapy! Like Dani said, I think I have been hiding too…behind therapy.

I'm so busy spouting off stuff like, "mentally healthy, processing events, and other, no offense Denise, but therapist lingo, that I think I lost touch with "real living."

Like the way Dani asks raw questions…the way Holly looks when a raw question is asked…the way Lynn naturally helps people…the way Imani dresses so youthful and fresh…the way Karen comes in saying she's in the military, like it's nothing special, when it's AMAZING…the way Cheryl and Yvette open their mouths and their souls sing…lastly, the way Penny, a cop comes in here and bears herself to us…this is real living ladies.

Heck, any other time I would've been taking notes so I could go home and look things up in my MANY self-help books, but not anymore. I'm taking it all in while living! Yeah, this was the last two percent of recovery I was looking for! Penny, girl you are next!"

All heads turn to Penny…

"Well, I've never told so much about the way I see myself. I feel fucked up most of the time but somehow I keep on moving. Let me think on things…but I'm good…ok…ummm Dani."

"Well ya'll, I guess I'm feeling full and satisfied tonight! I can't describe it any other way. It's all good ya'll!

Holly, you're next!"

"Ok, so….ummm…tonight I actually felt my own thoughts in my head…ummm that's all.

Internal thoughts

Holly…I have no idea how to be right now…I'm always the last one picked!

Denise, smiling and starts to speak, but is interrupted by Dani.

"Wait Denise, can I lead the group in the relaxation exercise? I've been doing it at the end of each of my exercise classes!

I'd also like to thank you Denise for introducing me to relaxation exercises, but, I gotta tell you it's better with music."

"Ok, is that alright with the group?"

Everyone laughs and nods or says it's ok.

Dani pulls her cell phone from her jean's pocket and scans until she finds the song she's picked.

"This is some meditation music to help us along…ok, you know how we do…eyes closed…palms flat on our thighs…breathe in and hold it…"

Pimp Gene's shame…

Squidget didn't open the first closed door, but crept down the hall and looked through Good and Plenty's rooms. They left most of their stuff behind, but it was clear they were long gone.

Squidget goes back to the kitchen and through the living room. On the dining room table she sees a DVD player.

Yo, I can get some money from this! Naw, I'll keep it for myself so I can finally watch some movies!

Wait something is in it…Squidget plays the DVD and half-way through she falls off the chair laughing.

Then she hears…"Who the fuck in there? You better get yo ass in here and help me outta these mutha fuckin cuffs!"

Squidget stands up and leans over so she can continue to see the video in its entirety. Old nasty Pimp Gene got a golden shower!!!

Yeah, that's what I'm talking about!

She turns and goes to the closed door and knocks, "Hey Gene you in there?"

"Who the hell is that?"

Squidget opens the door and pisses her pants laughing! "Damn Gene your ass stinks! Did you shit yourself? Damn man!"

She goes to the bathroom and turns on the exhaust fan.

"That ain't gonna help, but for real, yo ass stinks! How long you been like this?"

"Squidget is that you? Did you do this to me? I'm gonna fuck you up when I get out of this! Unlock me bitch!"

"Now, hold on, you long-legged mother fucker; First I ain't your bitch...second I didn't do shit to you...third yeah it's me Squidget.

Now if you want my help you gotta promise not to try nuthin when I get you outta this."

Pimp Gene closes his eyes and weighs his options, "Ok, I ain't gonna do nuthin to you if you help me outta this...'cmon girl find a key or something."

Squidget looks all around the room, but can't find a key and the fumes coming from Pimp Gene's shitty ass don't help, because her eyes keep watering.

Squidget gets an idea, "Hold on Pimp Gene, I'm gonna look at the video and see if I can see where they put the key."

Squidget runs back to the dining room where she left the DVD player.

Gene says out loud, "What video?"

Squidget watches every move the ninja freak makes during the torture of poor old Pimp Gene. I mean moving around in all black like that...must've been a ninja!

Wait, when the person leans in toward the DVD player it looks like they are stopping the machine but something is in the right hand. Squidget turns the DVD player over and the key is stuck under black electrical tape.

 I'm a fucking genius!!!

"Hey Pimp Gene, I got it!"

Squidget runs back into the bedroom and once again is hit by Pimp Gene's body odor and whatever else he's secreted.

"Ok, I'm gonna undo your feet first...then your wrists."

Pimp Gene waits for Squidget to unlock all the cuffs before trying to rise up in the bed.

"OWWWWW something is pulling my shit!"

"What you mean something pulling yo shit? I ain't going up your ass to unlock a damned thing!"

"No bitch, something is pulling my dick!"

Squidget walks to the end of the bed and peers over at Pimp Gene's genital area.

"Ummm, Pimp Gene, looks like the glue they used is now hard as cement and your dick is glued to your thigh. What the fuck, man who did you piss off?"

"WHAT YOU MEAN THEY USED GLUE ON MY DICK!?"

Squidget runs out the room and retrieves the DVD player. She comes back into the bedroom and plays it for Pimp Gene.

He can't believe it and tells her to rewind it. She does and they watch it together three more times. Then, unbelievably, *Mack Daddy*, *Pimp Daddy* & *Big Dick Willie* begins to cry and pisses down his thigh.

At the end of his shift the police officer who took the unanimous call about Pimp Gene looks at the post-it and decides to drive by Gene's apartment before calling it a night.

He arrives and knocks. A thin black girl dressed in a robe answers the door.

Squidget had to change out of her clothes after cleaning up Pimp Gene. Those few nurse's aide classes in high school paid off, because if not, I don't think I could've rolled his nasty ass around and cleaned him up.

177

Can you imagine if this cop came here and found him shitty and pissy?

"Yeah Mr. Officer, can I help you?"

Ma'am we got a call that someone was tied up and needed some help."

"Yeah, he's here but he ain't tied up no more.

One of his bitches ran a game on him, but he's alright now…come on you can see for yourself."

The officer follows Squidget into the apartment. It smells like two day old shit, but the apartment is clean and decently furnished.

"He's still in bed, as you can guess, since he had an ordeal today.

Gene this officer wants to know if you alright now."

"Mr. Gene…sorry sir, I don't know your last name. I'm Officer Conklin and I'm here to check on you."

"Officer it don't matter now I'm alright and don't need no help."

"Well ok, but I still need your last name so I can file a report."

"Squidget, bring me that Ajax can over there on the toilet bowl top."

Squidget gets the can and brings it to Gene. She and the officer watch in disbelief as Pimp Gene unscrews the bottom of the can and pulls out a wad of money.

"Look here Officer whatever your name is…here's $500 for you to forget all about filing a report."

Pimp Gene hands the money toward the officer.

Squidget says, "Man you better take that money 'cause you know you ain't gonna get no raise this year!"

178

The officer hesitates for two seconds, snatches the money and walks very briskly out the apartment.

Squidget follows him and closes the door. She locks the dead bolt and the knob lock.

"Ok, Pimp Gene, let's get your dick unglued!"

"Oh Lawd what you gone do to get this off me?"

"Well they say finger nail polish remover is the only way to get hard glue off. I'll go see if the girls left any."

"What you mean if they left any? Good and Plenty should be out on the street this time of night."

"Gene those girls got the hell outta dodge when they found you like this. If not for me you would be on your way to the hospital and the whole block would know about this."

Squidget finds two bottles of polish remover and cotton balls in Wendy's bathroom.

"Ok, so I'm gonna soak a cotton ball and let it sit for a few minutes. I'm not sure how long it will take. You want something to eat or drink?"

"Yeah, look in the fridge and bring me that bottle of Thunderbird and see if those hos left me some chicken wings. I'm starvin like Marvin.

I can't believe those ungrateful bitches left me like this! Can't trust nobody these days!"

Squidget leaves the nail polish soaked cotton ball on Pimp Gene's stuck dick and heads to the kitchen.

She takes out the Thunderbird and wings, putting them on the counter.

"Hey Pimp Gene where are the glasses?"

"Girl, I don't need no damn glass! My dick is stuck to my leg! Just bring me that bottle! And don't worry about heating those wings either."

Squidget takes the wine and chicken back into the bedroom.

Gene unscrews the wine bottle top and takes a long deep gulp of the wine. He has managed to prop himself up on his elbows without too much discomfort.

"How's it looking down there?"

"Well it's softening up but I don't want to pull it yet."

"What you planning on pulling!" cries Gene and takes another long gulp of wine.

"Well at some point I've got to start pulling at it so more nail polish can eat through the glue."

The bottle crashes to the floor...Pimp Gene has passed out cold!

Squidget laughs, takes another soaked cotton ball and dabs the glue between Gene's penis and his thigh. Then she retrieves the bottle of wine and takes a long drink, placing the bottle on the bedside table, so Gene can get it later. She then sits on the floor, where she had left the DVD on pause when she made her first attempt to remove Pimp Gene's glued dick. Squidget watches the DVD and eats some chicken wings.

Be careful what you ask for…

Mr. and Mrs. McCollin exit the garage elevator and are both shot in the upper body.

Their daughter Imani got the call from the Morganville police department just as she was getting out of the shower. She had just returned from one of Dani's aerobics classes. Barely dressed, she rushes out of her apartment toward the hospital.

Once there, she is directed to the ER family waiting room. Yvette is on duty and sees her sitting alone.

"Hey Imani, what are you doing here?"

Imani looks up a little dazed, "Yvette, hey I didn't even think about you being a nurse."

She lets the tears flow, "My parents were shot coming from the mall tonight. Who would do such a thing to them?"

Looking down at Imani Yvette says, "Can I call someone for you? Do you have other family members or friends nearby?"

Imani's face is make-up free and she looks like a teenager, "No, I don't have anyone except them! This is totally my fault! I wished and prayed for this!"

Internal dialogue…

Yvette…Yep that's just what I was thinking too!

"Shhhh now," says Yvette and she sits down next to Imani looking around to see if they were being overheard.

"The police will be in here in a minute and you can't tell them it's your fault. They won't look for the person who did this if they think you did it. So stop saying that ok?"

Imani continues to cry on Yvette's shoulder until the police arrive.

"Excuse me miss, I'm Det. Ruth Hill and this is Officer Conklin. I know this is a bad time but I need to ask you a few questions."

Imani lifts her head and tries to staunch the flow of tears but she can't.

Yvette says, "Officers, I'll go get some water for her and check on her parents."

"Ok, thanks Mrs. Dyson."

Yvette and Imani don't let on they know each other outside of this moment, but Det. Hill let's Yvette know she remembers her name.

Internal dialogue…

Yvette…No that bitch didn't just call my name out like that! Well fuck her!

"Miss McCollin, can you tell me where you were tonight?"

"Ummm, yeah, I went to the fitness X Club to an aerobics and spin class. I got home and took a shower then someone from the police station called me."

"Do you live alone?"

"Yes, I go to the university and my parents got me an apartment so I wouldn't be on the road all the time going from home to school."

"Can you think of any reason someone would want to shoot your parents?"

"No, I can't…they really are nice and decent people. I guess as a child you don't realize that until it's too late…"

Internal dialogue…

Imani…I can't believe I just said my parents are nice and decent people! I'm such a hypocrite after all the shit I've been talking

182

about them. If the police interview the women's group they will think I had motive to shoot them!

"Well it's not too late, your parents are still alive. Officer Conklin and I will leave you for a few minutes to check on some things. Do you want us to call someone for you?"

"No, there really isn't anyone I'd want here with me except my parents."

Imani closes her eyes and begins to do something she's never done before…ask God to keep her parents alive.

Walking toward the exit Ruth says to Officer Conklin, "Ok, Conklin, I'm gonna go to the crime scene. You stay here, but just observe, ok? Anything comes up you call me."

Officer Conklin finds a chair to sit in where he can see the daughter without crowding her. She looks like she's praying. I've sure been praying ever since I got that $500 from Pimp Gene.

When I got the call to come in, I thought for sure my ass was grass! I gotta be smart about this and keep my cool.

Hey that nurse is back and she's fine as hell, but she's got that, "don't fuck with me look" so I'll just do what I've been told to do…watch.

"Here's some ice water, crackers and softer tissue," says Yvette.

Imani takes the items and says, "Thanks, can you sit for a minute?"

"Sure, I can. I found out your parents are in surgery and they were the only patients in here tonight, if you can believe it. So the docs were able to take them straight up to surgery.

Usually this place is hoping with sick people, but, whenever there is a sports event at the college our shift is a piece of cake."

183

Two hours later…

"Nurse Dyson, excuse me, is this Miss McCollin?"

Yvette and Imani stand and look at the doctor.

"Yes, sir I'm Imani. How are my parents?"

The doctor takes a deep breath and says…

"Your parents were shot, but no vital organs were hit and the bullet was a small caliber. They are going to be fine."

Imani drops to the floor and hugs Yvette's legs. Yvette sits down with her on the floor and holds Imani while she cries tears she's held for too long.

Det. Hill arrives at the crime scene while forensics is just finishing up.

"Anything guys?"

"Nope Det., nothing…we think the perp stood just beside that cement pillar and waited for the elevator door to open. Two shots through and through…no casings found…no images on the tape either according to the security guard."

"Wait, who interviewed the security guard?"

"Hold on, don't get territorial, no one did, he came up here wanting to see a "real live murder scene." He told us he watched the video after he got a call that shots were fired."

Ruth's head snaps up from the patch of ground she was inspecting for missed evidence. "Someone called it in? Was it recorded?"

"Yeah, but he says it sounded like a mechanical voice not human."

"Where is the security guard now?"

184

"He's downstairs still in the booth."

Ruth ran down the stairs two at a time.

The security guard was on the phone telling someone, "I'm telling you nothing but blood!"

"Excuse me, can you hang up the phone please?" Ruth flashed her badge.

"I gotta go, the Chief of Police wants to interview me."

"I'm not the Chief of police, I'm Det. Hill and your name is?"

"Oh, ummm, I'm Officer Medley."

"Ok, Officer Medley, tell me what happened here."

"So I was watching the WV game and a call came in that said there were gunshots on level 3. I knew that was the skywalk that leads from the movie theater to the parking garage. I thought maybe there were some bangers or something up there. I called 911 and requested assistance.

Then I started looking at my monitors for anything suspicious."

"Did you see anything?"

"Yeah I saw a two people, man and a woman lying half in and half out of the elevator. I called 911 again and told them to hurry two people were down. Then I waited."

"Tell me about the person who called you. Were they male/female...old/young?"

"Sorry, but the voice wasn't human, more like a robot or something. Probably one of those voice changers you can get at the mall. My kids had one for Halloween one year. It makes them sound funny like that movie where the guy was cutting up those kids and …"

185

"Ok, yeah, I got it. Did you see any other cars leave here around the time they were shot?"

"No, sorry, nothing, most of the cars left early, I guess to see the game. Do you think it was a robbery?"

"Not sure, yet we've still got to investigate."

Ruth thanks Officer Medley and leaves for the hospital. On the way Officer Conklin calls and says the McCollins will survive.

The hospital put them in the same room and provided a cot for their daughter. Since there isn't much for Ruth to do, she decides to go home. She tells Officer Conklin to call it a night as well.

As she's turning on her street, Penny calls.

"Hey partner how ya been?"

Ruth says, "I'm good, but, truth be told I'm missing you and your worrisome ass!"

"Well thanks for that and for hearing my daily voicemail and not pushing me by calling back."

"Figured you needed some space Penns so I respected that and laid low.

Now why are you calling tonight?

You left a message of "Hey bitch, I'm ok and hope you are too" earlier today. I will make you pay for using such derogatory language toward me as soon as you get back!"

"I'm calling because I've been doing a lot of thinking and I'm really trying to change. I just wanted you to know that."

Penny hangs up and the connection is lost.

Ruth says to the broken connection, "Good night partner."

The next day the other support group members see the news and call Denise. Denise promises to reach out to Imani and send well wishes.

Denise gets through to Imani's cell phone, just as Imani is leaving the hospital.

"Hello, Imani, this is Denise."

"Oh hi Denise, I guess you saw the news uh?"

"Yeah and so did the ladies. They have all called me, except Yvette, but I bet that's because she was on duty last night."

"As a matter of fact she was and she was amazing! She stayed with me until my parents were settled in ICU and she made sure the hospital provided me a cot so I could sleep there with them."

Internal dialogue…

Denise…Nice to see Yvette can be appropriate at times!

"Wonderful, I'm glad she was there for you. I understand your parents are expected to make a full recovery?"

"Yep they are! Tell the group my parents have been stepped down to a regular room and hopefully will be home in a few days.

Tell them I will be at the next session and will tell them everything. Thank them for me for being so supportive."

"Ok, will do and I'm glad your parents are going to be ok."

"Yeah the doctor said they were shot in the right place, there are no major organs hit and no vital arteries were nicked.

I'm really thankful…you know I came so close to them dying and I couldn't imagine my life without them. I've been a really stupid girl."

"Well let's process this in group. If you need to talk call our hotline ok?"

"Thanks again Denise for being there for all of us."

"You are very welcome and call our hotline 24/7 if you need to talk, bye."

They disconnect and Denise starts sending off identical email to each of the support group members.

After a day...

Squidget was successful in getting Pimp Gene's penis unglued from his thigh. Unfortunately, he was left with a very raw penis and he fainted several times when he attempted to urinate or if wind blew across the exposed area.

Squidget moved her things in the apartment after Pimp Gene fainted the first time.

Her movements around the room caused a slight breeze that hit that spot and he hit the floor again.

Squidget learned to just let him lay there as she moved slowly about, until his constitution returned. She kept the raw areas covered with an antibacterial cream.

When she finally ran out of cream she had to go to the store to get more. There she saw Wendy aka Good trying to get her attention.

"Hey Squidget, I heard you moved in with Pimp Daddy...he alright?"

"Yeah that fool is alright. I got his shit unstuck and now I'm trying to keep it from getting infected."

"Why are you helping him Squidget? He was always mean to you."

"Girl it's gonna be cold soon and I'm tired of whoring in the winter. I'm gonna use that DVD to get me a warm place to stay.

Pimp Gene is too old to make a full recovery from this so he's gonna need somebody to look after his nasty ass. He got money too, so I'm gonna help him spend it.

Now what you and that nasty bitch Plenty up to?"

"Tina left town and I haven't heard from her since she left the apartment. I'm about to leave today with a friend of mine. We're headed down south to live with some of his people until we get on our feet."

"Well good luck to you and good riddance to Plenty!

Anything you want me to tell Pimp Gene? I think he is real broke up ya'll just left him like that."

Wendy thinks for a minute, chewing on her bottom lip…"Yeah tell him we are grateful for all he did for us and we're glad he didn't die. Tell him it was just time for all of us to move on."

"Ok, cool I'll tell him. Look I gotta get back with some cream or his ass may fall out just thinking about that sore on his dick!"

They fist bump and Squidget saunters down the aisle marked "first aid."

Wendy pays for her items and runs out the store to the open door of Brian's car. She wasn't completely honest with Squidget, guess cause she didn't want to be looking over her shoulder once Pimp Daddy got better.

Wendy and Brian are moving to a little town called LaPlata MD. Brian said he followed a news story last year about a terrorist attack that happened at the A-Z Emporium. He pulled it up online for Wendy and they both liked the town's look. Brian applied for four medical technician positions and Wendy applied for a cashier position at the A-Z Emporium.

Everyone is seated and Denise asks Imani if she'd like to address the group.

"Yes, thanks, well as you all have seen on TV, both of my parents were shot, each in the chest. They needed surgery and were in ICU for a few days, but now they are home.

Outside of the pain they are doing ok. No major organs were damaged and they didn't lose too much blood or anything. They were very lucky and so was I. I almost lost them."

"Well honey sometimes it takes a tragedy for us to realize what's really important," says Dawn.

"I agree," says Dani. "I knew all along you didn't really want your parents dead. You were just hurting cause they betrayed your trust."

"I guess I didn't really want them dead, uh? No I realize now I really didn't want them dead." Imani says sheepishly.

"Well if you didn't you shouldn't have kept spouting off that you did!"

Everyone, including Denise, look at Penny like she had yelled out the zombie apocalypse is here.

Internal dialogue…

Karen…Penny is crazy and I love it! My friends are going to eat this shit up!

Lynn…Oh, no Penny don't do this to Imani. No…

Holly…I feel sorry for Imani! I would die if Penny came after me like that!

"WTF Penny!" says Dani.

"What the fuck you say? Well I'll tell you what the fuck! I'm sick and tired of people always giving mixed messages, like, oh my goodness bad things happen to good people and God won't give you more than you can handle.

Also, I can wish they weren't born so they couldn't hurt me, but I can't wish I wasn't born so I wouldn't be the one they hurt?

Ya'll sit in here telling me not to give up on living because "they" will win…win what? They already won! He won my life the minute he raped me! I'm a fucking corpse walking around and I know it.

But lil Miss Imani here with parents who love her and are truly sorry, she wants them dead. Now that they aren't dead, she's sorry she was just what? Immature and feeling sorry for herself?

Well Dani, what the fuck about her parents? They've spent years in hell because she wouldn't let them love her, let them say sorry and actually show the sorrow they felt."

Penny stops and shakes her head…she continues to glare at Imani.

Denise clears her throat and says, "Penny I must admit I'm shocked by the anger you've verbalized in group tonight. Can you speak to where it's coming from since it's apparent something in Imani's situation has triggered this response from you."

"Sure Denise, I can "speak to it." I've spent my adult life waiting for my cousin Rory to say he was sorry. I've spent my adult life waiting for my fucking mother to actually give a shit about me. But it never came, so here I am still waiting.

Imani almost gets what she wants…her parents dead…or at least what she *says* she wants and what…she fucking wimps out and changes her tune!"

"Now hold on Penny!" shouts Imani, "I didn't wimp out or change my mind."

"Oh you still want your parents dead?" Penny shouts right back at her.

Internal dialogue…

Denise…Where is this anger coming from tonight?

Cheryl…Is this supposed to be therapy?

Dawn…Now our little group is getting into some dark waters…perfect…it's about time.

"Well, no, I don't…but I realized they are the only family I have. They really do have my back and I guess I realized that if I let go of the hate, I am able to forgive them.

When the police officer called and said my parents were shot and I needed to meet them at the hospital, all I could think of was getting there to see them. I never thought about the molestation or my anger. I just thought about my parents being hurt and I needed to be there."

Penny looks into Denise's face and says, "Well Denise isn't that some freakin insight!, I'd like the group to discuss a few things tonight giving up vs. acceptance and forgiving vs knowing you'll never get a "sorry.""

Penny sits back and watches the group.

Denise takes a small sip of water and says, "Well Penny has opened our group up in a way we have not experienced before. She has laid bare her feelings tonight and I'm sure it feels uncomfortable, but I will ask you all to give some thought to what she has said. When and if you're comfortable, please speak up with your thoughts."

Denise sits and allows the group to process…after 12 minutes…

Internal dialogue…

Imani…I'm so embarrassed…Penny is right, but I can't believe she actually called me on it. I thought it might be Cheryl since Yvette had been so good to me the other night. I wonder what they all think of me now?

Holly…People can change their minds right? Maybe Imani is such a good person she changed her mean thoughts about her parents to good thoughts. I wish people would change their thoughts about me. But maybe they can't because I'm really as messed up as they think I am.

Karen…Why haven't I felt angry about what happened to me?

Lynn…Forgiveness is a choice and as young as Imani is, she might be stronger than all of us. She learned how to forgive while she's young. Maybe she'll have a better life than us old-timers. Who are just marking time without moving forward.

Dani…This is absolutely awful tonight and Denise should do something besides sitting there.

Yvette…If all we're gonna do is sit here in silence I can take my ass home. I've got to work a double shift tomorrow and I need my rest.

Cheryl says, "Well Penny, I guess I have accepted that I'll never get a sorry from Gerald, my brother-in-law."

"But if you've accepted that, then why are you so angry Cheryl?" asks Penny.

"Shit, I'm angry because he took something from me that I can't get back. Plus he's dead and I can't have revenge on his ass."

"So you accept that he took something from you?"

"Yeah Penny, I was there when he raped me. I know he took my body from me! I used to be confident in the way I looked and he took that from me too."

"Aren't you still confident? You look confident to me," says Lynn.

"No Lynn, I'm not confident, I'm fucking angry! I'm angry that I'm faking being confident so it won't look like he's still taking something from me!

This is some fucked up shit! Last week I felt so good when I left here and then I went home and realized wasn't a damned thing changed. I still wear my anger like a "don't fuck with me" shield. I wear clothes that are functional but not flattering.

No, I'm not confident anymore about any aspect of my life and it makes me fucking crazy angry!"

Internal dialogue…

Dawn…I know about that…I dress in tunics and leggings most of the time. I've gotten fat…maybe so I'm not attractive and then not a target.

Dani…I feel confident in my new body, but sometimes I think it comes across wrong cause guys just act like they want to jump my bones!

Karen…Damn! Cheryl had me fooled, but I can see what she means. People look at me and see one thing, but I feel like another.

Imani…Well I'm opposite from Cheryl…I dress sexy so I'll have the upper hand! I got what they want and I feel powerful shutting them down!

Holly…My stomach hurts and I feel a hang nail I need to bite off…is anyone looking at me?

Karen says, "I'm not sure how to respond to Penny's question, but I do feel I've accepted that I had a role to play in what happened to me.

Yeah, ok so don't look so crazy at me. I was coming on to him and I did tell him I had on crotch-less panties.

Internal dialogue…

Yvette…Yep yo ass was asking for it! Bitch get outta here!

Lynn…Why would a young lady wear crotch-less panties outside of the house?

Holly…If there is no crotch then how does she keep her panty liner in place?

Cheryl…Freak!

I didn't think about pressing charges until I told another female shipmate and she got all wigged out about it so I did too. I'm trying to also deal with accepting that I could allow someone to alter my perception so much that I almost ruined my career and his too. And nothing to say about our families, hell, I feel like I owe him an apology."

Internal dialogue…

Yvette…Yeah, ya think?

Dawn…She's got to develop her own mind.

Holly…Maybe Karen and I could be friends…I don't know what to think either. Naw, she wouldn't pick me for a friend…no one does.

Penny…Yeah her charges wouldn't have stuck.

Holly asks, "Will you give him and apology?"

"I'm not sure…up until last week I thought I was assaulted.

Honestly, I can't say what I'll do, think or feel any given day."

"That's weird, but not weird I guess," says Holly.

Yvette looks at Imani and says, "I was with you when your folks were brought in."

"Yeah, and I can't thank you enough for being there with me and making sure the hospital allowed me to sleep in the room with my parents. I will never forget your kindness."

"No problem, that's my job, but I agree sort of with Penny.

Imani's smile of gratitude turns to ashen stone.

You were in here talking about your parents being dead like it was nothing. I mean you went toe-to-toe with Ayda over it.

I guess my question is what if they say or do something you don't like again…will you wish them dead again?"

"Oh my GOD Yvette you were with me that night! Where is this coming from?"

"It's coming from me Imani. Yeah I was with you that night and I did my job. But we're in the group now so I'm not the nurse. I'm a group member who just asked you a question."

"I think you and Penny are being too harsh on Imani tonight!" says Lynn.

"No, I think we're being honest and real for a change," says Yvette.

"This group is ending soon and I want to get some of the real shit out in the open. We've been playing nice and that won't get us anywhere," says Yvette.

"I don't know how I'll feel later on, but for now I love them. I can't see myself ever wanting them dead again.

You and Penny may not believe it, but I was scared and still am scared that I'll lose them. I've always loved them, but I felt like they should show me how miserable they were for what happened.

I wanted them to pay for what they did! I wanted my mom to be on my side and leave him! I wanted my father to try something dramatic like trying to kill himself to prove to me he was sorry!

I didn't want to feel like a loser for loving them." Imani starts to cry.

"What do you mean "feel like a loser for loving them"? asks Holly.

"What kind of person can love the man who molested you? How can I possibly love my mom after she knew and stayed with him? If I love them, then aren't I accepting what they did to me was alright? No one fought for me so I was fighting for me." Imani wipes at the tears streaming down her face.

The group is silent once more.

Denise clears her throat, but before she can speak, Yvette says, "Naw Denise, we got this tonight ok?"

Denise, wide eyed says, "Ummm, ok Yvette, I'll defer to the group to work through this."

"Yeah, so let's stop pissing around and put some stuff out there. Penny opened the door wide…now who's ready to walk through?"

Dawn says, "Well Yvette why don't you go through it? You seem anxious to get something off your chest tonight as well."

"Maybe I am Dawn! I'm angry tonight because we're sitting in here and another generation of "us" is being made as we speak!

In the newspaper there was a 14 year old girl molested by a 26 year old man! He contacted her on one of those apps and she got off the bus at her middle school to meet him!

She waited for him in the nearby woods and when she saw his car she ran to meet him. He drove them to a local motel where he had sex with her for several hours.

Nasty muther fucker must have stolen his daddy's Viagra!

Anyway, she got caught trying to sneak back in school and told the whole story. They got him and he was convicted and given 10 years, but all of it 'cept 18 months was suspended!

What kind of shit is that? Is that all her life is worth, 18 months? He'll do less than that and then get out."

"Yeah I read that," said Cheryl. "He'll have to register as a sex offender and will have five years of supervised probation. I wish his ass was assigned to me! It would be the worse five years of his life!"

"Right, but Cheryl he'll have five years of what kind of life? No one will know who he is and what he did. He probably won't get any counseling and last I checked there weren't any pills to fix his nasty ass! I also read he has another pending charge for underage sex with a 14 year old girl."

"I'm not condoning what he did, but what if he does get some counseling and what if he is remorseful?" asks Holly.

Yvette, Penny and Cheryl glare at her...

Penny is the first to respond, "I'm a cop remember? I see it time and again, people like that don't change."

"Yeah," agrees Cheryl. "I've got a caseload full of repeat sex offenders."

Holly, squeaks out, "But Imani's dad did."

Cheryl says, "Well Holly I guess that makes her father a man who made a real mistake and is not a predator. All the more reason for Imani not to want him dead!

Holly, have you ever looked up the guy who sexually assaulted you to see if he has a history?

And if you don't find anything, is that because he only did it once to you or is it because no one has ever reported him?

If he only did it to you, then why did he pick you?

And if he does it to someone else and you didn't tell, could you have stopped him by reporting him?

See, these are the type of questions that float through the mind of a rape victim. I've heard them in my own head and I've read statements from victims that say the same thing." Cheryl takes a deep breath and drinks some water.

Holly says, "I don't know, I never looked him up but I guess it's my fault if Danny Clark sexually assaults someone else since I didn't tell on him?"

Penny says, "No, his actions aren't your fault but the consequences you feel for not telling and you find out he did assault someone else will feel like your "fault."

I never told on my cousin Rory and I heard he had raped a girl at our school the next year. My other cousin in the car, Jayson, told me and said he would go to the sheriff's office and tell what happened to me, but I was too scared.

I'd already lost my best friend, my mom, and my dad. I was too afraid of what more I would lose, so I kept my mouth shut. As I got older, I found that more people than I thought knew what he had done to me and none of them ever said anything to me.

No one tried to comfort me or fight for me either Imani. So I chose to believe I wasn't worth it. I felt like I made people uncomfortable because they knew what happened and somehow I was the freak."

"I know Penny, that part about feeling like a freak," says Lynn. "Once my co-workers heard about the rape, they were initially shocked and supportive.

I was on family medical leave for a month and I received cards, food, flowers, email messages and calls. Once I returned to work it was different. My supervisor kept coming by to "check on me." My co-workers would say they were there if I needed them, but no one invited me to coffee or lunch.

When I walked into the file room, anyone in there would stop talking until I left. I felt like people were watching me all the time.

Once I laughed out loud during a holiday party and the room got quiet. I apologized and someone near me said, "Glad to hear you can laugh again."

I had no idea I wasn't supposed to laugh again.

After the trial, things got a little better, but by then I had been moved to another social services agency in another county.

Of course they had heard, I could tell by how they treated me."

"Lynn, how do you know it was because of that and not just because you were new?" asks Holly.

"I'm asking 'cause I feel like everybody can see that something happened to me and they judge me according to how they feel about it."

Karen asks, "What do you mean about how they feel about it?"

"Well they might think I asked for it…sorry Karen no offense to you. Or they might think I'm a wuss and weak.

201

The guys will want to mess with me 'cause they know about me. It sounds crazy when I say it out loud, but it's what I think."

"Let's see…if anyone hasn't felt what Holly described, raise your hand." Dawn looks around and doesn't see a hand go up.

Dawn continues, "See Holly, you're not alone. I used to think there was a bull's eye on my forehead that told everyone that I was damaged and easy pickings. Whenever something bad happened to me, I felt it was because I was a marked woman.

Even small things like, not finding a close parking spot or getting caught in the rain made me feel like the universe was out to get me!

I laugh now at how stupid I was, but working with my therapist helped me to see I had constructed a negative view of myself. I thought bad things would happen to me because I was a bad person that only attracted negative things.

I couldn't even stand getting a compliment from a stranger! That was the worst! I would get scared that they were going to come after me or something. They knew I wouldn't be able to fight back.

So I was a bad penny that only bad men wanted to mess with and I really didn't deserve anything better."

Dawn shakes her head at the memory of feeling so helpless and scared. She drinks her coffee and gobbles a cookie.

Denise says, "I'm sorry, but we are at the end of our group session, any last thoughts before we close?"

Penny says, "Well since I kinda started things I'd like to end it with…I feel like I live in the grey area of life…nothing is as it should be or as it seems." She picks up her purse from the floor and leaves.

The group looks in shock at the back of Penny as she storms out the door.

"Well that was fucking weird…right?" asks Cheryl.

"Ok, well…I'll see you all next week for our second to last session." Denise says.

She doesn't offer to de-stress the group because she is too keyed up by Penny's reactions tonight. What is going on with Penny? Should she call someone or just wait and let Penny work through whatever she's feeling?

Imani and Lynn walk out together…Cheryl, Karen and Dawn talk as they head to the nearest coffee shop…Dani and Holly leave for a spin class…Imani heads to the hospital to visit her parents…Yvette stands outside the building smoking a cigarette and watching.

Holly...

Holly has a difficult time sleeping after the group session, even though she and Dani completed an hour spinning set.

Dani had declined dinner saying she had to get home to her fiancé or he would think she'd run away from him.

It must be nice to have a man to go home to. Dani has been married and now has a new man! I'm 26 years old and never even been on a date. It's just not fair. How come some people seem to get everything they want and people like me don't get anything they want?

I don't want to admit I agree with Penny but I understand some of what she said in group.

Dani is nice and all, but she got her husband put in jail, got the house and money, now she's got a fiancé who treats her like a princess!

OMG, and her body is AMAZING! I'm so jealous...shit I shouldn't be jealous of the only friend I've had since Annie in second grade.

I remember playing on the playground with Annie and feeling like she and I would be friends forever, but forever didn't last that long. We grew up and apart like all the good things in my life, our relationship came to an end.

I am reminded of my old carefree and happy personality when I'm around Dani, but when she leaves me and I'm left with just "me," and no direction.

Holly runs a bath filled with lavender scented Epsom salts. She brings her pizza and beer with her.

If Dani saw it she would freak, but Dani is home with her man so lad-di-da!

She gingerly eases herself into the bath, finds a comfortable spot against the tub and starts to sip her beer.

Tonight was a crazy kind of group but it's got her thinking over her life and the choices she's made. Have I been too crazy to get out of my own way?

I mean I'm not like Imani, I do call my parents once a week and go back to Virginia to see them during the Christmas holiday. I've never EVER wished them dead!

In Virginia I was attending J. Sergeant Reynolds Community College and working on getting a Radiology certification.

I'd just finished my first semester when one of my professors recommended me for a paid internship at the local hospital. He only picked four students out of 50!

I was stoked and my parents were so proud of me!

I was going to be an assistant to the respiratory technician and hopefully make a good enough impression they would offer me a job after I completed the certification program.

Well that sure never happened!

Holly takes a bite of her pizza and stares at the fluffy bubbles in her water. I never noticed the Epsom salt stuff made bubbles. Is that normal?

Maybe it's a bad batch...she sloshes in the water and reaches for the bag and realizes she's poured in the wrong thing!

Shit, I poured in the bubble bath instead of the salts...I'm such a goof ball!

So she slides back down into the water, takes another bite of pizza and goes back in time.

I can see it so clearly, me being so excited that I was wearing a real lab coat with my ID badge swinging. I felt like a real professional and a grown up.

Most of my classmates were afraid to do actual work with patients, but not me. My mom had always said I was "an old soul" and unafraid of anything.

Well that went out the window the night I met Daniel Clark, one of the janitors.

I was cleaning up the tech room when Danny came in to buff the floor. He and I hit it off immediately.

Danny was 26 and I was 20. We liked the same music, food and movies...I thought we were going to be friends, but I guess he had other ideas.

Alone again one evening, cleaning up the tech room, Danny came in.

"Hey Danny, I thought you were off tonight!"

"Yeah, but I wanted to come and see my girl" he says, words slurring.

"Well, that's nice of you, but I'm running a little late. I'm supposed to babysit my little cousins tonight while my aunt goes to a concert with my mom."

Danny grabbed my arm as I walked past him. The bag of trash I was carrying dropped to the floor.

"What are you doing? I say, suddenly afraid.

"Shhhh, Holly it's ok, I want to be your first."

"My first what?" I ask him.

I can't believe this is happening, but I'm not sure for real what is happening.

"You're a virgin right? So I want to be your first. I want to pop your cherry."

He leans in and licks my ear.

"Danny, I don't know what's wrong with you tonight. You smell like beer and stuff."

I pull away from him, but I'm backing up in the wrong direction. He's standing between me and the door to freedom.

"Look dude, I like you, but not like that ok? I need to leave now…my mom…"

"Well Holly, this won't take long. I'm sure your tight pussy will make me cum real quick!"

He lunges for me and I run around the equipment falling over some of the cords. Danny comes down on top of me. He turns me over and from somewhere he produces a knife.

"Holly, I'm gonna fuck you, but I don't want to cut you ok?

Now pull down your scrubs and panties so I can get into some of that sweet tight pussy."

I don't know why I didn't fight. I just did what he told me to do. I felt the knife against my throat as he came down into me.

I tried to scream, but his other hand was over my mouth. He kept kissing my neck and licking my ear.

I was crying and my whole body was shaking.

He didn't take long.

I was only a few minutes late getting home even though I took a shower in the employee locker room with Danny. He made me shower with him so he could scrub all his evidence off me.

He kept telling me how now no one would believe me, so I better never say anything or I'd lose my internship and never work in this town.

He was right…I refused to go back to school and I didn't return to my internship. I told my parents I wanted to move away cause of a boy and a break-up.

I never saw Danny again.

My mom was grateful when her sister, my Aunt Muriel could get me a job in the courthouse where she worked in Morganville.

My parents just wanted me to be a strong and independent woman.

Little do they know…

Holly drains her beer and nibbles on the remaining pizza crust.

What would've happened if I had fought back more? I mean he didn't have the knife on my neck the whole time. I could've picked up something and hit him.

I should've been fast enough to get to the door and run out.

I shouldn't have been trying to be friends with him in the first place. He was older than me and we were always alone in that section of the hospital.

I should've been more careful.

Why did this happen to me? Danny seemed like a nice guy…maybe I did something to make him go bad.

He knew I was a virgin, but how?

Since I haven't had sex again, does that make me a virgin again?

Shit, I don't know anything…wait I do know some things…I will never take a shower again with a guy and I will never be alone with a guy; lastly, if I'm ever in that situation again, I'll kill him before I allow him to rape me.

Holly stands and steps out of the tub then dries off. She takes her plate, knife and beer glass to the kitchen.

She's lived in this apartment since she left her aunt's house. She stayed with Aunt Muriel for four months and then with the help of her parents, she moved into this apartment.

She has brown colored black-out curtains at every window so no one can see in. The apartment has a nice sized bedroom decorated with just a bed and matching dressers, but Holly sleeps on the futon that doubles as a sofa in the living room.

She has one of an expensive set of six steak knives situated throughout her apartment. One in the bathroom magazine rack, one under her futon mattress, one under the bedroom mattress, one taped to the side of the microwave, one in the pocket of her old lab coat hanging next to the front door (she moves it when her parents come to visit.) and lastly she carries one around the apartment with her at all times.

I know, I'm a nut case for having knives all around the apartment, but I can't help it.

I don't know when or where it will happen, but I believe something bad is going to happen to me again and I NEED to be ready!

As Cheryl would say, fuck it!

Holly puts down the knife long enough to get some ice-cream in a bowl.

She picks up the bowl and knife then heads to the futon and a movie.

Squidget and Gene…

"Look Gene I think we can do it. You've got the cash and I've got the where-with-a- fuck to help you make something of it."

"Squidget look, I'm down with you being my bottom babe and shit but…"

"Naw mutha fucker, ain't no bottom babe shit up in here! I'm talking about being partners. Anything else and you can take your glued dick on somewhere!"

"See why you gotta talk about that, and lower your damn voice girl, the window is open!

I'm just saying that's a lot of money and I don't know if I want to go spending it like that. Hell Pimp Daddy ain't getting no younger."

"Reality-check ok, you are so far from being a Pimp Daddy that it ain't even funny.

Your hos is gone and your ass too old and broke down from that glue and piss episode to be out on the street again!

 Face facts man!"

"Girl lower yo damn voice…I told you the window is open. Ok, so let's say we do this thang…what's in it for you?

 I mean Squidget we ain't for real ever been friends and all. I don't know why you, even with the glue thang, helped me after I made you suck my dick and took all you money but $5."

"See Gene that's the difference between me and you…I'm always looking to the future and making my glory! You feel me?

So this is what's in it for me…I help you run the bar that old man Ray left and you pay me 25 percent of the profit after you pay the bills.

Also, you let me live here rent free and I'll cook and clean for your ass. But I will NOT FUCK you! Understood?"

"So I get to keep everything after paying off the rent and 25% to yo ass?"

"Yep you sure can."

"And you want to stay here with me?"

"Yep I sure do. This is the nicest place I've ever lived in. We can turn one of the bedrooms into an office so we can do the books and stuff."

"Oh, so now you wanna do the books with ole Pimp Daddy?"

"Gene if you think I'm gonna let you cheat me you got another thing coming.

Mutha fucker, I will put that video of you on the internet so fast!

Yeah, I've kept the disc and it's in the bank vault and shit. I gave a copy of the key to someone and put their name on the box so let my ass go missing or something.

You gonna be drinking that golden piss all over the internet! Viral baby!!"

Internal dialogue…

Squidget…I heard that shit on TV about giving a key to someone, but old Gene so scared he don't question it too much!

Pimp Gene's nuts try to hide inside him…

"Look Squidget…"

"Let's start our partnership off with this…I'm no more Squidget, my name is Kim…Kim Swann. You better start using it because I'm gonna be getting it put on all our paperwork."

"Yo name is Kim Swann?"

"Yeah mutha fucker what's wrong with that?"

"What's your momma's name?"

"Susan Louise Swann, why?"

"Oh, I was worried!

Ole Pimp Daddy used to fuck a Swann back in the day and I was scurd it was your momma!"

"You one sick bastard Gene, that meant you could've been my daddy! Yuck!"

"Naw, I got my shit fixed the day I decided to be a pimp. I was all about making money not no damn babies. Lil assholes costs too much and I don't need to hear no yapping from them or their mommas."

"So, Gene we gonna do this? Oh, yeah, I ain't calling you nuthin but Gene from now on so what's your last name anyway?"

Gene sits up tall in the chair, clears his throat and says, "My full name is Alowishus Eugene Cartwright III."

Squidget aka Kim Swann falls out her chair laughing and peeing down her leg!

Gene's nuts were on their way down but decided to stay up instead…

Gene and Kim go to the bank the next day and start the paperwork to buy Ray's Bar.

Seems Ray owned the bar outright and he left it to his niece Yvette Dyson.

The bank is going to send the owner a certified letter with Gene and Kim's offer.

"What if they don't want to sell to us Gene? I mean what if they want to keep the building but rent it to us? You open to that shit?"

"I don't know 'bout that shit. I've never worked for no one in my damn life. But what I know about life is this...just be patient and what's up will be what's up."

Yvette received the certified letter from the bank notifying her that she is the sole owner of great-uncle Ray's bar. The letter also notifies her of an offer for the building of $50,000! Yvette and her husband discuss it and decide to take the money.

They agree not to tell anyone in the family. Hands will be out looking for a piece.

Yvette has no desire to EVER go into the building where that man lived and worked.

Yvette and her husband call the bank and make an appointment to meet with the bank manager. Yvette wants to sign the papers without the new owners knowing who she is.

Yvette doesn't want anyone outside of the family and group to know she's related to that man.

But then Det. Ruth Hill knows it too.

If the detective finds out about the sale of the building will she think its motive for me to have killed old Ray after all these years?

Should I call her and tell her I've been given the property and I'm selling it?

No, why should I tell her anything. It's a free country and I don't have anything to hide.

Plus it's none of the detective's damn business!

Yvette signs the forms and the bank manager promises to send her the certified check for the balance minus, bank fees and taxes. She and her husband should expect a check for $44,980.57.

What would the group say about this? Would Imani ask if I feel like I'm selling out to Ray? Am I? Hell no, I'm being practical, he left it to me and someone wants to buy it.

Fuck Ray! He didn't owe me shit, but I sure hope he paid for what he did to me.

I heard that ass whipping my great uncles put on him was enough to keep him on the straight and narrow for the rest of his life.

Maybe if not for that he would've ended up back in jail again.

Ayda would've loved this shit…my sacrifice helped to turn his life around!

I hadn't thought about her until now, and that's wrong.

She was a pain in the ass though. Always using religion to explain everything and deal with nothing. I bet she got raped by a priest or a nun…an altar boy or someone else "holy" in her eyes.

Shame she died before we could find out for sure. But for real, I'm not sure it was a shame she died…she really seemed unhappy about her situation.

Why in the hell am I thinking about Ayda?

My husband and I gotta find a nice restaurant to celebrate our windfall of money!

"Wow that was some meeting honey! The ladies got really raw and said stuff I never expected to hear."

Dawn's husband nods his head and says, "Sounds like some good work happened?"

Her husband is an avid fisherman and while Dawn is making him sandwiches for a fishing trip, he's trying to pack his tackle box.

"Yeah, a lot of talk about anger, misrepresentation, consequences and responsibilities…it was an amazing and frightening night."

"Why was it frightening?"

"Some of the ladies were really angry and I felt scared for them. I know what it's like to be so angry at someone that you somehow turn it on yourself."

"Well you're not feeding into their issues are you? You know I worried about you doing a group when you've come so far in your recovery."

Dawn stops packing the lunchbox and looks at her husband. Frank has always been a support to Dawn.

And when she told him she was raped after their third month of dating, Frank had immediately researched the effects of rape on the victim and her family.

He and Dawn were married two years later.

They both attended therapy for over, three years, but Dawn seemed unable to stop.

Frank was, at first, concerned that Dawn was buying every self-help book she could find and wanted to continue therapy even after her therapist told her she could cut back. Dawn still continued to see Dr. Lee three times a month for "maintenance therapy."

Dr. Lee encouraged Dawn to attend the support group as a way to challenge herself and to see how far she's come in her recovery.

Frank thinks it's to get a break from Dawn and her, "Dr. Lee what do you think about…" sessions. Dawn has notebooks filled with session notes. It's a wonder she can pay attention to what Dr. Lee says and take such precise notes at the same time.

Dawn says, "Don't worry Frank, I'm good baby. I'm not feeling any worse about things. I'm just amazed at the stuff they think. I mean suicide and homicide never dominated my thoughts past the first year after the rape and even then I never really wanted Johnny dead."

"Well, you know how I feel about "the guy who tried to kill my wife's spirit" and what happened to him. No sympathy at all do I feel for that sucker!"

"Now Frank you know better! He got his in the end, but we don't gloat over it! We'll just chuck it up to karma!"

"Yeah, well my dear, karma got his behind didn't it? He thought he got off lightly by only getting probation and no actual jail time."

"Well back then there weren't harsh sentences for college rapes."

Frank snorts, "Have you been watching the news? There still aren't harsh sentences for college rapes or any other rapes for that matter."

"Well, he got his in the end I guess," says Dawn.

You know the rumor goes…he didn't pay a hooker and her pimp beat his ass. He never walked right again.

I thought maybe we'd heard the last of him until last year when his name popped up during that terrorist and hostage situation in LaPlata, Maryland."

"Yeah, Johnny was sitting in his wheelchair and got shot in the head.

216

Looked like he was going to survive the hostage situation, but BAM! Shot to the head and that's all he wrote.

When there is no justice, just wait on karma to even out the universe," says Frank, as he snaps his tackle box closed.

"Ok, karma!" says Dawn, "All I know is you and Wayne better catch me some fish for dinner tonight!"

Dr. Wayne Ellis, medical examiner and Frank have been best friends for over 20 years.

"Hey, ask Wayne if he can tell us anything about Ray, you know that bar owner found dead a few weeks ago. One of the ladies in the group is related to him.

Also ask him about a lady named Ayda. She was in our group and drowned recently."

"Your group is related to two recent deaths? Dawn what kind of group did you sign up for?"

Dawn kisses her husband and pushes him toward the door.

"Death is random honey! Nothing weird going on or at least I don't think so that's why you gotta get Wayne to spill the beans!

Now go and have a great time! I love you!"

Dawn stands on the porch and watches Frank drive away. She continues to stand there until she sees Miss Stephanie coming down the street.

Dawn rushes back into her house and locks the door.

She leans against the closed door and thinks, please don't let her recognize me!

Regrets...

Penny woke the morning after the group with a major sized hangover. I can't believe I drank a whole bottle of wine by myself.

I must be going crazy!

Did I really say all that stuff to the group?

I know I meant it, but I can't believe I actually said it. They must think I'm a loony bird or something.

What came over me? I know what came over me, I'm feeling sorry for myself and I took it out on Imani.

I'm envious that she has a family and a future. What do I have? This apartment and a job I'm not even sure I want anymore. I have no idea who I am or where I'm going.

Death would really be easier, but what would it really solve?

Rory's ass is still walking around and living his life. If he weren't around would I feel better?

Really, what is my problem? I know shit happens to good and bad people. I know that not everyone gets justice so why am I so stuck on dying?

Why don't I feel I'm worth the effort of living? Wait, I do feel like I'm worth the effort, I just feel like I've had enough pain and I don't want anymore. Death is the only way to feel safe again. But I haven't had anything bad happen to me since the rape and daddy's death. Well aren't those two things enough for a lifetime?

What about mom…she has all but forgotten she has a daughter. I wonder if, like Imani, I can forgive her for abandoning me. Maybe she and I could start over…just begin now and build from there.

Maybe I can…who am I kidding? Once I have a little happy in my life, I bet something will come along and take it away.

Ok, this is too much for a mind and body that has had a whole bottle of wine.

Penny gets out of bed and takes a shower. While her coffee is perking, she leaves a voice mail message for Ruth, "Hey partner, how are things shaking? All good here so don't worry."

She hangs up and considers calling Denise to apologize for last night but it's too much to handle without at least two cups of coffee first.

The weekend after group...Richmond Virginia...

"Danny is that you?" asks a woman he's never seen before.

"Ummm, yeah, who are you?"

"Oh, you don't remember me from the hospital? I used to volunteer there years ago, but I guess since I worked near the director's office you don't remember me. But I sure remember you because I thought you were really cute"

"Yeah! Well honey, I can't believe I don't remember seeing you around. What you up to tonight?"

"Not much, just looking for a little action. You know where I can find some?"

"Hell yeah, I'll give you all the action you can handle. You want to hook up or what?"

"Really, you would hook up with me after all these years?"

"Sure, looks like Danny-boy needs to make up for some lost time. Where you want to go?"

"I don't know somewhere quiet and very private. I've got a boyfriend and I don't want any of my family blabbing my business."

"Yeah cool, I get what you sayin...hell, I got married a few years back, but the bitch don't mean much to me. She got pregnant and I got trapped. Look, follow me to a spot."

Danny leads the way down Richmond-Petersburg Turnpike and takes the exit to Bryan Park. He drives deep into the park bringing them to a secluded spot behind a snack stand.

He gets out of his car and walks toward her car.

"So what do you think, is this quiet and secluded enough for us to get our freak on?"

Getting out of the car she says, "I can't believe you are this easy!"

"What you mean I'm easy? Honey, a piece as fine as you can have me anytime and anyway!"

"Well I'm glad you feel that way Danny. Let me just get a condom out of my purse."

"Yeah right! I love a girl who's prepared. Hey I got a blanket in the trunk of my car. I'll get it so we can relax on the ground and take our time."

"Yeah, you get the blanket baby...I'll be right there."

Danny opens the trunk to his car and moves around the various items he's kept in it. A car vacuum, an emergency pull-up that his stupid wife insisted he keep in case the baby had an accident, and a lot of other useless stuff.

Now where is that blanket?

"Hey Danny..."

Danny turns around and is hit in the forehead by a hammer.

When he comes to he's handcuffed to the steering wheel of his car.

His head feels like he was hit by a hammer! Wait he was hit by a damn hammer.

"Hey stud you awake?

Damn Danny, you've been out for over an hour. Your wife is gonna wonder where you are."

Danny shakes his head to try and clear away the cobwebs, but finds the pain instead. What the fuck is going on?

"Ummm, did you hit me in the head with a hammer?"

Laughing, she says, "Yeah Danny, I did indeed hit you in the head with a hammer. Do you want to know why?"

"Yeah…ummm…shit my head is killing me."

"Well we don't want your head to kill you…that's why I'm here."

"For real you're gonna kill me?! Why? I don't even remember you! What the fuck is this? Take these fucking cuffs off me."

Danny struggles to get lose, but he can't, all the struggling does is make his head hurt more.

Blood trickles down his face and he blinks really fast in an attempt to keep the blood from getting in his eyes. His head is pounding!

"Awww honey let me wipe that blood off your face. I don't want it to get in your eyes because I want you to see everything I'm going to do to you."

Danny's face is wiped with a moist toilette.

"Now I gotta be honest with you Danny, you don't know me. I lied just to talk to you. I had no idea you would want to go to first base immediately! Now, I'm not complaining because I really did want to get this done and over as quickly as possible; so for that, thank you."

"Ummm, you're welcome I guess," says Danny, not really sure what he should say.

"Hey Danny, do you remember a girl named Holly Chism?"

Danny's eyes grow wide and he becomes completely still.

"Well do you remember her? Please don't lie because I really won't like it."

"Well…ummm…let me see…"

"If you ever want to see again with those eyes you better tell me the truth or I'll take this knife and pluck each eye out."

Danny looks at the knife. It is small but looks really sharp.

Speaking really fast, "Yeah I know Holly Chism, but I haven't seen her in years. She moved from around here and I hear she comes to visit her parents, but no one ever really sees her…ok?"

"Yes, Danny, that was excellent!

So listen first let me explain about my knife. It's called a paring knife. It's used for making garnishes…you know when they make flowers out of radishes and stuff.

Well these knives are good when you want the blade of the knife to perform with precision. You know, so you don't mess up."

Danny never takes his eyes off the little knife. If he wasn't so sure it was going to hurt him he might have liked the little knife. Danny likes knives at least 'til now.

Where in the hell is his knife? Shit it's in the front right pocket of his jeans. Wait, where are his jeans?

"So look Danny, I don't have all night, but I do have just enough time to make you pay for what you did to Holly."

"What do you mean what I did to Holly Chism and what the fuck do you mean I gotta pay? Look I don't have no money so I don't know what you want from me."

"Danny, you raped Holly and I want you to apologize for it."

"Did she say that? Lying bitch! She can't prove a thing. What's her proof huh?"

Before he can think of another stupid remark his penis is exposed by a quick swipe of the knife to his boxers.

223

"Hey bitch, what the fuck you doing? I'll…"

"Danny…Danny…Danny you're gonna sit here and lie to me about Holly?

Really? Well alright then…let me show you how this paring knife works."

A piece of duct tape is slapped over Danny's mouth before he can say anything else.

The paring knife cuts into his left testicle and Danny's mute screams are only heard by the crickets, frogs and other animals along the park's edge.

She stands back and surveys her work…removes the duct tape from Danny's wet mouth. He's been crying and has snot running EVERYWHERE.

"Ok, now see how beautiful that is? Really does look like a flower doesn't it? Ok, a wilted one but…ok, so now let's get back to that apology you owe Holly. Wait, I have something else for you."

A nose spray tip is placed inside Danny's left nostril. She squeezes the bottle twice releasing two hits of cocaine.

Danny takes a deep breath and his whole body soon relaxes.

"See coke makes everything better doesn't it? Now tell me about Holly."

"Yeah…see…me and Holly became friends when she worked at the hospital. She was, you know, young and dumb. My buddies and I had a pool going on who was gonna pop that cherry first!

Yeah so one night I did. She was scared but I talked her into it."

Danny sniffles and lays his head back on the headrest. He has forgotten all about his left testicle being cut to look like a flower.

"So did you really put a knife to her throat and make her take a shower with you afterwards? You know to get all the evidence off? Man that was smart thinking."

"You know right? Yeah, I keep a knife on me so you know I used it to keep her from backing out. There was like $50 bucks in the pool and I wanted that money!

Then the shower thing came about because of those, you know, cop shows that come on TV. They're always talking about evidence and shit."

"Yeah…those cop shows…ok, so Danny, I'm outta here, but first I gotta finish decorating your other ball ok?"

After placing another strip of tape over Danny's mouth, the next flower is carved. Danny's cocaine high was lost as soon as the knife made the first cut.

"See Danny this is how you use a knife on someone! Don't show it unless you've got the balls…sorry…the guts to use it."

Danny's right leg is pulled outward and his femoral artery is stabbed. Danny begins to gush blood.

"So look, thanks for the truth and no remorse. You made this way too easy. I'm gonna leave you cuffed and your mouth taped…ok?

You deserve to die because Holly died that night. You took more than her pussy from her…you took her spirit. Maybe your death will give a little of it back to her…see ya in hell."

She closes the door on an already dead Danny.

Miss Stephanie and Roxie tell a tale…

Ruth is furious! It's Sunday and she decides to finally do some laundry and wouldn't you know it, she doesn't have any dryer sheets.

So she's going up and down the parking lot of A-Z Emporium looking for a spot. Everyone and their extended family must be here today! Are they giving away gold or something?

Finally she parks, in what seems like another country, and starts her long walk to the entrance of the store. After asking three store clerks where they've moved the dryer sheets, Ruth finds them.

As she's making her way through the crowd toward the self check-out lanes she hears a familiar voice calling her name.

Ruth looks around and sees Miss Stephanie and Roxie standing near a display of jelly beans.

"Hello Miss Stephanie, how are you today?"

"I'm real good Det. Hill and so is Roxie. What, are you doing your clothes today?"

Looking down at the box of dryer sheets Ruth says, "Very perceptive Miss Stephanie! Yes, I ran out of them so I had to come here to get some more but it seems like the entire town is in here today."

"Yeah, folks come in here after church. It's like they gotta shop out the religion they just got!" She laughs really loud and several people turn to stare at her or maybe it's the stuffed dog she has in the dog carrier that draws the attention.

"Well, I outta be getting home so I can finish that laundry."

Ruth turns to walk away when Miss Stephanie says, "I saw the back of the woman that was coming from Ray's bar that night."

Ruth drops the box of dryer sheets.

226

Ruth turns back and says, "You saw a woman that night?"

"Yeah, me and Roxie were going to Mr. Iswara's store for some chunky chocolate and gummy bear ice-cream. You know he's the only store that orders it!

I love the way you gotta take a lot of time to chew the gummy bears and by the time you get back to eating the ice-cream it's gotten soft and creamy.

Roxie likes to lick the gummy bears but she don't actually eat them. I don't give her chocolate because it's not good for dogs."

Ruth is standing there with her mouth slightly open and she just can't believe she's listening to this crazy ass woman!

"Ok, so you and Roxie were going to Mr. I's store for ice-cream...then what did you see?"

"Well, it was dark down the alley next to Ray's bar, but when a car went by, I looked down the alley to, you know, make sure nobody was gonna try and grab me. So, anyways, I see the back of a woman walking away from Ray's back door."

"How do you know it was a woman if it was dark?"

"Well you know the difference between how a woman walks and a man walks right? Besides, the walk kinda reminded me of someone, but I can't say who."

"Are you sure Miss Stephanie you didn't see who it was?"

"No, I don't know, her, but I did see that same back and that walk again somewhere..."

"Where?! Asks Ruth who has stepped right up in Miss Stephanie's face.

"Stop growling Roxie, the detective ain't gonna hurt momma."

227

"Sorry Roxie…but Miss Stephanie, where did you see this person again?"

"I can't remember, but when I do, I will call you on the number you gave me on your card. Now we have to go now…the bus will be back soon and Roxie can't decide on which flavor of jelly beans she wants for tonight. We're watching a bootleg copy of the Luther Prince concert.

Take care detective and don't forget to pick up your dryer sheets."

Miss Stephanie turns and a lively conversation is had between her and Roxie.

On the way home Ruth is feeling hopeful…finally a clue into the death of Ray Jones. It's a small clue, but more than she had before. Should she call Penny and tell her…naw it's best to respect her leave of absence and keep her out of this.

But, wouldn't it be the shit if Ruth could close this case before Penny comes back!!

The remaining group members arrive and take their seats. Penny is the last to arrive and she has difficulty making eye contact with any of the ladies.

Denise takes the last available seat and opens the session.

"Well hello ladies. It's nice to see you all back here tonight. This is our next to last meeting so I'll keep my comments brief so you will have time to discuss anything on your minds. I do want to remind you to think about how you want the last meeting to be…a regular meeting with a potluck after or something else…just let me know.

As for educational material…some of you have contacted me and requested materials related to post traumatic stress disorder, managing anger and journaling. If there are any other topics you would like to have, please let me know no later than noon before the last session.

Any questions?"

"Yes, Denise, when you talk about a potluck. How would we heat up food?"

"Great question Lynn; through those doors is a small kitchen with two microwaves."

"Well I don't mean to be rude, but I don't want to participate in a potluck," says Yvette.

"Why not?" asks Lynn.

"Lynn you seem nice and all but I don't have to give you a reason. I said it and you heard it…right?" Yvette takes a sip of her water never taking her eyes off Lynn.

"Well fine Yvette, you sure don't have to participate!" fires off Lynn. "But the rest of us sure can! Well, let's vote and see what we want."

"Ok, all who want a potluck raise your hand," instructs Denise.

Holly, Dani, Lynn and Karen raise their hands.

Dawn says, "I'd rather just have coffee and conversation. I'm not sure I can eat this late at night and then go home and sleep. My metabolism ain't what it used to be!"

Everyone lightens up and the tension falls a few degrees.

"Well, I want to wait until this session is over before I cast my vote," says Cheryl.

"Why is that," asks Imani."

"I just want to see how people act is all."

"What people are you talking about Cheryl?" asks Penny.

"Well of course you, Yvette, and Imani…let's not pretend we all don't want to see what happens next."

Denise interjects before anyone can respond, "Cheryl that is a great segway into our group tonight.

Penny what's going on with you tonight?"

"Well, I'm very embarrassed for the way I acted last week. I want to say I'm very sorry for attacking Imani the way I did. I was just so confused about everything."

"Ok, Penny, can you be more specific about what was confusing to you and why you feel the need to apologize."

"Well I said some…"

"Please Penny it will help you and the group if you can talk very specifically about your feelings."

"I'm...ok, I will...I was angry that Imani had a decent life and she was throwing it away.

I guess I had been angry since the first time she said she hated her parents and wanted them dead.

At first, I thought my anger came out of me being a cop and how I hate to hear about violence and stuff.

But as time went on, I realized it was because I was jealous of her life. She doesn't have to work for anything and she's still so bitter and unhappy."

"Ok, but what tipped you over the edge and made you decide to speak up?" asks Denise.

"Her parents were shot and they lived."

Holly's bottle of water slipped out of her hand.

Everyone jumped and Holly starting sweating through her shirt.

"Sorry...I just can't believe Penny just said that!"

"Well, let me finish before the sky falls," says Penny sarcastically.

"Imani's parents were shot and they survived. Her dad molested her, she treated him like shit and God still lets her have a dad!

My father was an amazing man and if I had the chance to tell him what Rory did I know he would've taken care of me!

I'm angry because I tried to do everything right and what do I have to show for it?"

"What do you want Penny?" asks Lynn.

"I want my life back! I was happy once and now I've lost it all!

What about you Lynn, do you feel like you've lost more than you got?" cries Penny.

"I don't know what I lost because at the time I didn't know what I had. Does that make sense to you, any of you?

I was young and I wasn't in the same place I am now."

Lynn continues, "I know that when I came to this group I was still afraid from being raped. I was afraid because the man who raped me was in jail and I knew he'd get out one day. But now he's dead...so I've been questioning if I'm still afraid.

I don't think I've been actively afraid since he went to prison...but I've been so used to saying I was afraid it became like a habit.

I lived like I should be afraid, but I hadn't taken the time to really ask myself if I was really *feeling* afraid."

Lynn looks at Imani, "When Imani talked about being faced with almost losing her parents and, what I heard her say was, she really didn't want them dead. Then I heard myself admit I wasn't still afraid."

"But Lynn, Penny asked you about loss," said Cheryl.

"Yeah, I've lost but it's things I didn't know I would have.

How do I know who I would've been if he hadn't done that to me? I might still be the same person just without a traumatic event in my history. I mean I wanted to help people before the rape not because of it."

Dani says, "I often wonder who I would be if I hadn't married my ex-husband. Would I still have become a rape victim?

I mean is it the smell of "potential victim" on me that caused this man to be attracted to me?"

"Well maybe he had something in his past that caused him to do what he did," says Karen.

"After the last group, I looked up some stuff and there are a lot of people like us out there. I mean, I'm still torn about my part, but he didn't have the right to touch me without my permission even if I did tell him I had on crotch-less panties.

But some guys have been abused themselves and they hurt other people because of it."

Cheryl says, "I read that all the time in the profiles of the offenders on my case load.

But I call bullshit!

If you have been a victim why would you want to do the same thing to someone else and fuck up their lives?"

"Because when they were "getting over it" something happened to them and they decided to become the dragon instead of the dragon slayer," says Dani.

"Well I think we are simplifying this…there is more to the psyche of a sexual offender than what we've touched on," says Dawn. "But quite frankly, I couldn't care less about them. Can we go back to talking about us?"

Holly's cell phone rings and she yells out, "Yikes…what the…"

Jumping up and pulling her phone out her back pocket, Holly apologizes as she runs out the door.

"Sorry it's my mom calling," she says over her shoulder.

Denise asks, "Do you want to take a break and wait for Holly or continue your discussion?"

"I'd like to continue the discussion," says Cheryl.

"I bet you would" murmurs Lynn under her breath.

Dani says, "Holly wouldn't want us to stop on her account. I think it would make her feel bad if she thought we stopped because of her."

Everyone nods in agreement and they continue…

"Imani how are your parents dear?" asks Lynn. "I should've asked the moment group started, but I didn't get the chance." She says looking over at Penny.

"Thanks Lynn and I understand. Our group really isn't about my parents well being. But I do appreciate your concern.

They are home and doing well with their physical therapy. I've moved back home to help out. I wanted to take the semester off from school but they wouldn't hear of it.

My dad always has the "education is the one thing people can't take away from you and it will help you to have a strong footing in America" speech prepared and waiting for delivery whenever I get ready to quit school. So of course he said it to me the moment I mentioned taking some time off to help them out.

If all goes well they should be back to their normal routines within the next three weeks."

Everyone except Penny and Yvette verbalize well wishes.

Karen asks, "So Penny, are you still angry at Imani?"

"Karen I never said I was angry *at* Imani…I was jealous, quite frankly, of how easy she seems to have it."

"I just don't get that Penny," says Dani.

"You and all of us know it's no cake walk after being assaulted by someone you know and love! What is this jealous thing? It seems really childish to me that you would think like that." Dani rolls her eyes at Penny and takes a sip of water.

234

"Well childish or not, it's how I feel."

Penny's voice rises and her eyes brim with tears. "Of course you wouldn't understand since you're Miss, "my ex-husband went to jail and my new man treats me so well!

Did you ever stop to think how that makes others feel?

Ya'll flaunt your successful relationships all around and what do I have?!

NOTHING! That's what I have!"

"Well whose fucking fault is that Penny?" says Cheryl.

"You are not going to tell me they trust you with a gun?" says Yvette with disdain.

"What did you just say to me Yvette?

"You heard me Penny! How do you separate this "victim Penny" from the "cop Penny"? Or do you…I sure hope so.

"Yes, I am able to shelf my depressive side and do the job, what of it?"

"Well, why haven't you been able to carve out a shelf for a relationship?"

Holly rushes back in and takes her seat.

"Sorry, that was my mom and it was an emergency."

Denise asks, "Is everything alright?"

"Ummm…she pulls at a cuticle with her other hand. "Yeah, but I guess Danny Clark got killed and his body was found a few hours ago."

"Oh my Lord," says Lynn. "This is too much!"

235

"Are you alright?" asks Dani.

"Why wouldn't she be alright?" asks Yvette.

"Yeah," says Cheryl.

Dawn looks at Cheryl and Yvette and shakes her head. She says to herself, these two have ice water for blood!

"I don't know how I feel…ummm, I guess shocked is what I'm feeling right now."

"Do you want to continue the group or would you like to be alone?" asks Denise.

"I'd like to stay if that's alright…"

"Of course dear it's alright," says Lynn.

Dawn agrees and gets up getting a bottle of water for Holly.

"Here honey, drink this and know we are here for you."

Internal dialogue…

Dawn…Wait till I tell my husband this shit!

Denise says, "Let's explore feelings of jealousy, anger, guilt and triggers tonight.

Penny said her "trigger" last week was the feeling that Imani was "winning" again and she feels she's lost so much. Is that an accurate summary Penny?"

"Yes, I'm sorry to say but yes…"

"Well I feel like my trigger is people feeling sorry for themselves," says Yvette.

"I just think you're your own worst enemy if you give in to the shit that was done to you.

So what? It's been a long time since Ray touched me. Hell, I don't really even remember anything that he did to me.

I'm not a little girl anymore and he for damn sure ain't putting his hands on me anymore. Why would I stay stuck in that past? I decided to make my own future, hell, it's my life!"

"I hear you Yvette," says Cheryl. "Since I've been coming here and hearing all of you, plus my own voice, I feel like I've been so stupid for staying angry all the time.

I mean I am still angry that I can't have my brother-in-law meet me today like I am! I would put his ass down like a fat person putting down a hunk of cake! Fast and without delay!

But also Yvette, I think it's easy to say we've moved on with our lives, but I think you're wrong if you think the past hasn't left a scar on you. You can't see it, maybe, but we can."

"Oh I don't need anyone to tell me about me ok? I see the "scar" as you say, but I chose to use it as a reminder that I should never give up on what I want. For better or worse, Ray was determined to get what he wanted from me and he did.

I've turned that around to something positive…I get what I want. I say what I want and do what I want.

I've had something very precious taken from me…never again."

After a few moments of silence…

Dani says, "Penny it seems like you are more focused on what you've lost and what you think other people have. I was raped by my husband, a man that I loved and thought he loved me.

I was an adult and you were a child…I was able to press charges and you chose not to tell because it was best for you at the time. Seems to me you are really angry at yourself for not telling on your cousin.

237

It's not my fault I dealt with my ordeal differently than you did. I deal with things in my life my way!

Someone took something from all of us and some of you are in here fussing about the way some of us have taken back our control.

I think Penny is jealous because some of us are living an actual life and not just pretending to go through the motions of living."

"Those are hurtful and powerful statements Dani," says Dawn.

"Whatever," says Yvette, "For once I agree with Dani."

"So do you think I'm pretending too?" asks Holly.

Internal dialogue…

Holly…What am I doing? Now they are going to focus on me! Stupid…stupid…

"I think you are still very afraid and that fear keeps you from being your true self," says Dani.

"Well, I don't know who my true self is."

"Ok, well let me ask some questions and you just answer them honestly…ok," says Dawn.

"Ummm, ok, sure…I guess," answers Holly.

"Say the first thing that comes to your mind, about yourself, ok?

My therapist used to do this with me whenever I acted like I didn't know something about myself.

Ok, so first question…what's your favorite thing to do?"

"Ummm, I guess I love to read."

"Where would you like to travel to?"

"I guess…it sounds silly, but…I want to go to Savannah Georgia…it looks pretty and safe."

"So you do know something about yourself and even though it seems simple, it at least gives you a foundation to work from.

My therapist says that even though I feel like my foundation is cracked and damaged, as long as I can see my way toward something… that is all hope is."

Internal dialogue…

Yvette…I knew she couldn't get through one session without quoting her damn therapist!

Crying, Dani says, "Dawn that is so beautiful and thank you for sharing that with us…with me. I'm always trying to portray being bubbly and fun but honestly, Holly, there are times when I just shut down and cry.

I eat too much ice-cream and chocolate chip cookies for my own good, but I just need something to make me feel safe and happy. Yeah, I admit I'm not all exercise and happy!

Penny, no one is perfect and none of us, I don't, have it easy…just different ways that we present ourselves to the world."

Cheryl says, "Yeah, Penny, I know you think I've got it made because I got married to my husband even after the rape. But have you ever considered how difficult it was to go through with the marriage after being raped?!

I mean by my husband's own brother! Shit they even look alike minus the fucked up crack mouth his brother had!

I had to decide if I wanted to live with the rape more than I wanted to live with my soul mate…I chose my husband Steven and I've never regretted it.

239

He has been so supportive without even understanding why I had mood swings. Sometimes I would bite his head off and other times I couldn't stop crying.

There have been times in our marriage that I haven't had sex with him. He was hurt and frustrated, but you know what, he stood by me."

"Why didn't you tell him what happened?" asks Penny.

"I didn't want him to pity me. I knew he would be the only pure relationship I'd ever have. I've loved him since the first time we met at church.

Yeah, my foul mouth used to go to church. It's a shame ole Ayda ain't here to hear me say it; rest in peace Ayda." She makes the sign of the cross.

"Steven and I became fast friends and lovers soon after. Honestly, I've never loved anyone the way I love that man. I feel complete with him and I trust him.

He is the most loyal person I've ever met. I don't want that compromised because of his fucking brother."

The group falls silent…

"I'm not sorry Danny is dead Holly," says Penny.

Holly's head shoots up and she is again floored by Penny's comments.

"I know I'm a cop, but…well I'm not even sure I am a cop anymore.

Don't get me wrong, I don't want to promote killing or revenge, but since someone killed him, why not be glad he's gone? He hurt you and now he won't hurt anyone else again."

"But Penny, yes he's gone, but Holly's distress remains, doesn't it Holly?" asks Lynn.

Holly says, "I guess nothing about how I see myself has changed…ummm, whether he's dead or not, I guess doesn't change the fact he sexually assaulted me.

I don't know if I'll keep being anxious…I mean I haven't been anxious about him, but it's been the thought that something else is going to happen to me.

I'm not sure his death makes that go away for me."

"See that's why people kill themselves," says Yvette. "Right Penny; because they don't think anything will make the feelings they have go away?"

Penny looks directly into Yvette's eyes and says, "You have no idea what it feels like to really want to die. If you did you wouldn't ask.

It's a dark, cold, empty, void where your soul goes and there are no sounds or sights that can penetrate it.

There isn't any love that you can draw on that will keep you holding on to wanting to live."

Penny closes her eyes and continues.

"It feels like the only thing you can do for those that love you. They are worried all the time that you are not happy and may hurt yourself.

They can't understand why you don't see yourself as they do.

They tell you to stay strong when all you feel is weak.

They tell you to talk to someone when you can't find the words to describe the void where you now live.

The void is all consuming…you are there all the time.

When you are around people, it's like they are on the other side of Plexiglas and I'm inside the void all alone.

241

Laughter, drama, tears none of it can penetrate the barrier between you and the outside world.

There doesn't seem like real air in the void…I mean I can't feel myself breathe…I feel like I'm awake but already dead…like all I need to do is finish it and then I'll find the peace that has been illusive to me all my adult life."

Penny opens her eyes and looks at their staring faces.

"Shit…," says Cheryl.

"Oh my merciful Lord," says Lynn who is openly crying.

"Penny…I'm so sorry you have felt that way," cries Dawn.

"I guess I really haven't been suicidal," says Yvette. "That's such a awful way to live…if that's what you call living."

Denise clears her throat and asks, "Penny are you alright?"

"I don't know what I am, but alright," she laughs. "Denise, what does that even mean?"

"I'm asking if you are going to be safe when you leave here tonight."

"Honestly, I don't know."

Silence…

"Ladies this has been the most intense night I've ever experienced, except my parent's shooting," says Imani.

"I don't know where my relationship with my parents will go from here, but I am glad that I was coming here before they were shot or I don't know if I would've been able to move forward. I know it's not the last session, but I wanted to say thank you now."

Silence…

242

Internal dialogue…

Cheryl…Penny is crazy as hell!

Yvette…These folks are fucked up! Imani is a little bitch. Penny, damn girl, just shoot yourself already cause you're fucked.

Dawn…OMG, wait until I tell my husband about tonight!

Lynn…I will never come to a group again. I wasn't angry until I came here. Wait, is that a bad thing? Maybe I should've been angry.

Dani…Poor Holly, Imani, and Penny…just so much going on for them; I hope they get into treatment cause if not I'm worried about what will happen to them.

Karen…Damn! What the fuck is going on in this group? Some of these bitches are crazy, but damn, fucked by your cousin, uncle, brother-in-law, and father…shit there are some fucked up individuals in the world.

Imani…I wonder what mommy and daddy are doing?

Holly…I knew they wouldn't like me…said it the first day of group…next week is it and I didn't make any friends. The only kind of friend I attract are people like Danny. Danny is dead! What happened? I can't wait to get outta here and call momma.

Penny…I'm empty…

Denise…I'm going to call the police precinct and request a welfare check on Penny. She is worrying me and I don't want her to kill herself.

"Does anyone have anything else to say tonight?" asks Denise.

Lynn says, "Yes, I do. Holly, if you want to get together sometime here's my cell number. You can call me and we can talk. I mean you and I have something in common besides the assaults right?

Our guys were killed and no one else can know what that feel like but us. I know I'm older than you and everything...but I just wanted to offer."

She leans behind Dawn and hands Holly her number.

"Thanks Lynn, I don't know what to say except thank you very much. I will call, I promise. And, Lynn...you're older than me yes, but so what? They say age ain't nothing but a number right?"

Internal dialogue...

Holly...Lynn likes me!

Everyone chuckles...

"I'd like to thank Dawn for the little exercise she did with me earlier. I've never been to a therapist, but I'm thinking tonight, for the first time, maybe I should go talk to someone...but I'm not sure yet...but we'll see...thanks."

Silence...

"Ok, well I guess we can discuss next week's agenda," says Denise.

Cheryl says, "Look these meetings have gotten way heavy and I for one don't want to hang around and smile afterwards. This has been a very stressful time for me so I'm not interested in a potluck or anything else."

They all start talking at once...

Finally, they decided that everyone would give Denise $5 and she would purchase gourmet pastries for the last session.

They all left with their thoughts...some more positive than others.

Internet streaming…news flash…

Today on WJLA we have follow-up on the death of Donovan Tate…Julie, what is coming out of the medical examiner's office?

"Well Leon, we have been here all day and the official cause of death for Donovan Tate was a gunshot wound to the head. To remind our viewers, Mr. Tate was convicted for the rape of a foster care worker over 20 years ago. He was recently released after serving 25 years in the state prison.

There was also something interesting that a source close to the case, who doesn't want to be identified, said, Donovan Tate had a piece of paper stuck down his throat. There were readable pieces left which seemed to explain Department of Social Services programs and resources.

This has authorities wondering if this was a revenge killing for the rape of a young social worker by Tate many years ago.

Also, there was an arm and leg bone found in the same lake. They were not Donovan Tate's but authorities think they are the bones of a male. No further information, Julie O'Shea reporting…back to you Leon."

The killer thinks…

YES!!!! The Department of Social Services fact sheet was still readable! That was such a nice touch if I do say so myself!

Tate was a broken man by the time he met me. I guess they fucked him up in jail cause all he did was drop to his knees and start praying.

And when I told him I was his niece, the one he molested back in the day, he started to cry.

I put a pillow over his face, and blew his brains out.

245

Bonus they found some bones of Petri's...one of my kills from last year. Hey baby!!! He was a good fuck...too bad...his ass is dead now.

Internet streaming NBC12 news @ 11 pm

"Earlier today, Brent Rudder was outside the Richmond coroner's office and he filed this report."

"Today we heard that the body of Daniel Clark was found at a secluded part of a Richmond area park. Mr. Clark was handcuffed to the steering wheel of his car. It appears his genitalia area was mutilated and his thumb was cut off and...I apologize for the graphic nature of this report...his thumb was then placed inside his anus.

When asked if there was any evidence this was a random killing, police said they are following up on several leads and will keep the public informed.

The coroner also stated there was evidence of cocaine use at the time of the sexual assault...this is Brent Rudder, NBC12 news."

The killer thinks...

Yeah...I bet they are following up on several leads! They don't have shit! But let's hope little Holly gets something out of this. If not, fuck her...it's almost time to end this damn thing.

Ruth is on the case…

Ruth is on her second cup of coffee when her office phone rings, "Yes this is Det. Hill, may I help you?"

"Yeah detective, this is Dr. Ellis, how are you this morning?"

"Fine doc and you?" says Ruth.

"I'm making it you know fair to middling, as my grandfather used to say. Anyway, the reason for the call is this; I received a flash message about a murder in Virginia.

After the murder of Mr. Raymond Jones and the manner in which his body was left, I put out a notification alert for any other murders with similar aspects."

"So, wait, Dr. Ellis are you telling me you got a hit? There has been another murder like ours?"

"Well, yes, that is what I was trying to tell you but you beat me to the punch."

"Sorry, Dr. Ellis, tell me everything."

"Well Det. Hill, another thing my grandfather used to say, "I can show you better than I can tell you." I'll email the information over to you immediately."

"Thanks doc, I really appreciate it! This case can use a real break."

Ruth spends the next 20 minutes reading and re-reading the investigation notes on the murder of Daniel Clark aka Danny. He was found dead in his vehicle parked at a secluded spot of Bryan Park in the Richmond Virginia area.

Mr. Clark was 32 years old and had worked for several of the local hospitals as a janitor. Mr. Clark lived in his deceased parent's mobile home, married, but also had numerous other relationships.

Mr. Clark has four children ranging in age from 20-12 years old. All the children live with their mothers (2). The older children state they have little to no contact with their father.

Mr. Clark was found with his pants down around his ankles, his testicles were cut in a manner that suggests the perpetrator was trying to torture Mr. Clark. Mr. Clark's right hand thumb was cut off and inserted into his rectum.

The cause of death was a stab wound to the femoral artery on the right leg.

There were no signs of a struggle and no fingerprints, other than the victim's, have been found on the driver's side of the door.

The victim's car trunk was raised, but it is uncertain why.

"Shit," says Ruth out loud. I've gotta get to Richmond and interview some of the locals myself. My gut tells me there is a link between these murders. It can't be a mere coincidence another severed finger crammed in a dead guy's ass!

She leaves her desk and goes into Lt. Brogan's office.

After telling him everything, Lt. Brogan calls the Richmond Police Department handling the Clark case and asks if Ruth can come down to interview some of Danny Clark's relatives and friends to see if there is a link to Raymond Jones' murder.

They agree, but remind him that she is not investigating their murder and is strongly encouraged not to interfere. Lt. Brogan passes this territorial message to Ruth as she runs out the door.

While Ruth is in the office with Lt. Brogan she gets a call that goes to her voicemail.

"Hello, my name is Denise Wallace and I'd like it if you would call me ASAP. I need to talk to you about some concerns I have. I can be reached at 304 555 9311, again that's 304 555 9311. Thank you very much for your time."

Well, thinks Denise, I've done all I can for the time being. Penny isn't returning my calls and I have no idea if she's alright.

Wait, here's a text from her. "I'm fine Denise, just need some quiet time alone. I promise…Penny."

Well I'm so relieved to have heard from her. It would be so unfortunate and such a waste if she killed herself!

In the neighborhood...

Squidget and Pimp Gene aka Kim and Eugene are now the proud owners of Ray Jones' bar.

They hire a cleaning service which Gene, as he wants to be called, is not happy about, but Kim tells him she ain't cleaning shit so he has to hire someone. He's able to find some broke college kids to do the cleaning for under $300 a week.

Gene is impressed with Kim's business sense and within days they have ordered a new bar sign which will read, "Good & Plenty." Both Gene and Kim agreed on the name since it really was the hos that paid for the bar and they had been good to ole Pimp Daddy.

He wishes them well and so does Kim just as long as they don't come around sniffing for a piece of the action. They both agree to let bygones be bygones but those hos better get the hell on!

All the bar equipment is in working order and the bar still has ample stocks of liquor, beer even peanuts! They have to order perishables like fruit and stuff but that's under control as well, Kim used to service a bartender from another part of the city and he agreed to help them for free. Well not free since he's looking for a job on this side of Morganville so he'll be closer to his girlfriend.

"Well Gene, it looks like things are going our way! What you say 'bout that?"

"I say, you sure you won't suck my dick at least one more time; C'mon girl for old time sake."

"I will fucking kill you if you ask me to touch that shriveled, glue and nail polish remover dick again!

I swear you are such a dog!

Now shut yo golden showered mouth the hell up and let's look at what kind of cable package we gonna need for the bar."

250

Gene's nuts go north again…

You can always come home...right?

"How did you get in my house?"

"Well momma, I used the key."

"I'm not your momma! Who are you? You gotta leave, you're upsetting Roxie."

"Old woman, that dog ain't even real. I don't want to hurt you while you're talking crazy, so sit back down on your bed and we'll just talk 'til you understand."

"No, I can't lie back down; I have to make breakfast for me and Roxie before 9 am so we can watch Let's Talk Live Morganville. We watch it every morning."

Miss Stephanie is shoved back down on the bed. Before she can react, her hands are zip tied together and her ankles are tied to the bedposts by rope.

An enema tube is placed inside Miss Stephanie's anus with little effort. The tube is attached to a bottle filled with a liquid substance.

Roxie is then placed at the foot of the bed facing Miss Stephanie.

"Now can you see Roxie real good?"

Internal dialogue...

Miss Stephanie...What is going on? Is this real or am I dreaming?

"Yes, Roxie honey, it's ok, stop barking honey, mommy is gonna get you ok?

"Now, if you scream, I'll take this knife and slit Roxie's throat. Do you understand?"

Miss Stephanie starts to cry, "So this is real! Yes...I do understand, but I don't know why you are doing this.

I mean I know it's your back right that I saw at the mall and down the alley near the bar of that man who got kilt right?"

"Oh Miss Steph, can I call you Steph?"

"Well I don't like people who make their names short, but since you asked and you got Roxie and that big knife, I guess it's alright."

"Well good, and thank you…so I'll sit in this chair next to your bed and I'm going to help you remember where you first saw me…ok?"

"….ummm….alright, but will it take long?"

"No, we'll do it over some cookies so it will only take as long as it takes for you to finish the cookies."

"What kind of cookies you got? I really shouldn't eat them before breakfast. Well unless you got some chocolate chip, then I can eat them anytime!"

"Ok, first question…how could you stand back and allow your husband to molest your only child?"

"Shit you say, I've never had any children or a no good husband! You got me mixed up with somebody else!"

The plastic enema bottle is squeezed…

"Oooooh, I think I'm gonna pee myself! Something cold is moving in me!"

"Well, I did promise you cookies remember? This is what is known as a cookie enema.

I saw you had this enema bag in your bathroom when I was in your house a few weeks ago. Why do you have an enema bag Miss Steph?"

"Sometimes the moo moos off the clearance rack are off size so instead of taking them back and maybe not finding the colors I want, I use the enema bag to lose a little water weight.

I saw it on one of those TV infomercials a few years ago.

Roxie, did you know someone was in our house? Did you smell a strange scent cause you didn't tell momma; bad dog!"

"Focus Miss Steph…you did have a daughter and a husband. You knew he was molesting her and instead of doing anything about it, you just acted like nothing was going on.

You continued to work, go to bars and clubs, grin with your girlfriends and let your husband have his way with your little girl.

Tell me why…"

"Nnnnow this sounds like one of them Life Happens TV movies or a talk show thing.

But I guess if a momma did something like that, it would be because she was scared of the man. Like he might beat her up or leave her alone with no way to fend for herself.

Is that what happened on the show?"

The bag is squeezed again…

"Holy cold shit up my ass!

What kind of cookies are these gonna be again, and when can we have them?"

"What was the last thing you ate last night?"

"Roxie and me had some of that chocolate chunk and gummy bear ice-cream from Mr. Iswara's store.

You kknow the store I'mmm talking about? Sorry, I got the stutters but my booty and parts feel ccold!"

"Yeah I know the store, and you're probably gonna have chocolate chunk cookies real soon so let's continue.

What do you think happened to the family we were talking about?"

"What family? The one on TV?"

"Sure…"

"Well I think the girl went away to live with her grandma or somebody else so maybe she don't tell on her daddy. Her daddy was probably feeling sorry for what he did, but didn't know what to say to the girl.

And on most of those shows the momma goes off by herself and starts her life over. Is that what happened on the show you saw?" asks Stephanie.

"Well yes on the movie that keeps playing over and over in my head…but it doesn't play anymore since I know how it's gonna end."

With a chastising look, Stephanie says, "What, did you skip ahead and watch the ending before you saw the whole thing? You know that's cheatin right? Roxie wants to see the ending of a movie, but I tell her no, we have to wait until the movie ends properly."

"Well I do agree with you on one account…movies should end properly.

So anyway in this movie, as you say, the girl was raised by her grandmother, who rescued the girl from mean relatives her momma and daddy had left her with.

Her grandma recognized that the little girl had been messed with because when the grandmother was about 15 years old her own father messed with her. She got pregnant.

Before she started to show, she met up with this guy that had liked her, but she never liked him. Grandma thought he was stupid and didn't have anything going for him in the looks department. But she needed someone who would take her and not question the early birth of their first child."

Stephanie says, "So the grandma married someone and passed the child off as his? Lawd have mercy! I wish I had seen this movie it sounds off the chain!"

The bag is squeezed empty…

"Well to make a long story short since it's almost time for the cookies to come out…the girl grew up with her grandparents and was mentored by a man she called "the toothpick man" because he always had a toothpick sticking out the corner of his mouth. She doesn't remember either her grandmother or "toothpick man" saying his real name.

He had been one of her grandmother's lovers, but he called off the affair after he went into the Army. When he came back, he took an interest in the granddaughter because she was very intelligent, ruthless, and could hit anything she aimed at with her grandfather's .22 caliber rifles. Her grandfather was always bragging on how good a shot she was and how fearless she was when they went hunting.

So when the girl graduated from high school, toothpick man paid for her college, without her knowledge. While in college she was recruited by an organization that recruits, trains, and hires assassins to support the CIA, MI6, FBI, and other nationally security agencies. Well this little abused girl became known as the "cream of the toppy top"!"

256

"Really? Well that's good for her right? She overcame all that stuff and moved on with her life. I bet she gets to go to lots of cool places. Roxie and I would love to travel, but there are some mean people out there and…ouch! My stomach is trying to hurt."

"Well, I better get ready to go, but before I do, would you like to know what happened to the little girl's family?"

"Ummm…owww…yeah, that would…owwww, be ok, and then I've gotta go to the bathroom and do a turd!"

Laughing, "Ok, well I don't want to be around for "doing a turd!"

Well, after a few years, the young woman found her father. He had remarried so she waited for him to be alone and then she killed him.

We're running out of time so I can't tell you how she did it but they had a reunion she would not soon forget. That reunion memory has replaced all the other bad memories she had of him molesting her."

"Well that's good…honey can you untie me? I don't feel so good."

"Sure, I'll untie you while I finish the story…when the girl left for college she stopped communicating with her grandparents. She was told by the agency she worked for they would die if she tried to reach them.

This was the first step in her indoctrination into the agency. They needn't worry; she never experienced homesickness and didn't even return to their funerals even after she was given permission. She vowed never to go back, unless it was to clean up something from the past so it wouldn't compromise her future.

So that's where we are now…Miss Steph"

The killer leans over Miss Stephanie's face and they stare at each other for a long moment.

"No! It can't be! It can't be! OWWWWWW!"

257

A cloth goes into Miss Stephanie's mouth, "Stop yelling cow! Or should I say mommy?"

"Fuck! Ok, what happened?"

"Lt. Brogan it's as I've already stated. The victim, Miss Stephanie, as she's known on the street was found with an enema hose near her rectum. The hose was still attached to an enema bag which was found in the deceased's right hand. It appears there was a complication and, well...something caused her intestines to explode out of her anus!

She died, I'm sure, very painfully, and it would've taken at least 10 minutes for the poor woman to expire."

"Shit! Does it look like a homicide or an accidental death?"

"I've got some questions, like why she was laying on the bed doing this, but the TV was on so maybe...but I'll know more once I complete the autopsy. I'll keep you posted lieutenant."

"Alright doc, I would appreciate that." Lt. Brogan hangs up the phone and reaches in his desk for a package of mini-donuts; its gonna be one of those days, I can feel it!

"Ok, let's get her body to the morgue so I can start the autopsy," Dr. Ellis says to his technicians.

While he's talking to a police officer, one of the techs says, "Shit, I'm never gonna be able to eat cookies again! Why does it smell like cookies in here?"

"You talking 'bout cookies what about eating gummy bears? That toy dog has a shit crusted gummy bear stuck to his damn eye!

258

I mean for real, why does a grown ass woman have a toy dog sitting there looking between her legs?! Man some freaks out in this here world!"

"Yeah, man you right!"

They place Miss Stephanie and all her internal parts in a body bag and slowly take her down the stairs to the wagon. Roxie is placed in a large plastic bag and the bag is tagged. The poop encrusted gummy bear remains stuck to Roxie's glass eye.

Ruth arrives in Richmond…

Ruth makes nice with the local police investigating Danny Clark's death and finds out the names of his babies mommas.

The first one is Heather Boyd, who has agreed to meet Ruth at a local coffee shop.

"Thanks for agreeing to meet with me Ms. Boyd; I promise not to take up much of your time, as I'm sure this is an awful time for you and your children."

"Well if you think that Det. Hill you drove all the way down here for nothing! No tears here from any of my kids, and I haven't heard from Danny in over 10 years. He was a no good son-of-a-bitch for sure!"

"Ok, then I'll keep this simple, anyone you know or have heard of that would have killed Danny?"

"Well it wasn't me, so no, I don't know anyone else who hated him more than me; well 'cept Gail. The mother of his other kids; she hates his ass too!"

"What about his family? How can I reach any of his immediate family?"

"Danny's parents died, and his only sister moved away, and ain't come back since."

"Why? Do you know what happened?"

"Naw, I don't know nuthin, sorry you came all this way for the nuthin I got for you.

Look I gotta go, I don't want to be late for work."

"Thank you Ms. Boyd, I appreciate you taking some time to speak with me. Can you tell me where I might find Gail Hartman-Clark?"

"Yeah, Gail don't work 'cause she hurt her back shoveling snow a few years ago. Here's her address…"

Ruth got into her car and punched in Gail's address into her GPS.

Maybe she'll get some answers from Gail Hartman-Clark, Danny's wife.

"Thanks for taking the time to see me Mrs. Hartman-Clark."

"Awww, no problem, but please call me Gail! Mrs. Hartman-Clark sounds so stuck up and formal! Besides, I'm going back to my maiden name as soon as my divorce from Danny is finalized. I'm just waiting for the papers to get signed but since he's dead I don't know what will happen now."

Ruth says, "Alright Gail, and I'm just Ruth to you."

Ok, Ruth, shoot…what do you want to know about Danny besides he was an asshole who didn't raise his kids and treated women like they were shit?"

"I completely understand, but honestly Gail, anything you can tell me is going to be a tremendous help!"

"Ok, so what I know is this…years ago while working as a janitor at the hospital, Danny supposedly raped a girl! She was an intern or volunteer or something. No charges were pressed by the girl. I heard she left the state and never came back."

Ruth shakes her head and checks her notes, "No wasn't that his sister who left home and didn't come back? Sounds like maybe the story has gotten muddled over the years."

"No Ruth, the sister did leave, but it was a few years after the girl was supposedly raped.

Rumor has it Danny got drunk and tried to rape his sister too! Their parents kicked him out of the house, but after a few weeks, his mother let him move back in. He had his mother wrapped around his little finger.

So when Danny's sister heard he was moving back in, she packed up when their parents were at the grocery store. She left them a note and hasn't been seen since."

"Do you think she would've killed her brother?" asks Ruth.

"No I don't...why would she do it now?" asks Gail.

"Yeah..." Ruth looks at her notes. "Well what about the girl he was supposed to have raped at the hospital? Do you know anything about her?"

"Yeah her name is Holly Chism, and I think she moved over to West Virginia...isn't that where you drove from?"

Ruth's eyes grow wide and her heart is thumping almost out of her chest.

"Do you know if Heather Boyd knows any of this?"

"Yeah she knows, but she's so proud! Doesn't want people to think she was messing around with a man who rapes women and wanted to rape his own sister.

I don't give a shit what people think about me. I slept with him and had two kids by him. Right or wrong, that's my life story."

Rising to leave, Ruth says, "Well Gail, thank you for your candor. And I hope you have a good day."

"Thanks Ruth and good luck to you with your investigation. I sure hope you catch whoever did that to Danny and Mr. Jones."

"I didn't say anything about Mr...."

"Girl, I'm not stupid…I looked your tail up the moment you called!

 I know you got a weird murder over there, so I figure you're trying to see if they have anything in common…am I right or am I wrong? I mean not too many times you find a finger in the ass of a dead person, right?"

"I like you Gail! If I could say it, I would say you're right, but unfortunately I can't discuss an open investigation."

Ruth laughs and leaves Gail giddy with laughter.

In the car Ruth says, I knew it! There is a connection between the deaths of Danny Clark and Raymond Jones! I've gotta get back to the office and put these pieces together.

Relationships lost…

Penny reads over a poem she wrote when she was in her early 20s called "*Looking forward to not looking back.*" I wonder when the day will come when I stop looking back over my past.

I should've told my grandparents what happened with Rory. As an adult I knew it was wrong and I needed some help. Why didn't I tell them? I know they would've understood and tried their best to help me understand why this happened to me.

But Rory was my grandmother's brother's only child and right after it happened I was fearful my grandmother would've picked her brother's side over mine. She really loved Uncle Wilbur and therefore loved Rory.

Even when everyone saw a change in me, I just couldn't tell them. Before my parents left for the mountains, my dad asked if I needed to talk. So I wouldn't chicken out, I told him we would talk when he got back.

He never came back and neither did my mom really.

Dad was the love of her life and she just fell completely apart when he vanished. I guess if it wasn't for grandma and granddaddy we would've both died.

I never knew my father's parents, but my maternal grandparents were the bomb! My grandma was always dressing in the latest styles and knew all the celebrity gossip.

My grandfather was a solid, loyal working man's man. He was always so patient with my mom after my dad died.

My grandmother, being the more flighty one would just say to my mother, "Honey listen…you got to keep it moving! Doug would want you to keep living so that way he keeps living too! You'll never stop being his wife and you sure as shootin ain't stop being Penny's mom."

But my mother did stop being my mom. We moved into my grandparents' home soon after my dad died. My grandfather helped my mom sell our house. She gave away all dad's clothes, shoes, tools, and his car was donated to a Veteran's organization.

Then my mom left me some money and moved away to Ohio. She would call occasionally to speak to her parents and I would get about a three minute check-in, then she'd hang up.

I last saw my mother when my grandparents died. They were killed instantly and I was thankful for that. I was a rookie cop at the time and heard about the motor vehicle fatality over the radio. When I arrived at the scene and saw it was their car, I screamed and fainted.

I woke several hours later in the hospital emergency room. My supervisor was there and said she understood after a check of the registration showed the owner of the vehicle and I lived at the same address.

My mom let me take care of all the funeral arrangements. She came for the funeral and stayed over a week to help with getting affairs in order. She wanted to sell the house, but I told her grandma and granddad had sold it to me a year before they died.

My mom didn't speak to me for two days. When she did speak, it was as she was about to leave the house, she had grown up in, forever, "Penny, I never wanted to have a child. I met your father and wanted to spend the rest of my life with him, but he wanted a child.

So to make him happy I had one. I have loved you, but I have not loved being a mom. I had to share my dad with my mom and everyone else he met. He, like your dad, was larger than life and never seemed to have enough time for me. Your unsympathetic grandmother always said I was "too needy" and I should get my "own life."

I had your father for three wonderful years…all to myself. Then you came along and you were cute, smart, inquisitive, fearless, popular and most importantly, you didn't need me after you learned how to pee in the pot on your own! I was your mom in name only.

So, finally, when your dad and I had the opportunity to go on vacation alone, I was ecstatic! You were sick but I knew your grandparents would take excellent care of you. Besides, you probably didn't need them to do much for you, as you have to be the most independent person I've ever met.

Anyway, as my luck goes, your dad went out for a walk and never returned. Why has God or whoever is in charge, mucked up my life every time I get a little of what I want?

Anyway, Penny, it's over…I'm going back to Ohio and you know how to reach me if you want."

"But mom, I need you now! How can you abandon me again like this? Don't you care at all about me?" I cried looking into my mother's cold brown eyes.

"Penny, I do care for you, but you have been the other woman in my relationship with my husband, and I can't forgive you for that. I've had to share my parents with you as well, and now, you own the home that should've been mine."

"If you want the house mom, you can have it! We can do the papers tomorrow!"

"No Penny, they chose you over me, so let's not try to re-write history, shall we?"

"But mom, I love you and I need you!!! Please, please mom, don't do this to us. We used to be so close and have such a wonderful relationship!

Don't you remember the times we would go to open houses and pretend we were looking for a new house? We used to eat the goodies, walk through the houses and pretend we lived there.

I loved those Saturday adventures with you. Remember when we'd cross the county line, we called ourselves "outlaws?"

I was never in competition with you! I loved you mom!"

Coldly my mother says, "Penny, perhaps we weren't as close as you thought we were."

Then my mother turned and walked out of my life for good. That was over six years ago. Well it's time I had a heart-to-heart with my dear mother.

Talking to parents…

Tony and Rosie McCollin are recovering well.

They are both itching to get back to their regular routine of work, long walks after dinner and playing golf on Saturdays with their best friends Ted and Debra Northcault.

Imani comes into the living room, sits on the chair ottoman, and faces her parents who, are sitting in their matching recliner chairs.

"Mom, dad, I need to talk to you both, if you're up to it."

Her parents look at each other and her dad says, "Sure honey, if you want to talk to us we are always ready to listen."

"Ummm…ok…I'm not sure how this will sound but I want to…no, I need to get it out so just let me dump ok, before you say anything or ask any questions…ok?"

Her parents nod their head in agreement.

"I've told myself and anyone who would listen that I hate my parents. I know it sounds awful and I can't imagine what it feels like for you to hear your only child say such a thing.

I can't describe all the stuff I was feeling for all those years, except I felt like I was broken and nothing could fix me. I felt like all you wanted to do was buy my silence. That if you felt like you paid for your mistake through gifts, trips, and stuff, it would make it alright.

Daddy, it will never be alright. I don't know how mom could forgive you for what you did to me. I don't know how you can forgive yourself for almost killing my heart and my ability to trust.

I've tried to hurt you both by acting out and sleeping around. I thought that I wasn't good enough and that's why you hated me so much that you did that to me.

I wanted to be dirty and nasty, cause then my upstanding father would never want someone who was beneath him.

I admit, I had sex with older men who didn't want anything but my body under or on top of them. I imagined mom walking in and finding me having sex with some old dude and wondering if that's what it looked like when her man was on top of me.

The more you two gave me, the more I hated you! I wanted daddy to kill himself and leave a note explaining that he couldn't live with himself anymore because of what he did to me.

I wanted mommy to sneak away with me, after dad left for work, where we would change our identities and start over.

I wanted to have a normal relationship with my friends, instead of feeling like you two were always watching me. Supposedly keeping me safe, but it was with you, dad that I was unsafe!

Then you were both shot and I forgot all that stuff. I was praying to God to have mercy on both of you. I wanted you both healed and I promised God I would learn to practice forgiveness.

I can't make up the way I've treated you, no more than you can make up for what happened. All, I think, we can do is to try and go on from here.

So with that I have only one request…will you both join me in going to family counseling?

I have made an appointment for tomorrow at 10 am, if you're up to it.

I promise it's not going to be a bashing session or anything. I just really and truly with all my heart want to be a family."

Through tears, her mother says, "Imani not even another bullet can stop us from coming with you tomorrow!"

Imani rises and very gently hugs both her parents. They all get on the oversized sofa and fall asleep together.

Holly and her mother talk for hours and finally her mother answers all the questions she can about Danny's death. She is curious as to why Holly is so upset about his death. Holly explains that she knew Danny when she worked at the hospital and she's never known anyone who was murdered.

Her mother is so happy to have a conversation with her daughter that lasts for more than 10 minutes and enjoys the conversation so much she doesn't ask too many questions.

But later, she wonders why Holly seemed to take Danny's death so hard. Maybe he was the boyfriend she broke up with that caused her to move away.

Well, I sure hope not, because Danny was not a nice boy. Rumors have been following him for years. Some say he even raped some girls he worked with at those hospitals.

Holly's mom stops rinsing the cold cream from her face and stares in the mirror in shock. Could my Holly have been one of those girls? Is that why she left and hardly ever comes home? And when she does come home she never leaves the house.

Doesn't call or visit any old friends. When she's gone, and I run into her friends, they say they haven't heard from Holly since she left Richmond.

Holly's mother rinses her face and pauses for a long time, she plans to ask her daughter if she has a secret.

Talking it out…

After work Karen stops in at the newly opened "Good & Plenty Bar." There's a nice vibe which is surprising. Everything is chilled, not loud like it was before. Karen is meeting Dawn and Cheryl here for drinks. Funny they sent text messages to each other simultaneously asking to get together to talk about the last group session.

After placing their drink orders and starting in on fresh roasted peanuts in the shell, they begin processing their thoughts and feelings.

Dawn says, "Ok, I can't hold it any longer! What in the world happened the other night? What did you all take away from it?"

Cheryl says, "I took away, that Penny should be taken away! I mean damn she's crazy!"

"Aww, she's not crazy, just doesn't know how to deal with what has happened to her," says Karen, as she cracks open a peanut.

"Yeah well, I don't mean to talk about people, but Yvette is a nasty piece of work," says Dawn. "I don't know why she's even in our group."

"She's there same as all the rest of us, but I understand her more," says Cheryl. "Yvette is like me, she's developed this hard exterior to protect the soft vulnerable part of herself."

Karen shakes her head, "I don't know about that Cheryl! Yvette is one cold be-iach! I mean, you bad and all I give you that, but I'd like to have Yvette on my side than against me. I bet if I showed her the guy who felt me up she'd kick his ass!"

"Yeah, maybe she found Lynn and Holly's guys and killed them!" laughs Dawn.

"Well she sure didn't knock off my brother-in-law, crack did that for me! But for real, would you like the person who fucked with you to die?

That's some heavy shit to carry around…karma is a bitch. I wouldn't want that on my heart, you know what I'm saying?"

"Yeah that's probably why Imani changed her tune once she was faced with her parents almost dying. I mean, can you imagine how messed up she would be if she wished them dead and then they died! Holy cow shit that would be awful!" says Karen.

"Yeah, I find myself thinking about my life and the choices I've made," said Dawn. I've spent my adult life in therapy! I could've paid off my house if I had saved those co-pays!

I mean what am I looking for?"

"How will you know you've found it?" ask Cheryl.

Dawn says, "Girl, I have no idea! I'm not even sure I'm really looking or I've just been so caught up in the "process" that I got too scared to actually live. I mean, I can't make a decision without first checking in with my therapist.

Even my husband asks me, "have you spoken to Dr. Lee about this?" For real a stranger has more clout over my life decisions than my husband or for real, my own mind. I've become some kinda neurotic therapy junkie!"

Shaking her head, Dawn continues, "I hate to admit it, but I've been writing letters to my therapist after every group session."

"What the hell for?" asks Cheryl.

"Since I can't see her until after this group is over, I wanted to write down the stuff I was feeling so we can process it together."

"Dawn, look, I like you but girl you really have an addiction to therapy. What are you so afraid of? I mean are you afraid to make your own choices or something?"

Leaning close, so as not to be overheard, Dawn says, "When I was in college, I was so independent and made all my own decisions. I was a leader in my classes and I was determined to graduate one semester early to save my parents some money. But then I made the choice to go to a party, drink and walk home alone.

I was pulled into a brush and raped by some guy. Everyone, including my parents, questioned my "decisions" that night. I've been questioning my decisions ever since."

"But how do you get anything done if you don't trust yourself?" asks Karen, while licking at the salt on her margarita glass.

"I probably do more pre-planning than a military general! That way, by the time I get to an event or need to do something, I know for sure it's right.

I used to see my therapist weekly, for years, but lately she's been booked when I try to make my weekly appointments. I guess she's really popular and people are flocking to her."

"Maybe, she's just telling you she's full so she doesn't hurt your feelings. I had a friend who was a therapist and she would do that to her "frequent flyers," you know patients that kept coming back all the time for no real reason."

"I don't think Dr. Lee would do that to me or any client for that matter. Is that even legal?"

Cheryl says, "Yeah they can as long as you're not suicidal or something. Hell, it's their schedule and their money! Dawn do you have an appointment scheduled right after group ends?"

"Not yet, my husband and I are going on a vacation to London for two weeks. I'll make an appointment when I get back. The journaling has been ok, so I can wait to see Dr. Lee until I get back."

"Well I have no intention of going into therapy," says Karen. "This group has been plenty for me! I really don't feel I have anything more to say about this mess."

Cheryl smacks her lips, "Man, there is nuthin like an ice cold beer!

Karen, now for real, tell us and just between us…why didn't you want to press charges against this sailor dude who stuck his hand in your coochy?"

"Seriously, it's like I said, I talked to some other people and it just isn't worth it. I know it's 2016, but for real, the military has made some changes with regards to their rules and severity of the punishment, but they haven't done anything about the hearts of the sailors that just devalue women.

I mean, I still hear sexist comments every day. Like one of the female supervisors told a maintenance chief the plane wasn't ready for pre-flight so you know what he did? He waited for her to go to lunch, called one of her junior male workers down and told them to inspect it. Said she was probably on the rag and wasn't thinking clearly. The plane needed to go and they didn't want to blow the mission time."

"Well what happened?" asked Dawn.

"The junior sailor understood what they were asking him to do, which was go behind his supervisor's back. But that would mean he would be in her sights from now on and seen as a traitor to her. So when he went to get his tools, he called her on his cell phone and told her what he was doing. She told him to go ahead check the equipment and she'd deal with the chief when she got back."

"Did he say the plane was ok to fly or pre-whatever?" asks Cheryl.

"No, he agreed with his supervisor's assessment and the chief had the item repaired. The plane left about 20 minutes late, but the mission was successful."

"What did the supervisor do? I bet she cussed them out!" said Cheryl.

"No, she didn't. See, she understands the game so she didn't say anything. She allows them to think they have the upper hand while she maintains her dignity and respect of the sailors in her shop. She protects them from fall-out from the higher ups and they protect her.

It's a dance, and most times it's not clear who is leading the dance, but if you try to buck the system, you come out in the end jacked up.

No matter what the nice framed, mounted on the wall, guidelines say, when the investigators are gone, you are left with those same people."

"I thought the military had changed, I mean the way they talk about taking care of their veterans and stuff makes being in the service seem cool," says Dawn.

"Dawn, what kind of work do you do?" asks Karen.

"I'm a principal at one of the middle schools."

"Ok, so if I look up your school's website, will your classrooms actually look like the pictures I'd see?"

"Girl no! We don't have that kind of fancy furniture and no one working there looks like those well dressed polished people on the web!"

"So what's it like working there? Do you have factions and cliques?"

"Karen, you are so right...nothing is what it seems anymore," says Dawn, as she takes a bite of her fried pickle.

"Who is running this kitchen in this place?" asks Dawn. "I mean to say these fried pickles are the BOMB!"

"Maybe we should order some for our last meeting!" says Cheryl.

Dawn says, "Naw you can't eat these with just anything, I mean these things need liquor with them to bring out the flavor! And I don't think Denise will allow liquor in the meeting!"

"What do ya'll think about Denise?" asks Karen.

Cheryl says, "I mean she's alright I guess. She doesn't say a lot, but I guess that's her role in all this. I wonder what her story is?"

Dawn asks, "Why do you think she was a rape victim too?"

"Why would you think that?" asks Karen.

Cheryl takes a sip of her beer and says, "Well most addiction counselors are recovering addicts themselves, so I'm just wondering if she was raped or something and that's how she got into this business. I mean this is some tough shit to listen to every day and all day! I wonder if she has a therapist too."

Dawn says, "I'm gonna bring it up in the next group!"

"You are not!" exclaims Karen.

"Why not? Watch me do it! Now, I want to know who this person is that's listening to our stories. Why shouldn't we expect her to share something with us?"

Speaking into a recorder…

"The autopsy of Ayda Espina is complete. Hispanic female, weight 195.3 pounds, height 5 feet 2 inches, obese, dyed black hair, no apparent previous surgeries, all adult teeth and left foot shows signs of a bunion.

Stomach contents include: crab and guacamole dip, tortilla chips, flat bread, cherry pastry, 10 ounces of a red wine and four Alprazolam, also known as Xanax.

Lungs had approximately 0.3 teaspoons of water in each; noting time of death, it appears most of the water was released into the bloodstream prior to body being found.

It is my opinion that Ayda Espina's death is ruled as an accidental overdose of Alprazolam which caused her to fall off the floating lounge chair into the pool water; whereby she breathed in pool water, and being unconscious she drowned.

Autopsy signed, Dr. Wayne Ellis, NPI number 1112020304, Medical Examiner, Morganville West Virginia."

Dr. Ellis hits send and his notes will be transcribed by a service the county employs. Once it's typed, a copy of the report will be sent to the Morganville police department and they will close their case.

Dr. Ellis' last action with Ayda Espina is to sign and record her death certificate.

Once that's done, he takes out his cell phone and calls Frank Walsh.

"Hey, tell that nosey wife of yours that there is no homicide. Miss Espina died from and accidental overdose of Xanax and then she fell in the pool. Remind her she better not repeat it to anyone or there will be no more fish fries! Yeah dude, keep your woman in check! Night!"

Dr. Ellis drops the Ayda Espina's death certificate in his secretary's "to do" bin and leaves for the night, thinking about the dozy of an autopsy he has tomorrow! Guts all out of her ass! Jesus, what is going on in this town?

Paradigm shift…

Sitting on the front porch watching humming birds enjoying their nectar, Lynn is drinking a cup of Oolong tea and thinks over the past seven weeks of group. So many things have changed, yet nothing really has changed. How can that be?

No, Lynn, you've got to be honest with yourself this one time! How do you really feel about Donovan Tate's death? So many emotions have surfaced within me. I really don't feel glad he's dead. I mean, he didn't kill me or anything.

But he did kinda kill my spirit right?

Lynn has been searching for everything she can on Donovan. Seems by all accounts he was a changed man. He served all his time without requesting parole and he never filed an appeal.

One site has an interview from his daughter, the same little girl I was trying to reunify him with.

She said, "My dad was a hateful man before he went to prison. I didn't want to visit him but when I turned 21 years old I felt it was time. I asked him why he hurt that foster care worker when she was just trying to get us back together.

My father didn't have an answer for me but he said he himself had been raped while in jail and he guess now he really understood what he did and how wrong it was."

When asked if she forgives her father, his daughter replied, "It's not for me to forgive him. I would ask his victim if she was ever able to forgive him."

So Lynn sits and ponders that question… Can I forgive him for what he's done to me? Can I separate out what the consequences of that day are versus the choices I've made for myself? Can I really, honestly say that the wrong choices I've made are Donovan's fault?

I've had a good life all-in-all haven't I? A loving and trustworthy husband, three beautiful, strong and independent children, two wonderfully spoiled grandchildren! Our home is paid off, we have good health…so what is so wrong with my life?

I was raped that's what's wrong…Lynn places her cup on the table and stands. She walks around the outside of her house and continues to think. After several trips around the house she has made a decision about her life.

It's my fault that I'm so sensitive…no it's my choice I'm sensitive and I let people get to me.

I am a helpful person because I want to help people. The rape didn't take that away from me.

I am hurt more than I am angry…that is a choice too…right?

I've never taken medication, but maybe I should, to help with this anxiety. I have to start admitting I'm the one that can or can't fix something that I feel is wrong with me. I've been blaming all my choices on Donovan and him raping me.

That man doesn't know anything about who I became. I don't know him either. I don't know anything about his daughter and what became of her.

But I do know my kids and I know I've loved them, educated them and taught them to give back to their communities. My kids don't even know I was raped. They love and respect me for being the person I am.

He didn't break my spirit because I didn't allow him to.

Why haven't I been able to see that before now?

Why am I so worried about pleasing other people then? I want people to like me. I want them to let me take care of them.

Where does that come from?

Lynn continues to walk around her home. She remembers snippets from her childhood.

Lynn grew up 10 miles from her current home. She was three of eight children and her family was always doing something in the community. Lynn can't remember a time when her parents weren't hauling them down the dirt road to town so they could help out a neighbor.

Lynn and her siblings used to sit in the back of the truck and sing songs and play games or if they had any left, throw crumbs to the birds and squirrels.

Lynn stops and looks up to the sky…Donovan Tate, I forgive you for making your choice my problem all those years ago…but now it's time for me to also forgive myself for being the person I am.

Maybe if I embrace myself, perceived flaws and all, I'll feel freer to be Lynn Febus…who ever that may be.

So you've got nothing to hide…right?

Holly comes home from work and has take-out from the steak place near her apartment. She loves their garlic red mashed potatoes and cheesy broccoli. She plans to wash it all down with an ice cold soda.

No workout tonight since Dani and her "man" have plans. They have to meet with the wedding planner for some final decisions.

It's not like I'm angry or anything, just jealous, I guess. I bet Dani doesn't invite me to her wedding. She comes off like we're friends, but she doesn't include me in any of the wedding stuff. I'd like to be invited and I would get her a nice gift from the A-Z Emporium too.

But, I'm never included in stuff. I know people feel something is wrong with me…that's why Danny Clark picked me to rape.

There's a knock at the door…who can that be? Nobody comes to visit me except my mom and she didn't say she was coming anytime soon.

"Miss Chism, it's Det. Hill, Morganville PD."

Cops! What the hell do they want from me? I bet it's about Danny! What am I gonna do?

Holly pees a little in her panty liner and starts to bite her thumbnail.

"Miss Chism, are you there? I won't take up much of your time."

With knife in hand, Holly goes to the door and says, "Can you please put your ID up to the peep hole, please?"

Ruth pulls her badge and places it in front of the peep hole.

Holly reads the badge and says, "Hold on please, I need to pull on some pants."

She runs to her cell phone and calls the police department.

"I have someone at my door who says she's Det. Hill, badge number is 0497; before I open the door I want to confirm she is who she says she is!

I work at the courthouse and we had a training that said we should do this before just opening our door to someone who says they're the cops. I mean these days a girl…"

"Miss, please! It's alright Det. Ruth Hill is a current officer with our department."

"Oh…ummm, thanks for that." Holly hangs up and goes back to the front door. She opens it to a smiling Ruth Hill.

"Sorry for that, I wasn't expecting anyone and I just got home from work. Ummm… what is this about?"

"May I come in Miss Chism? I promise it won't take long. I just have some questions about Daniel Clark."

Holly's stomach goes queasy and there will be no steak and cheesy broccoli tonight.

"Ummm…ok, yeah…come in please…sorry…do you want to stand or sit…I mean you can sit if you want."

Ruth chooses to sit in the kitchen nook since the apartment is sparsely furnished. Ruth pulls out a chair and sits. Holly takes the other chair.

"Were you about to cook?" asks Ruth.

"Cook? No…why do you ask?"

"You have a knife in your hand," says Ruth, nodding toward the knife in Holly's right hand.

Holly looks down and drops the knife on the table. "Oh my God I am so sorry! Please don't shoot me or anything! I'm sorry…I was scared and had the knife!"

Holly jumps up and puts the knife in the kitchen sink. She returns to the table and takes her seat.

"Please calm down Miss Chism! I just want to ask you a few questions about Daniel Clark.

Do you live alone Miss Chism?" asks Ruth, looking around the small apartment.

"Yes ma'am I do. Ummm...I haven't seen Danny, that's what we called him back home for a lot of years. Sorry I can't help you."

Holly starts biting her thumb skin. She has been putting Neosporin on her fingers every night to help them heal from the skin picking she did after the last group meeting.

They stopped bleeding, but are still very sensitive and they hurt when she bends her thumb, index, and middle fingers on both hands. But right now, she doesn't care and starts to pick at a small area on her thumb.

Ruth watches her carefully and proceeds...

"Miss Chism, is it true Daniel, or as you know him, Danny Clark raped you when you were an intern at Richmond Memorial hospital?"

Holly pees in her panty liner...

"What in the world kind of question is that officer, I mean detective...ummm...wait what? Why would you ask me such a thing?"

"Miss Chism, I promise you I'm just trying to investigate a murder and I need to get some background information."

"Well...why...I mean Danny didn't live in Morganville. My mom told me he was killed in Richmond, so why does it matter to you?

I'm not trying to be a smarty or anything, I'm just asking."

"Fair enough, but please answer my questions, then I'll answer your questions."

"Ummm….I don't want anyone to know it ok?"

Internal dialogue…

Ruth…Yes! Tell it girl!

"Yes, I understand, and I will not disclose anything you tell me as long as it's not pertinent to my open investigation."

Internal dialogue…

Holly…What in the hell did she just say?

"Ummm…I guess…ok…" biting more skin 'til the area starts to bleed. Holly looks horrified that Ruth is watching what she just did. Holly sits on her hands and looks at Ruth.

Finally I can tell…

Holly takes a deep breath and blurts out, "Danny Clark did put a knife to my throat and had sex with me. He put me in the shower and made me take a bath to wash away the evidence. I moved here and never told anyone. Not even the ladies in my group know the real truth. Danny said I didn't have any proof so I made up a story to the group that he just touched me, but that…"

Holly sits looking slack-jawed at Ruth. She can't believe she just blurted out her secret to a stranger!

"Sorry, but what kind of group are you talking about Miss Chism?"

The little hairs on the back of Ruth's neck stand at military attention.

"I go to a survivor's rape group at the Rape Crisis Center every week."

Ruth maintains a poker face, "Really, and has that been helpful to you?"

"Well, I don't know if helpful is the right word. I've met some other people like me and I guess that's a good thing.

I mean wait…I don't mean its good they are there or what happened to them was good…"

"It's ok, I understand what you meant, please continue."

"Well our group started off with 10 members but now we're down to nine. But we still have good talks and the next meeting is our last cause, it'll be over."

"During the group, did you discuss Danny and how you felt about him?"

"Well sort of, but not fully…I never really talked about my true feelings."

Ruth asks, "Why not, if that's not too personal for you to answer?"

"Well, I guess 'cause I don't feel comfortable talking about it. I guess I feel like a freak and I don't want to see it in other people's eyes.

It's kinda hard to explain…I don't talk or express myself as well as some of the other women."

"Miss Chism do you know of anyone who would want to hurt Danny?

Do you know if he raped any other young women?"

"No, I don't know nuthin about Danny after I left Richmond. I never even talked about him, for real, until my mom called, right in the middle of our last group session.

I stepped out and took the call. I didn't want to stay gone from the meeting too long, so I told my mom I would call her back. She doesn't know I'm attending meetings, so I told her I was working late and my boss was nearby."

"Well you sure came up with a quick enough story Miss Chism. Are you always so quick on your feet?"

"I guess…if I'm scared enough…what I mean is…I was afraid I would get into trouble for being out of the group for too long.

The ladies, especially Penny, were really pissed that night!

Penny and Yvette were jumping on everybody! I didn't want them to get on me! So I…"

"Wait, you said Penny and Yvette? What are their last names?"

"Ummm…I said their names?

Sorry, we aren't supposed to identify people outside the group!

Shit! I'm sorry officer…I mean Det. Hill."

"I understand Holly, and I shouldn't have asked you their names. I have a degree in counseling, and I should know better myself. Let's do this part another way ok?"

"Ok…"

"Did you kill Danny?"

"No way! I was at work every day! You can check my job! But please, don't tell them why you're doing it ok?

It would be so embarrassing if they knew about the rape and stuff."

"Wouldn't it be more embarrassing if they thought you were involved in a murder investigation?"

"Well...no...the rape is more embarrassing! Please Det. Hill can I go now?"

"Well, Miss Chism, you are home, so you don't have to ask to go!

I'm almost done, just let me ask this, how did your group react when you told them Danny was dead?"

"Well, Lynn was shocked cause her guy was killed too! After he got out of jail he was shot in the head.

I looked him up on the internet, so I wouldn't have to ask Lynn for details and upset her.

I'm sure if Ayda was alive she would've told me to pray or something!"

Holly starts laughing and says, "But all in all, they were all supportive. Even the lady who is a co...sorry someone in your line of work, thought it wasn't so bad he was dead."

Ruth's mind is going a hundred miles per minute. Holly, not only put some of the pieces together, but has outlined the entire puzzle. These murders are somehow connected to this group. I bet my life on it!

Pieces come together…

Ruth picks up a salad and heads back to the office after questioning Holly. It's a shame that girl is so slow…she gave me the names of four group members after having a near heart attack just moments before for slipping out one name. So there is an "Yvette, Lynn, Ayda and Penny."

Ok, so let's look at this…Ruth goes to the white board near her desk and starts to write it all out…

Y – uncle killed

A – ?

L – rapist killed

H – rapist killed

P –

Before she can put anything next to "P"… one of the desk officers says, "Det. there is a lady here to see you about Det. Darling."

Ruth goes to the front desk and the woman is pointed out.

"Yes, ma'am may I help you? I'm Det. Ruth Hill."

They shake hands and the woman says, "Well my name is Denise Wallace and I'm concerned about Det. Penny Darling."

Ruth and Denise leave the building and take a short walk behind the building to the smoking and relaxation area. They are alone…

"Well Det. Hill, I'm sorry to bother you, but I'm facilitating a group of women at the Rape Crisis Center. I hate to break a confidence, but…"

"It's ok, Miss Wallace," says Ruth. "I know Penny attends a group there."

289

"Really; well great, and please, call me Denise!"

"Ok, Denise, what is your concern?"

"Well Penny has verbalized some very negative self talk recently and I was worried she would hurt herself. She did send me a text message saying she's ok, but I am still worried.

I left you a voice mail message after our last group and when I didn't hear from you I thought I'd better come in person and follow-up."

"Sorry, Denise, I haven't had the chance to listen to my voicemail. I've been investigating a murder here that took me out of town. But anyway I'm back, and I do have a few questions that I hope you can answer."

"I'll try…as long as I don't have to break anymore confidences!"

"Ok, I'll ask this and you just say yes or no…ok?"

"Let's hear the question detective."

"Has your group experienced deaths? Meaning, a member died and or any of the women's rapists died since this group started?"

Denise looks around the area and seeing no one says, "Yes, yes we have had deaths."

After thanking Denise for her concern for Penny, Ruth returns back to the white board in her office.

One of the ladies in the rape support group is a killer…I just know it! But who…what do I do if it's my partner, Penny?"

Denise goes home and rethinks her conversation with Det. Hill. I don't regret verbalizing my concerns about Penny…it was time.

Day of the last group…

Penny calls her mom, "Mom, it's me Penny…how are you?"

"I'm fine Penelopie. How are you? How's the house…I mean *your* house?"

"Mom, look, I have a meeting tonight but I'd like to come up there and see you tomorrow if that's alright."

"Why do you want to see me Penny? I really am not up to fighting with you over the phone or face to face."

"No, mom I don't want to fight. I want to say some very important things to you, but face to face.

It's just time mom for us to move on with our relationship. Don't you agree?"

"No, I don't agree Penelopie! But when has that ever stopped you from having your selfish way? Fine come up here if you want, but don't plan to stay too long alright.

In case you forgot, the anniversary of your father's death is in two days or doesn't he matter to you anymore?"

Damn! Penny had forgotten her mother picked this date to mark his death, but she wasn't going to tell her mother that. Since her father's body was never found they have no idea what really happened to him or when; her mother changes the "death date" and Penny feels it's to keep him all to herself and not allow Penny to mourn with her. Her mother is really fucked up.

"Mom, I'll see you tomorrow." Penny hung up the phone and walked to the bathroom. Time to get ready for the group…

Ruth tried to call Penny, but it went straight to voicemail.

Looking at the clock and noting the time; she's probably getting ready for the last group meeting. Maybe I'll just wait until tomorrow to speak with her. She's been in the group and has a better take on those ladies than I do. I refuse to believe Penny has anything to do with these killings.

If anyone in that group is psycho and angry enough to kill someone, it's Yvette Dyson.

I'm gonna check that chick out some more.

Denise prepares the table with gourmet cupcakes, bottles of juice, teas, sparkling water, along with the regular staple of coffee and bottled water.

She arranges the chairs with a little more space in between so people don't feel too boxed in. The final meetings can be very emotional for people. They have come to feel safe with each other and often times can feel that when a group ends there also goes a moment in their lives that was, for the first time, raw and honest.

Without fail, Holly is the first to arrive.

"Hi Denise, ummm, is it alright that I bought some flowers for the table?"

"Awww, Holly that is so thoughtful of you! Yes of course, place them right in the middle of the table."

"I just wanted to say thank you to all the ladies, but I couldn't think of what to get each of them. Besides, I don't have that much money this month. I kinda ordered quite a few new movies on the demand movie channel."

She hangs her head and starts to pick at her thumb with her index finger.

"Holly, a nice gesture doesn't have to be large or even manifest outwardly. The fact you wanted to do something to say thank you is enough."

Holly, smiles and stops picking at her thumb and say, "Do you think people will think something bad about me that I bought the flowers and they didn't bring anything?

Some people get mad or feel some kinda way when you give them a gift and they don't have one for you."

"Holly, what someone else feels is their business. You are only responsible for your feelings. Speaking of feelings…how are you doing with the death of that guy who sexually assaulted you?"

"Well…ummm…I'm ok, I guess…I do have something to say to the group about it. I haven't been completely honest with them…or with myself, I guess."

"Well it sounds like a consequence of his death is it has allowed you to move forward in your recovery."

"I guess…and I may have helped the police too." Holly says picking up a cupcake.

"Really! How?"

"Well there was this detective that came to my apartment and was asking me questions about Danny. She said she was in Richmond because she was investigating a murder here and something about it made her go to down to Richmond. Well she didn't actually say she went to Richmond, just that she was out of town.

I guess she thinks they may be related, but I told her I didn't kill Danny or anyone else. I sure hope she believes me."

Holly doesn't think it's important to add she was also questioned about members of the group. Besides, there's Dani!

Holly moves to stand next to Dani as she signs in, "Hey Dani how did the wedding planner meeting go?"

Denise's eyes follow Holly and Dani to their seats. Denise continues to set-up but she is wondering if it was Det. Hill who questioned Holly and what murder is being investigated in Morganville that may be related to a Richmond, Virginia murder.

Yvette is the last to arrive and she'll have sit next to Holly and Denise. Oh joy!!!

She knew she would have to sit by somebody stupid! That's what she gets for not taking clothes to work with her. There is no way I'm coming in here in my scrubs! Hell I'm in those things enough during the day.

Denise opens the group by saying what a humbling experience it has been observing the changes each woman has exhibited throughout this process. I would like to encourage everyone to partake of the goodies! If you don't eat them here, please take them home with you.

Imani thinks she'll take some home to her parents. The counseling session went better than either of them expected. For once she is hopeful, but not crazy enough to share it with some of these judgmental bitches!

Dawn, Karen, and Cheryl are sitting next to each other and they sure didn't need any encouragement about eating! Each of them has three cupcakes and three bottles of sparkling waters; looks like they are getting their $5 worth of goodies.

Denise says, "Ok, so I'd like to begin discussing Ayda with the group. We really haven't talked a lot about her death."

Lynn says, "The newspaper says it was a possible accidental drowning."

Dawn says, "Well, I can't say who told me, but someone I know who is close to the investigation, said she accidently overdosed on Xanax and fell into the water. Then she drowned cause she was asleep."

"Really! Man Dawn you holding out on us!" says Cheryl.

"No I'm not! I just found out and I was asked not to spread it around. So I'm trusting my group to be careful with the information, until it comes out in the paper."

Denise says, "Well thank you Dawn for giving us closure with regard to what happened to Ayda. Anyone have anything to say about how they feel now that there is a cause of death?"

Silence...

"Ok, well I'll speak," says Penny.

"I feel like when Ayda talked about what happened to her was a sin against God I felt confused. Wasn't God supposed to protect us from evil? Why did he allow this stuff to happen to us? Where was He?"

Lynn clears her throat and says, "Ayda understood that God has a plan for us and it's our responsibility to accept His plan. I guess she was having trouble with accepting it like most of us."

Dawn says, "Yeah Lynn, I agree with you, but it also seemed like Ayda blamed herself for what happened. She just seemed so unhappy. Do you think the overdose was really accidental? I don't want to speak ill of the dead..."

Yvette says, "Well Dawn you got it straight from "someone close to the investigation" right? So if they say it was accidental that's all we know.

We can't know the mind of Ayda when she was taking those pills. Maybe she was addicted to them and became hyper-religious as a result of her "high". No way to know for sure."

"So, Yvette does religion or spirituality have a place in your recovery?" asks Denise.

"That's my business alright? What I personally believe and how it affects my life isn't for this group." Yvette takes a bite of her cookie and glares at Denise.

Dani says, "Well since this is the last group, I just gotta ask Yvette, have you achieved your goal for coming here? The reason I ask is because you point things out but you don't share a lot!

Like you *just* told us your uncle, the one who molested you, was murdered recently!"

Everyone starts to talk at once except Yvette who is staring at Dani like she's going to rip her eye lids off!

"What the fuck do you know about it, or *need* to know about it?" snarls Yvette.

"Well like Dawn, I know people too! When you sold the bar it was sent to the courthouse and I have friends who work there. They told me the bar would be open soon because some guy named Gene paid cash for it.

They said, "Yeah, I wish I were friends with Yvette Dyson, cause I bet she's gonna party and shop with all that money!" So I did an internet search and got your picture to go with the name.

Now how's that for a blond bimbo? Yeah I heard you going to your car after the third group...I guess you were talking on the phone to someone and telling them about the group members. Since I'm the only blond, I must also be the bimbo!"

Before Denise can interject...

"That's right on all accounts Dani…you're blond and I think a bimbo! Ray was my great uncle and he did molest me. He left me his fucking bar and I sold it.

What?!"

Dani is spent from her declaration and didn't prepare for a comeback. She sips her water and looks down at the floor. Yvette is fucking scary!

Cheryl says, "Yvette, girl you are something else! I know why you didn't tell us about the bar…'oh, cause it wasn't none of our business…right?"

"That's right it isn't!" Yvette looks angrily around the group.

Imani says, "Yvette can I ask you the same question you asked me…"

Yvette is ready for Imani's question and replies, "No Imani I don't feel like I sold myself. I didn't ask for the bar but I'll be damned if I was gonna let that money just roll out the door without me.

Fuck Ray, and fuck anyone who thinks otherwise!"

Denise says, "Ok, Yvette let's calm down some and focus on why we are here."

Yvette whirls around to face Denise, "Why are we here Denise?" asks Yvette.

"To talk about Ayda who died weeks ago! You should've asked us about how we felt then not at the end." Yvette finishes off her cookie and reaches for another.

Karen says, "She did ask us before…don't be mean to Denise! She's been really nice to us."

"She's paid to be nice to us Karen! I, on the other hand, am not paid to be nice to anyone after my nursing shift!"

"Ok, alright…does anyone have anything else to add about Ayda?" says a visibly shaken Denise.

Karen raises her hand, "Actually, I do…I just want to say that sometimes it's difficult to really acknowledge the negative stuff I feel because of my faith.

Sometimes it seems my faith hinders me because, like Ayda said, you feel guilty for being angry and questioning why something bad happened. That's all I have to say…thanks."

Silence…

Denise says, "Ok, let's review the goal statements you all made on the first night of group."

Denise grabs her clipboard from the floor and reads from a typed list.

Penny you stated your goal was to "not feel broken and used by a family member" how are you feeling tonight?"

Penny takes a long sip of her coffee and thinks, I'm not sure I want to die, but I still want to stop feeling this way.

She says, "Well, I'm not sure each day if it's worth it to get up, but I haven't tried to kill myself since this group started.

I admit that I think about death a lot and I wonder what life would be like without me in it. I have a lot to work on and I didn't realize how much until I came here and started to listen to my own voice sounding crazy as hell!"

You got that shit right, you are crazy as hell! Thinks everyone in the room except Denise.

"Thanks for your candor Penny. Can you talk a little more about why you have thought about self-inflicted death?"

"I told you all that last time…it's so cold and dark that it hurts to live in it. I don't know how to find meaning in my life! I don't believe it will get better or change! I just can't seem to make my mind think any other way!" wails Penny.

"Do you want to?" asks Lynn.

Penny just stares at her and then says, "I don't know what I want, but isn't it ironic that I'm a cop and I'm supposed to protect and serve…but I can't protect myself."

Imani asks, "Penny do you have any family or close friends that you can let in?"

"I have a mom who lives in Ohio, but she doesn't want in.

Please leave me alone for a little bit and move to the next person." Penny drinks her coffee and picks at an already bleeding hangnail.

"Cheryl you're next…your goal was to "decide if I should tell my husband about what happened"…have you decided?"

"Yeah, and I'd like to thank everyone for their contributions to the group meetings, but Karen helped me the most.

Yeah you! Don't look so surprised! Just hearing you talk about the consequences of telling really got me thinking about what I will lose and what is to be gained.

I've decided that this secret is going to the grave with me!

But what I can do now is work on this anger thang! I can't keep making my man pay for the actions of his brother."

Dani asks, "What are you going to do about your anger?"

"Dani I don't know for sure, but I'm going to start by thinking a little more before I speak and act.

I'm also gonna keep hanging out with Dawn and Karen! Those ladies are very smart, funny and...I've never had real girl friends before this group." Cheryl begins to cry.

"It feels good to be unafraid of the feelings inside my head. Karen and Dawn understand my outbursts, but will still challenge my ass if I'm too far outta character!

Thanks Dawn and Karen for being there."

Dawn and Karen come over and they hug Cheryl.

After they return to their seats, Denise asks Dawn if she has accomplished her goal of "moving to the next level of good mental health."

"I'm addicted to therapy! I know everyone probably knows it, but I need to say it out loud for myself.

I'm 56 years old and I have no idea what I'm still dealing with from 20 something years ago! I go to my therapist because I never forgave myself for getting drunk and walking back to the dorm alone.

My parents and school officials were angry and disappointed in my "poor decision" that night. I have been scared to make an independent decision ever since. For me it's not so much about the guy who raped me as it is the way I saw myself. I felt like I was so stupid and irresponsible for allowing myself to be in that situation.

Anyway like Lynn, Holly and Yvette...my offender is dead too. He was killed during that hostage thing at the Maryland A-Z Emporium.

Ya'll heard about it I guess."

Denise was drinking water and it spewed out of her mouth.

Choking, Denise says, "I'm sorry but that is a shocking thing to hear! I mean four of you ladies have experienced the death of your

300

rapist. I think that's some kind of weird anomaly…right Penny? Isn't that like, too much of a coincidence?"

Penny looks up and says, "No not really…death comes to us all." She closes her eyes and rocks in the chair.

Again they all think…Penny is crazy as hell!

Silence…

"Ok, Imani…your goal was to "try and feel what it's like to believe your life is really good," so where are you with that now?"

"Well, I'll keep it brief and hopefully not incur any judgments." She looks at Denise, but everyone knows she's directing her comments to Yvette and Penny.

"My feelings about my life are more positive. I'm really appreciative of all the support and feedback I got from the group.

But honestly, if my parents hadn't been shot, I'm not sure if I would feel this way. Or maybe I wouldn't be admitting it." Imani wanted to add…*I'm glad I came and honestly I'm glad this is the last meeting too…it's very intense in here sometimes and I don't feel like I'm equipped to deal with all of it.*

And no offense but Penny you are scary. But she doesn't…she just smiles and accepts a back rub from Lynn.

"Ayda's goal was to "be able to say it out loud," but she wasn't able to do that. It is my hope she found some peace while attending the group," says Denise.

Silence…

Internal dialogue…

Yvette…I think Ayda got messed with by a woman or something, cause she was tripping.

301

Cheryl…Maybe it was bestiality or something cause she was crying like some really bad shit happened to her!

Holly realizes she's holding her breath…please don't let them start fighting again about Ayda! It ain't right to fight and argue about a dead person. Awww, shut up Holly, you ain't gonna tell them that.

"Karen, you told us your decision was not to report the assault and making that decision was your goal. How do you feel about your decision and achieving your goal? asks Denise.

"I feel really good about my decision and I'm proud of myself for achieving my goal! I'm really glad I came to the group and met all of you.

Dawn and Cheryl are strong ladies, and I hope to continue to learn from them."

Denise says, "Ok, now it's your turn Holly…your goal was to "not be so nervous all the time"…how do you feel tonight?"

Internal dialogue…

Holly…Shit! Shit! Shit! I'm still nervous! I failed to reach my goal! I knew I wouldn't get it right. Everyone else got it right…'cept maybe Penny.

"Well…ummm…I guess I'm still kinda nervous, but maybe not as much as before.

I did ask some questions right? So I must not have been too nervous all the time." She looks around the group for confirmation that she is better.

They all nod their heads in encouragement.

"I do want to say something…it's kinda my new goal…see…ummm…ok, well, I didn't tell the complete truth about me and Danny. I guess I can say his name now since he's dead

302

right? Danny Clark didn't just feel me up and almost put his thing in me...he put a knife to my throat and made me have sex with him!"

Holly pees into her panty liner again. In anticipation, she is wearing a thicker pad tonight...just in case she's so nervous she really pisses her pants!

Dani is the first to respond, "Holly! Why didn't you tell us the truth about what happened to you? Oh my goodness you poor thing, why did you feel you needed to lie so much?"

Holly starts to tear up and says, "I never told anyone what happened. He made me take a shower so there wouldn't be any evidence on my body.

I just never thought anyone would believe me, so I just didn't say the whole truth. I told the intake girl just enough to get in this group."

Denise asks, "Why Holly? Why did you want to come to this group?"

"Because I'm tired of being sick and tired; I'm tired of being so scared I can hardly move about my own apartment!

I just want to feel normal...like when I'm in the gym with Dani...I feel like a real person; not someone who had "evidence" inside her, but can't prove what was done to her."

Silence...then Dawn starts to clap...Dani follows...then Cheryl, Imani, Karen, Lynn, Yvette and lastly Penny, all give Holly a sitting down clap ovation!

Holly just stares at them and then begins to grin. She realizes she has spoken up and the world didn't fall on her head!

Also, she didn't pee anymore in her panty liner!

Way to go girl!

After everyone settles down and each person, except Yvette and Penny, give her a hug, Denise continues.

"Lynn you are next, your goal was "to work through your fear of your offender getting released.""

"Well, I must say I'm no longer afraid!" She receives a small hand clap of praise.

"I've been beating myself up and feeling afraid or at least telling myself I'm afraid for far too long. I lost sight of all the wonderful blessings and accomplishments in my life.

If I don't know anything else, I know this…Donovan Tate is dead and Lynn Beverly Febus is alive and kickin!!"

Everyone claps again for Lynn.

"I'm next ya'll! I remember going after Lynn! So I think I said my goal was to "try and be present in my own life," is that what I said Denise?

"Yes it is Dani; so where are you tonight?"

"Well I feel like I've really been making strides keeping myself honest and present. With that said, I do have a bomb shell to drop on the group nation!"

She looks around all wide eyed and silly!

"My fiancé and I have called off the wedding!"

Silence…

"I know ya'll are probably wondering why?"

Yvette thinks…no not really!

"Well, I just started feeling like I was just replacing my first husband, like I was scared to be on my own or something.

I left momma and daddy's house to take up with my first husband. I've never really lived on my own and I want to see what that is all about.

My fiancé Knic, couldn't understand my need to hold off on the wedding for a little longer so I gave him a little of Yvette and Cheryl…told him to get the fuck on!!"

Leaning in her chair to look at Dani, Yvette fell out of her chair…literally fell out the chair in shock!

She quickly recovered and jumped back into her seat.

She was embarrassed as hell!

"Yep Yvette…see you shouldn't judge a book by its cover honey! I may look like a sexy bimbo, but I got some depth and ass kickin to me!

People have always let my looks and bright smile fool them into thinking about me things that ain't true about my character.

Before I shut up, I do want to say to Holly…I know I haven't been around a lot and that probably hurt your feelings, but there was a part of me that was embarrassed that I was ending my relationship.

I had you thinking I was all that and a bag of kale chips!

I really needed to be my honest and true self without worrying if you would judge me. So I kept you at arm's length…I'm sorry and I hope you and I can hang out at the gym more often."

Holly is speechless as she watches Dani eat a cookie! So she is human after all!

Holly just nods her head yes. This is friggin amazing!

Taking in a deep breath, Denise exhales and says, "Yvette you're the last one to give feedback on your goal…which was "to identify my anger nuggets and find a way to deal with them" how are you feeling tonight?

Yvette looks around the room and has no idea what she is feeling. "I can't believe this, but I have to agree with Holly, some group sessions back...I have no idea what I'm feeling!

This is foreign to me and I'm at a loss for words. I don't think I have any understanding of where my anger comes from. I guess maybe I'm still angry at my great-uncle, my parents and my extended family. No one did a damn thing to help me!

They helped themselves by beating the hell outta him but what did that do for me?

He had a long life and now he's gone. But I'm still here and so are all of them...using me to have something to talk about amongst themselves.

Gossiping mother-...sorry. I guess Denise I still have to work toward my goal."

Lynn says, "Well Yvette I think you have moved toward your goal, 'cause a little while ago, you wouldn't have stopped yourself from saying mother fucker!"

Everyone hoots and hollers with laughter...even Yvette.

Dawn says, "Denise, before we move on...I was wondering if you were sexually assaulted."

Silence...

"Why do you ask Dawn?"

"Well substance abuse counselors are usually people who are in recovery, so I just thought..."

"Does this look like a substance abuse group? For real Dawn stop analyzing everybody!" says Yvette.

"Well there's our Yvette again…being her true self!" says Dani smiling.

Denise says, "Dawn it is not a qualification that someone have a personal history with sexual assault to work at the rape crisis center. I hope that answers your question."

Silence…

Denise says, "Well ladies we are coming to the last 30 minutes of our group. I have been humbled by the awesome faith you all put in me to facilitate your group."

Everyone claps and says thanks Denise.

"I wasn't looking for praise, but thank you! As we come to a close, I'd like to give each of you the opportunity to write down a negative self statement you have said about yourself while in group. I want you to write it down and leave it here. Every time you think about it, just know it is in this box and not in your heart."

Denise holds up a black cardboard box.

She passes around clipboards that have pen and paper attached. After you finish, you may stick around and talk or leave. I will keep the room available to you for 30 minutes pass our usual time.

I am so proud of each and every one of you for showing up no matter what you were feeling. You are all such strong, funny, and smart women…but more importantly, you are all survivors! Well done ladies!

Denise stands and claps toward each woman.

Group 8 of 8 is over...and in the black box…

"It's my dad's fault I can't keep a boyfriend. He ruined me."

"I'm worthless like this and I'll never feel anything else."

"A piece of my puzzle is missing and it pisses me off!"

"I don't feel connected to people cause I'm not as smart as they are."

"All people see is sex with me and they think I'm a dummy."

"I need people to like me and need me."

"I don't know my own mind most of the time. I'm such a squash head!"

"I'm a closed circuit and I can't let anyone in."

"I don't know who I can trust to help me make decisions about my situation."

Denise takes the comments out of the box and one-by-one shreds them.

…score one for the survivor's team…

Long time coming...

Penny rises early and drives to Ohio to see her mother.

Ruth arrives at the office so she can check out Yvette Dyson.

Cindy, Denise's assistant, reads an email in which her boss says she's taking the day off because group is over and she needs a mental health day!

Well alright boss, your day off is mine too! Cindy pulls up an online clothing site and starts shopping.

Penny arrives at her mother's house around 10:30 am. She knocks on the door and waits almost 15 minutes before Charlotte opens the door.

"Well you're early aren't you Penelopie? Why so early?

I'm retired so there is no need for me to get up early. But I guess all you care about is getting up here and in my face!"

No hug, no warm greeting...nothing maternal at all...but I've got to do this.

Penny takes off her jacket and puts it on the back of the sofa. Her mother glares, but doesn't say anything. Penny knows Charlotte hates to have clothes lying around on the furniture, but for once, her mother is right about her...she selfishly just wants to get this over with.

"Mom, please tell me why you hate me so much.

Dad was so loving and gentle! How could he love someone like you?"

If Penny expected her mother to explode, she was going to be disappointed.

Charlotte took her time responding…"Penny, I don't hate you. I've told you that a million times. I just don't want to be a mother to you. I don't know why you find that so difficult to understand and accept. I gave birth to you and I helped raise you. What more do you want?"

"I want a normal mother-daughter relationship with you! Mom, why is that so hard for you to understand and accept?"

"Penelopie, I'm just not made that way. I'm sorry, but I chose who to show love to…I loved my parents and I showed them. I loved your father, very much, and I showed him. I'm sorry, but I don't have any love left to show you.

I feel it for you, but honestly, I'm just not interested in showing you."

Penny feels like she's been hit by a dump truck.

"So we don't have this conversation again, let me tell you a little something about your daddy!"

Penny places her hands over her ears and yells, "NO! NO! NO! You can't take him from me! Stop it mom! Please don't take my daddy away from me again!"

"Penelopie, no one can take your father from you. You just need to know the truth."

Charlotte opens an envelope that Penny only just noticed on the table.

Charlotte hands a small yellowed note card to Penny. "Read it Penelopie and then I have one more thing to show you."

Penny reads the note, written in a beautiful flowing handwriting, that isn't her mother's, "Honey, I miss you and I would never tell anyone where you are. Please contact me when you can! The signature read… *Your loving Wife…*

Penny falls down into the nearest chair. Her father was married before? It couldn't be; someone would've told her!

Charlotte rises and gives her daughter a photo. In it she sees a young woman holding a toddler in her lap. The little girl is smiling at the camera. The woman holding her is laughing at something out of camera shot.

Penny turns the photo over and screams! No! It can't be! She can't be my sister!

"Yes, that's your older sister and her mother, StephanieAnne…"

But before Charlotte can finish, Penny runs out the door and jumps in her car.

Charlotte picks up the letter and picture. She goes to close the door when a foot sticks in from the outside and stops her.

No…

Ruth is unable to find any evidence that Yvette had anything to do with the murder of her great-uncle Ray, Danny Clark or Donovan Tate.

She's now in her car and decides to check in on Penny. Last night was the last group session, so Penny should be coming off leave any day.

At Penny's house, there is no answer to the bell. Ruth looks through the windows and can't believe what she sees in one of the bedrooms!

Ruth uses the key Penny gave her for emergencies and enters the house.

In the guest room she finds taped to the walls pictures of the dead men! Under their pictures their names are typed: Ray, Danny, and Donovan.

There is also the movie schedule for the night the McCollins were shot!

Shit! Shit! Typed below are the details for the ambush at the garage!

Ruth turns around and sees a box on the floor. She gingerly opens it with an ink pen from her pocket. In the box is a very sharp bloody knife! Looks like some kind of specialty knife, like a paring knife!

Oh my God is this the knife used to kill Ray Jones and mutilate Danny Clark! No I can't be! I don't believe Penny would do this!

She picks through the box and finds a DVD that says "Pimp Gene's Golden Shower."

She struggles to form the thoughts in her mind...what the fuck is going on with my damn partner?

As she rationalizes, she thinks, obviously Penny is experiencing a psychotic break with reality. Shit!! Shit!!

What am I gonna do now? Before Ruth's mind can come up with a plan, she notices a little black bottle in the bottom of the box. The label reads, "Sarin."

Holy shit, we are definitely fucked today!

Sarin is a goddamn nerve agent! What is Penny doing with it?"

Ruth runs from the house, barely taking time to lock the door. She jumps in her car and dials Penny's number.

"Ruth, look I don't have time to talk right now! I'm ok, but I have something to do."

"Penny where are you?"

"I'm in my car and I'm headed back to Morganville from my mother's house in Ohio. I'll call you when I get back."

"No, Penny I need to see you now, how long before you get into town?"

"Look, Ruth, I'm not back on the clock yet, so leave me alone. I can't talk about anything right now."

Penny hangs up and puts her phone on silent.

"Penny! Penny!" screams Ruth into her phone. What should she do? Call the captain, put out a bulletin…what?!

Before she can decide her phone rings…

"Hello Det. Hill, this is Dr. Ellis, can you please come by my office immediately!"

Ruth arrives at the medical examiner's office…

Not only is Lt. Brogan there, but so is the Chief of Police! What the fuck is going on?

"Awww, Det. Hill I was just explaining my autopsy findings on the body of Miss StephanieAnne Eubanks…the cause of death was Sarin poisoning!

Seems it was mixed in with milk and molasses for some undetermined reason!

My assistant did a search and it seems the mixture is called a "cookie enema," used by the Amish to move the bowels of farm animals! But without the Sarin, of course!"

Lt. Brogan starts breathing hard and looking for the exit.

Chief Ritchie says, "Det. Hill are you alright? You look like you've been running a marathon or something."

Ruth says, "Ummm…yes sir…I just rushed over here as fast as I could. Dr. Ellis sounded urgent on the phone."

"Well hell yeah, detective, Sarin is very urgent!"

"Yes, Wayne we know that! Pull your shit together and stop yelling it all over the building," says Chief Ritchie.

Lt. Brogan says, "Isn't Darling due back from extended leave today or is it tomorrow?"

Ruth blinks her eyes until her mind clears, "She's on duty tomorrow sir."

"Well fuck it, we need her today! Find her and tell her the Chief said to pull her shit together right damn now!"

"Yes sir," says Ruth, as she turns and runs out of the building.

Where the fuck is Penny and what is she going to do now?

Shit, why didn't I think of it before…thinks Ruth as she sits at a traffic light…pulling her car over at the next curb, she calls the station and asks for Det. Darling's cell phone GPS location.

Ruth makes a u-turn and heads to Penny's location.

Well it's over now…

"What do we do now?"

"I don't know."

"You've wanted to die for so long and now you're not sure are you?"

"No I'm not. Maybe I've allowed myself to think about finding peace. Lynn said something about finding peace and acceptance.

I used to think I had accepted my past, but I never had a feeling of peace with it.

I was always looking for a magic explanation to explain it all away. I thought if I were smart enough, thin enough, cute enough, have enough friends, I could make the rest go away to some place that made it all better.

But I could never find a place that could keep my insecurities at bay.

Do you understand? I know in some part of your heart you understand what I'm trying to say?"

"Yeah, I hear you, but no I don't understand.

You've been so abusive toward yourself instead of seeking revenge. You've caused more harm to yourself than your cousin could have.

Why didn't you embrace your power? I became strong enough to control my emotions, manipulate them in a way that always brings me pleasure.

I eat when I want, and not when I see something that looks good.

I fuck when I want to not, cause some fine ass man wants to.

I even kill when I want, because I feel they deserve it or because I want the money. I am not beholden to the person behind the money, hell, I'd kill them too if I wanted."

"Will you kill me?"

"Yes, because you can't do it for yourself."

"Even if I don't want to die anymore?"

"You will always have a part of you that wants to die."

"How do you figure that?"

"Just the look of you screams you don't want to live your life. You screamed it when you called your lunatic fucked up mother and let her demean you.

Penny you want to die...I'm trying to help you do it quickly, instead of letting you suffer any longer."

"How did you know I called my mom?"

"That's not important now is it?"

"Please don't, not before I tell you something very important."

"Ok, my friend, what's that?"

"We're sisters."

Before another word is spoken, Det. Ruth Hill rushes in, with her gun drawn and pointed directly at Penny.

"Hands up bitch or I'll blow your damn head off!"

Penny grabs for Ruth's gun and a shot rings out from the gun.

Penny's sister dives to the left, while pulling out Penny's .380 Firestorm pistol. Penny has been so preoccupied lately, she never noticed her weapon was missing.

Her sister fires, striking Ruth in her right shoulder.

Ruth, falling to the floor, drops her gun.

Ruth's gun is kicked away from Penny and Ruth's reach…

Penny drops to her partner's side and starts to apply pressure to the wound.

Penny asks, "Ruth why did you point your gun at me?"

Ruth is moaning, crying and bleeding copiously.

Penny wiggles off her jacket to hold over the wound.

"Please, let me call her an ambulance!"

"Aw sugar, she ain't gonna die, right Ruth? Ruth's a tough old school mother fucker, she'll be ok."

"Ruth looks with disdain at Penny and spits out, "You are a cop! How can you take justice into your own hands Penny? Why did you do it?"

Penny, looking from Ruth to her sister, "What are you talking about? What did I do?"

Her sister says, "Wait for it Ruth…all will be revealed in a few minutes."

To Penny she says, "Now finish your little story,"

"I wanted to talk with you alone not over my shot partner!"

"Well sometimes you gotta embrace flexibility. That's always been a flaw in your personality; you're stuck too often on the "shoulds…woulds…perfect time looks like…"

"That may be but…"

"I'm running out of patience Penny. Continue, NOW…"

317

"Well, it's simple, we were fathered by the same man, but have different mothers."

"That's it?"

"Well yeah, why don't you seem shocked?"

"Ok, Penny, tell me about your dad. What was he like? What were his hobbies and shit?

Then I'll tell you about *my* version of daddy."

"Ok, well daddy was…"

"You've got about 10 minutes for a condensed version or old Ruth is gonna lose that arm."

"Shit, sorry Ruth!

Ok, daddy was a very smart and funny man. He was compassionate and helped people on our street. He attended church and he donated his time to the local soup kitchen. He used to take me with him on the weekends.

I spent more time with him than I did with my mom, but I know they both loved me.

You know, my dad died during a trip my parents took one winter before Christmas when I was almost 16 years old. It was supposed to be a family pre-Christmas trip but I got pneumonia two days before we were due to leave.

Since my grandparents were coming for the holiday they came earlier to stay with me. Long story short, my parents went up to Bear Lodge at Massanutten Mountain and only my mother came back.

Dad used to like getting up before the rest of us and go for a walk. Mom said he left for his walk and never came back.

They searched for him, but never found a trace of him.

As for how I found out about us, well I was having it out with my mom and she showed me a letter from your mom, his first wife. As if that wasn't enough she showed me a picture of you and your mom. On the back of the picture it said, StephanieAnne and you when you were four years old.

So in a nutshell that's the story of who our father was and how I found out we were sisters.

Where is your mom? She kinda looked familiar but in my haste to get to you I just couldn't place her face.

Did you know he was dead? Is that why you befriended me, to find him?"

"Cute story, touching…and my mom's dead; no, I didn't use you to find out anything about him.

Yes, I knew he was dead; because I killed his ass!"

Ruth stills and looks from Penny to this woman she knows as Denise, the rape crisis center facilitator! Her mind can't quite comprehend what the fuck is going on!

"Oh, and Ruth, Penny didn't kill anyone…I did…I'm an assassin, not some fucking group leader! I'm just really good at pretending to be something I'm not.

I'm just here so I can tie up some family business."

"What? Why?" cries Penny. This can't be happening; she didn't expect any of this.

"Then who are you…?"

Laughing and shaking her head, Denise says, "Who the fuck knows anymore? My new name isn't important; I never keep them for long anyway.

319

See Penny, I don't exist. I haven't since *our* father changed me."

Denise leans against the wall, gun still pointed directly at Penny's head.

"Cause before he became "*Mr. Upstanding,*" he was a woman beater and a child molester.

We are related, that's true, but we are nothing alike. You went down one path and I the other.

I've often wondered why people make the choices they do. Why two people can share the same type of trauma yet make different life choices.

You're a "*goodie too shoes*" cop who internalizes EVERYTHING and me...I'm the judge and executioner...I don't internalize anything...anymore.

Let me tell you about my so called childhood, and for Ruth's sake, I'll keep it brief.

My first memory of the molestation is an incident at my paternal grandmother's house. Grandma gives me a hot bath and is whispering in my ear that I'd better not tell anybody about what happens when I come over her house. I don't understand what she means, but I know it's linked to whatever my uncle did to me.

Funny how memories get buried, then become cloudy and BOOM, everything comes rushing back and slaps you the fuck in the face! So when I was 19 years old I realized why I couldn't "see" what was happening to me because my uncle used to put a pillow over my face.

I don't know how long or how many times he assaulted me. I think he was around 14 years old at the time, but I'm not sure. No worries though, I took care of him in a satisfying way.

You know that dog that raped Lynn back in the day? Well Donovan Tate was the uncle that was allowed to rape me by my paternal grandmother.

I couldn't protect myself back then but I waited patiently for his release from prison. Then I blew his fucking brains out! I even put a pillow in front of his face like he used to do with me!"

Penny is too stunned to respond. She just can't make her brain process all this new information.

Internal dialogue…

Ruth…Damn! Crazy runs in this fucking family!

Denise continues, "While *our* uncle abused me, *our* father had a game of his own going on with me.

He would close the curtains to the bedroom window. He would tell me to close my eyes and not open them or a monster would come and get me.

I can still feel him kissing my neck and inserting his finger in my ass. I'm ashamed to say the episodes still sends a tingle through my body.

Isn't it sick how the body responds to sexual stimuli without our permission? Hell it's still the fastest way to turn me on…anyway for that reason; I have only allowed sex as a way to kill a mother fucker!

I used to wonder if it's because of him I like being kissed on the neck or is it because it's how I really feel.

Guess we'll never know since I was never given the opportunity to sexually mature on my own, without help from our perverted assed daddy!

See you thought you knew him, but he was an evil son-of-a-bitch!

321

Close your damn mouth and blink your eyes, before I shoot one of them out! You look like a leaf tailed gecko and it's freaking me out!"

Penny blinks, but can't for the life of her close her damn mouth.

Denise, continues, "See *my* daddy was the master of the seduction game. He even used props like the zodiac sign poster on the wall in the living room. It was a velvet poster of different sexual positions for each sign.

I even did an internet search of it to make sure it was real. It was hard there for awhile to tell reality from fiction. But when I found it, I cried for hours and felt sick to my stomach.

Seeing it also made all my memories real. Finally it felt like I wasn't just making it up in my head, cause that shit actually happened.

Anyway, he would ask me to close my eyes, point to a picture on the poster. Whichever one my finger landed on that's the position we would do.

I can remember doing the one where I had to sit on his lap with my chest to his chest. We did that one and the 69 position a lot.

My dreams were always very vivid and they lingered with me. If I had to remember more than what I did, I don't think I could've handled it.

But none of that matters now…I'm a survivor…right!"

Denise laughs and swipes at the lone tear running down her cheek.

"See I'm not crazy, I was made to be this angry person and then I was recruited to become a killer.

I became the monster daddy used to scare me about.

Penny, we are half of the same broken record, only I chose to become a killer and I'm as good at it as you were a cop. Maybe the reason you stopped wanting to be a cop is because you liked the little taste of the dark side you felt in group when you went off on Imani.

Might I add, bravo on that! You really expressed yourself and I was proud to be your sister! But that didn't last long, and once again, you showed your true colors.

Penny, you're weak. Just like your crazy mother, who, you don't have to thank me, I took care of after you left her this morning."

Penny's heart has just about stopped. Her mother is dead?

Ruth continues to moan and tries to reach down for her ankle weapon. Maybe Penny will notice her moaning and understand what she's trying to do. If only Ruth could get Penny to look down at her!

But before Penny can snap out of it and take the hint, Ruth is shot in the head.

Penny screams and lays Ruth on the floor screaming her name over and over. She is crying and covered in her partner's, no her friend's, blood and brains.

When Penny looks up and turns to Denise she also sees the gun pointed directly between her eyes.

"Now sis, we are alone and I'll tell you how your daddy really died...

Payback is a bitch!...

"Good you're waking up! I didn't want to start until you were fully awake. We should experience this together like all the other fun times we've shared."

Daddy becomes aware of his predicament. His arms are held by metal armbands and he can't move his legs. He's lying on his back with his head strapped between two cushions, like they were made to keep his head in place but gently.

The table feels weird next to his skin. So I must not have on a shirt he thinks. He's unable to tell what the table is made of, wood maybe, it feels unexpectedly comfortable as if it's been worn and the wood softened.

"Can you speak yet?" I ask my father. He can't see me, just knows my voice comes from the shadows.

He tries his voice and realizes he can indeed speak.

"Yes I'm awake and I can speak my darling daughter. He says looking around for me.

"Now since we've established that, I have every expectation that you will tell me what the fuck is going on!"

Laughing and coming into view, I lean over his face and say, "Well Pops, I'm here to show you how much I love you. Whatcha think about that?"

"Well, honestly, I'd really like that! We haven't spent quality time together since you were what four or five years old? I've often wondered how you got along."

My stomach tightens and I taste bile on the back of my throat, but I don't show my disgust. I feel snot trying to drip out my nostril, but I won't let it. It's an awful weakness of the body.

A tear or snot falls when I'm overly emotional. Could be anger, frustration, sadness or melancholy, and my body will have a small leak. It's stupid really and hard as hell to control.

Besides the leak, in a small corner of my heart, I had hoped he would take this opportunity to apologize for killing my spirit, my humanity all those years ago.

But he was a monster, the very monster he used to warn me about. I hear his threat so clearly, if I told what he was doing to me, the monster would come after me and kill me then gobble me whole.

"Well Pops, I've gotten along pretty well since we last spoke. Remember how you used to tell me stories about a monster that would kill me if I told our secret?

Well I made myself strong then I set out to meet that monster. I found him and now I'm going to gobble him whole."

Pops' smile disappears and he looks directly in my eyes.

His eyes widen and in Pops' fashion, he started to yell, cuss and threatens to beat the shit outta me when he gets free. He tried to move, but of course he couldn't. I've got him securely held to the wooden table that was identical to the dining room table we used to have in our house when I was a little girl.

It looks just like the table he used to bend me over so he could fuck me up the ass.

He would make me look at the wall with a poster of zodiac signs depicted in sexual positions. After a few pokes up the ass, he would allow me to pick a sign and we would do that sexual position on the table or on the dining room chair that he had also made me sit during meals.

I decided to share with him about the table and he goes quiet and still. He looks me in the eye and sees, for the first time, my eyes are just like his, brown with a splash of gold.

They are cold, unfeeling, dead, but more importantly, mine are deadly. People used to say I looked like my father, especially around the eyes.

He used to think it was funny when people would say I walked just like him too, never bending my knees. No one ever thought I walked stiffly because I was being molested, at four and five years old by a grown sadistic man.

I say to him, "Pops, you taught me that people can be controlled, manipulated and broken. I'm going to teach you those same lessons, but I'm going to add one more lesson to all that…people can change when they're being tortured and humiliated before dying.

 Are you ready for your lesson?"

His eyes follow me around the room. His lips have gone dry and there is a slight twitch to his right hand.

"I thought you'd like some music from your era to get you in the mood."

I put on the playlist.

 "I've made two hours of 60's music. That should be just enough teaching time."

Then I step out of his line of sight.

"Wait what are you doing?" Pops yells as he's shaking his head from side to side trying to see what I'm up to.

I arrive back to the table standing by his right side.

"Well I'm going to duct tape your balls to your dick so everything will be at attention. I remember your dick always being at attention when you showed it to me…right?

See, I really want to take you down memory lane Pops. If we don't understand the past we are going to repeat it right?

326

Well I've never understood why you had sex with little girls and why I was one of those little girls.

I don't understand what there was about me that you hated so much that you would ruin any chance I had of a normal life. I don't understand…so we are going to repeat the past until one of us understands."

I grab his shriveled up parts with one hand, and with the other I slap a long piece of duct tape around them.

"I've even gotten the tape with a camouflage pattern. That way we still keep what we're doing hidden and secret!"

I laugh cause this shit is funny!!! Camo so no one can see it!!!

"Don't you get it? Awww come on you used to have such a healthy sense of humor back in the day. Don't worry, no one will see what I do with your little weenie except maybe one other person, but we won't go there yet."

As the music plays, he's just lying there, not saying a word.

"Do you admire me Pops? Is that what you're thinking?"

I start wheeling the utility cart closer to the table.

"I don't know what to think, 'cept my little girl is crazy."

"Ding, ding, ding wrong answer Pops! I'm not crazy. I'm angry and extremely smart. Now, that's a potent combination in itself, but then I've sprinkled in a little revenge and wala! Here we are!"

"Oh and I'm also extremely methodical, so with that said, let us start at the bottom and work our way up to the prize spot.

No the prize spot is not your little pecker, I know to you that's your pride and joy, but for me, the prize spot is that empty space in your chest where your heart should've been.

He continues to stare at me and occasionally pulls at a piece of skin on his dry lips.

I've often wondered if you actually have a heart. I mean how could you have one and still do what you did to me? We'll find out together so just sit tight.

Oh, you are sitting tight because you can't move can you?!

"I gotta stop laughing at my own jokes and get serious here!"

Smiling, I say, "I forgot I got you lying down tight as a bug in a rug. Remember you used to say that to me the nights you put me to bed after mommy gave me a bath? Well I think it's a stupid saying."

Coming closer to his face, I say, very sweetly, "You know what, cause of that stupid saying, I kill every bug I see. I think that's how this past thing works. It stays with you unless it gets processed, picked apart and made to go away."

He blinks and I see tears forming in his eyes. We both know this is a choice moment…I can still turn back.

I pick up a pair of very sharp tree snipers and I snip off his right big toe. He yells and starts shaking all over. The blood is minimal and I'm a little disappointed. But his yells are very satisfying.

He never let me yell out.

"Well this big piggy ain't ever going to market!" I sing and throw his toe in the trash.

"I used to hate it when you sucked my big toes and fondled my clitoris.

Karma is a bitch…just saying."

Sobbing he says, "Wait baby, I can make this up to you! We can talk this through can't we?

What do you want me to say? I'll say it! I will," he says crying with snot falling out both his nostrils. His yellow tinged whites of his eyes are filled with tears. He's shaking all over.

For the first time in my life, I feel completely in charge. I have made the monster cry. I'm the shit!

No, I'm now his monster!

"I'll consider it, but I can't promise I will deviate from the lesson plan. Now tell me how you're gonna make up my childhood and all my life to this point up to me?"

He starts to speak, falters and then he tries again. "I'm sorry, ok; I didn't mean to hurt you. I had no idea you even remembered those things.

But wait a minute are you sure it was me? I mean, wait ok, not calling you a liar, but you were very small and kids have funny recollections.

I could've been someone who looked like me. Why don't you let me up and together we'll go find the son-of-a-bitch.

We can even bring him back here and together make him pay for what he did to my 'lil girl. How does that sound baby?"

"Like a pathetic unremorseful asshole." I say with my nostrils flaring and, I hate to admit it that damn one piece of snot is about to fall.

"Let's get back to the lesson, shall we?"

He looks at me and takes a deep breath. "Sweetheart, I don't think you're listening to me. I'm sorry you were hurt but…"

"Remember those ass fucks you used to give me before the, as you would say, "love making" began?"

He looks like he's been frozen, nothing moves.

329

"Ok, so here's my version" I pick up an extendable metal baton for him to see. I extend it to its full 12 inches and let him take it all in.

"Now I'm gonna give this to you on a curve ok? Not the whole 12 inches, since your shit wasn't but what…6 inches fully erect?"

He starts struggling against the board again, his head thrashing from side to side with mucus streaming out his nose.

"What the fuck are you gonna do with that goddamn thing?

Now listen girl you better stop this shit right fucking now and let me outta here! You hear me? You better not put that goddamn thing near me or my ass!"

I put cocoa butter all over the extended portion of the baton. "I've always loved the smell of cocoa butter and most suppositories have a cocoa butter base, so as you insert them, it melts and doesn't hurt when inserted.

I've had to use sooooooo many suppositories over the years because all that ass fuckin really messed me up. Did you know that?"

Pops goes still again and he stares at me like he's just really seeing me for the first time.

In a much quieter voice, he says, "Baby girl, I'm really sorry for what I did to you. I don't have an excuse for it except I was an angry man.

 I was angry at your mother for a betrayal I couldn't forgive her for and baby, God help me, I took it out on you."

"Really, that's it? Mommy pissed you off and you started fucking me? I mean for YEARS!"

I lean in over his face and say just as quietly as his declaration, "That's not good enough. I don't believe you.

Why were you the type of man who takes his anger out on a little girl, especially sexually, cause he's mad at his woman? You're a fucking animal!"

Then, I move from over his face to stand at his feet. He looks down at me and I see the dawning acceptance that this is going to be his life for the next couple hours.

Then, I find the sweet spot and ram the baton in over and over again.

Grace and mercy finds him and he is allowed to faint.

While he's out, I take a large straw, insert it in his penis hole and pour some hot sauce in the hole. He always liked his sausages with hot sauce.

I'm Pops little girl and I want everything to be as he would want it.

After torturing him for two hours...I'll save you the rest of the gory details cause I don't think I want to share them with you. They are my private sweet memories.

Anyway, before I cut him up, I took my mom out of the trunk and let her see what had become of the man she loved more than me.

I had plans for her too, but she had some kind of mental break and started babbling. I dropped her off on the side of the road after I left his parts in the woods for nature to do the clean-up.

Any questions...sis?"

Penny never answers; she's dead before she can process anything she's heard.

Shot by Ruth's gun...

Epilogue...

"What happened here?" asked Police Chief Ritchie while Lt. Brogan looks on.

Denise, crying and pretending to shake all over, "Det. Hill came in and told Det. Darling to drop her weapon.

Det. Darling shot Det. Hill in the shoulder.

Det. Hill's gun fell out her hand and slid across toward me. Penny was so crazed she didn't notice the gun, so I picked it up and hid it behind my back.

While Det. Hill was lying on the floor, Penny bent over her and tried to cover her with her jacket. She was crying and saying how sorry she was. She said things got out of hand and she could make it all better she just needed more time.

Then Penny pointed her gun at me. She was going to kill me!

I was aiming Det. Hill's gun at her shoulder so she would drop her gun but I accidently shot her in the face!

My hands were shaking so badly, Det. Hill was bleeding and Penny, sorry Det. Darling was screaming at me about our father. I guess I just closed my eyes and pulled the trigger. I'm so sorry!"

Chief Ritchie says, "It's ok, you don't have to do this right now Miss Wallace."

"No sir, I need to make some sense of this. Why would she do this? I thought we were close and I felt it was the right time to talk to her about being biological sisters. See we had the same father.

When I told her, she said she knew, but then she got angry and pulled her gun.

Det. Hill came in and tried to talk some sense in her, but she just started crying and waiving her gun all around."

332

"Miss, it seems Det. Darling has been heading to this day for quite some time. Just between you and me, Det. Darling has attempted suicide several times.

Since Det. Hill had a degree in counseling, leadership felt they could partner her up and Det. Hill could have a positive effect on Darling's moods.

In all honestly, we just didn't want to lose Det. Darling on the street because she was the best detective our force has.

Internal dialogue…

Lt. Brogan…Why did I just say all that? Shit we're gonna get sued for sure! Two cops dead! Fuck!

Is there anyone we can call for you?

"No sir, I just want to go home and forget any of this ever happened."

"Ok, I'll have one of our officers drive you home after you finish writing your statement."

"No sir, I won't need a ride. I have my car, if that's alright?"

"Sure, I'll just have an officer follow you home just to be sure you get there safely."

"Ok and here's my statement. I really wanted to get it all down before I forget it. You see I plan to forget this night ever happened.

I tell my clients how important it is not to carry negative events around, and I am definitely going to do everything I can to let this night go before it consumes me."

Denise lowers her head and pretends to cry.

Epilogue…

Tina, formerly Plenty, takes $2,000 of her money and makes $150,000 in Vegas! Seems the bank manager she used to screw every Sunday morning, while his wife was at church, knew what he was talking about when it came to reading people at the poker table. Tina used the information to increase her little nest egg. She even has enough to buy a run-down hotel and hopes to turns it into a bed and breakfast.

Wendy, formerly Good, loves living in LaPlata Maryland…she is working at A-Z Emporium, managing the lingerie section…she has self-published a book of poems & plans to marry Brian.

Gene and Kim, formerly known as Squidget and Pimp Gene, continue to live together and make a nice living running the bar.

Somehow, the Golden Shower DVD was unanimously released online…it went viral in 30 minutes!

A new pimp is in town and her name is Irma Lomax…she plans to offer the locals some "stud loving." Irma and Gene have much to discuss.

Gene's other hos have left the business too…one by death the other went into rehab.

Lynn continues to volunteer in her community and is at peace. She and Holly have lunch together often.

Imani and her parents just returned from a family cruise; Imani met a cute guy that her parents like too…they continue family therapy.

Yvette continues to work at the hospital and tries not to snap off but…

Cheryl, Dawn and Karen remain friends; they go on weekend trips together and are moving forward…Dawn has quit therapy!

Dani continues to work-out and while at A-Z Emporium she ran into her ex-husband; he attempted to hug Dani and she flipped him onto his back. He was fired immediately and Dani was given a $500 gift card for her inconvenience.

Holly continues to work at the courthouse and walks around with knives in her apartment; she stopped working out with Dani because she felt guys were looking at Dani and therefore looking at her too; Holly is in therapy and down to wearing only three band aids a day. She enjoys spending time with Lynn and goes home more often now that she's told her mom the whole story.

Press conference held four days after Penny and Ruth's death...

"It is with a heavy heart that I have to report Det. Penelopie Darling and Det. Ruth Hill were killed in the line of duty.

Both officers were exemplary officers and will be remembered for their tireless efforts to serve the community; however Det. Darling, suffering from a mental illness, fired upon her partner, Det. Ruth Hill...striking her in the head and killing her instantly.

Det. Darling then turned to fire on a witness but the witness was able to secure Det. Hill's weapon and fire first; striking and killing Det. Darling.

We are also investigating Det. Darling's potential involvement in other homicides to include that of her mother.

For now, we have no further information.

Moving on…

"Alright, now can we focus on the new tasks at hand please? We've supported your little family holiday…now it's time to get back to work. We have been missing our best assassin."

"Awww, daddy…I mean boss…I'm back and ready…who do I kill next?!"

Internal dialogue…

Assassin…Ok, girl jettison this shit and move on.

Ray shouldn't have purged his soul to you that night at the bar. When he found out I was supposed to be a therapist he just unloaded. Sorry for him! He told the wrong bitch!

Poor nasty ass Danny Clark…well I had to kill him to tie Penny into shit.

I really didn't want to kill Ruth but shit got crazy at the end so I had to improvise! I'm one BAD ASS BITCH!

Those ladies in the group have no idea how close they came to being on the dead list too!

Mom and Dad dead…check

Sister dead…check

Sister's mom dead…check

Uncle dead…check

Rapists dead…Danny and Ray…check…check

"Well it's finally time to deal with someone we let live last year, Benjamin Sydnor. Here's his portfolio, review it and let's talk about the best way to kill this traitor!"

"It would be my pleasure!"

Last thoughts…

It is my hope that this fictionalized story will give all readers a glimpse into some of the emotions felt by sexual assault victims after the event(s) occurred.

I can't speak for all victims, but I just wanted to give "voice" to the "thoughts, traits, and behaviors" that I have had to adopt in order to just make it through one day.

Many of us have stumbled down the path toward recovery, not knowing that's what we were doing.

Waking up can feel like punishment instead of a blessing.

Admittedly, I attempted suicide as an option…I was, thankfully, unsuccessful.

And I admit, I wanted my offenders to die…thankfully, I wasn't willing to go that far.

I am not advocating for violence; just not ignoring that the violent feelings are real.

I **NEVER** thought I would find myself accepting the traumas and incorporating them into my life, my soul in a way that would bring me to this shameless moment.

For those of you living with this, I pray you acknowledge the abuse or assault; accept that it happened to you for no other reason than you were chosen by a sick or evil asshole!

Or were you chosen because God wants to use you for His glory?

I don't know the answer…you'll have to make that peace for yourself.

Acceptance doesn't mean you agree with what happened, just that you don't DENY what happened.

Then, after acceptance, develop changes you MUST make to survive…start with forgiving yourself!

Most importantly, you MUST LIVE!

Please reach out for help to a trusted friend, family member, community rape crisis center, women's health center, hotline, or all of these safe havens.

If you aren't at that place, then please write it all down…everything you remember and feel…just let it out, don't hold it inside.

Say it out loud, alone in a room; the universe is big enough to hold it until you can deal with the enormity of your pain.

I wasn't there when it happened to you…but today and everyday…I'm sending you power nuggets and love…

Toki